I0822813

The Art of Detachment

By

Joe Manzello

Published by Book Writing Maestros

www.bookwritingmaestros.com

Dedication

For my son, Joey.

You are the first soul I ever fought for harder than myself.
The boy who taught me what it means to rise even when I'm broken.
The one who unknowingly pulled me out of the darkest chapters of my life simply by needing a father worthy of you.

Every page of this book was written with you in mind.
Not so you would carry my pain,
but so you would one day understand the man I had to become to give you a life built on strength instead of wounds.

I want you to know this:

A man can lose everything—his money, his business, his pride, his plans, even the woman he loves— and still come back stronger than anyone thought possible.
A man can fail, fall apart, start over, break open,
and rise into someone unrecognizable… someone better.

And I want you to watch me do it.
Not for admiration,
but so you'll never be afraid of your own fire.

You will never walk this world without a man at your back.
You will never question whether your father loves you.
You will never stand at the edge of the unknown alone.

If you inherit anything from me, let it be my strength, not my scars— my courage, not my collapse— my discipline, not my demons— my sovereignty, not my survival mode.

May you grow into a man who stands tall, loves deeply, and fights honorably, and carries his heart like a weapon and a compass.
And if you ever lose yourself, may these pages guide you home.

For you, my son.
My legacy.
My why.

Acknowledgment

There are chapters in a man's life that he cannot walk through alone. This book was forged during one of those seasons.

To Liz, thank you for standing with me through a transition most people would have run from. You never asked for a role, never applied pressure, never tried to shape the path. You simply wanted what was best for me and showed up sincerely when I had nothing to offer in return. That kind of presence leaves its mark. I'm grateful for you.

To my mother, thank you for doing everything you could to help me, even when I didn't always communicate well, even when I pulled away to fight battles that didn't make sense from the outside. Your love was steady, even when I wasn't.

To my Group Chat brothers — the men who stayed steady through the fire, who didn't flinch when I fell off the edge, and who reminded me who the hell I was when the world went dark. Every man needs a tribe. You were mine.

And finally, to every reader who now carries these pages into their own battles, I honor you. This book was born from collapse, but it was written for resurrection. If one man rises because of it, the pain was worth it.

— J.M.

About the Author

Joe Manzello is a forged man, rebuilt from fire, discipline, collapse, and the long, brutal path back to himself. His life's work centers on the masculine journey: heartbreak as initiation, adversity as alchemy, and sovereignty as the inevitable destiny of a man who refuses to stay broken.

A devoted father, Joe tries to lead his son by example, choosing discipline, integrity, and emotional strength as the language of legacy. As a fighter, he shapes the body and the mind with the same conviction, knowing a man's physical edge sharpens his spiritual one.

As a writer, Joe explores the inner war men face but rarely articulate, identity fractures, attachment wounds, heartbreak, addiction, and the long road back to self-respect. His writing blends mythic masculinity with psychological precision, giving men language for battles they have fought in silence.

As an entrepreneur, he first built himself from the ground up and then rebuilt himself from rock bottom after business failure, financial ruin, and the kind of life collapse that would have buried a lesser man.

And as a masculine coach, Joe guides men toward discipline, sovereignty, self-loyalty, and the internal structure required to build a life worthy of their potential.

He writes, fights, fathers, coaches, and lives with one purpose:

The Art of Detachment

To help boys become men and men become the strongest, clearest, most sovereign version of themselves—in body, in mind, in spirit, and in legacy.

Table of Contents

REQUIEM

For the woman who brought me to the edge of myself—
who amplified my strength until it felt like I could carry the world,
and then, just as violently, exposed the cracks I had spent years
pretending weren't there.
The cracks I tried to hide from everyone, even myself.

There were seasons when we were aligned,
and in those seasons we felt unstoppable —
like the universe had bent its rules for us.
Two storms that never collided,
yet somehow merged into something ferocious, alive, and
undeniable.
We laughed until our ribs ached,
we argued until our voices broke,
and somehow, it never broke the bond.
In those moments, the world wasn't just conquerable —
it seemed irrelevant, waiting for us to decide its fate.

And there were seasons when we fell out of alignment —
and in those seasons we became dangerous to ourselves,
not because the love was weak,
but because the current between us was too electric,
too raw for two broken halves still carrying their private wars.
I remember nights where silence between us roared louder than
any fight.
I remember the sharp, quiet anger,
the way a look could wound deeper than words.
I remember wondering if love had ever been enough — or if it
was always just a test.

Before you, I thought love was endurance,
a slow burn, a ledger of loyalty and patience.
With you, I realized love is revelation —
it strips you bare, forces you to confront the parts of yourself
you've spent a lifetime avoiding.
After you, I had no choice but to become the man
I had only pretended to be,
the man I had lied to myself about,
the man capable of holding more than my own illusions.

If there are a thousand realities,
in nine hundred ninety-nine of them
I believe we made it —
just not in this one.
And maybe it's hubris to think any reality could hold us.

In this reality, you were not the destination.
You were the descent.
The mirror I didn't want to face.
The initiation I didn't ask for,
but desperately needed.

You shattered me, and in the shards, I glimpsed myself —
a self I hadn't been brave enough to meet before.
I do not bury you —
I bury the man who could not yet carry
the weight of what he demanded from the world
or from love itself.

This is not longing.
This is not bitterness.
This is trembling gratitude after fire,

honor after loss,
a bow to the love that forced the forge to exist.
A bow to the nights that made me question,
the mornings that reminded me I had survived,
and the quiet, trembling realization
that I am, finally, more than I was.

“It is the struggle that defines us.”
Not goodbye —
requiem.

AUTHOR'S NOTE

If you're reading this, there's a good chance no one actually knows you're hurting.

Men like us don't get the luxury of collapsing where people can see it.
We don't fall apart in public.
We break in silence — behind locked doors, in parked cars, in showers where the water can hide what the world says shouldn't exist on our faces.
We break where no one can measure what holding everyone else together has taken from us.

You probably haven't told anyone how bad it really is.
You might not even have the language for it yet.
All you know is that something heavy has settled inside you, something that didn't used to be there,
and you're carrying it alone because that's what men like us were taught to do.

I know that place.
Not from theory.
From living it.
From being the man no one checked on,
the one everyone trusted to be "fine,"
the one they leaned on while I was quietly bleeding behind a ribcage that looked solid from the outside.

I didn't need advice.
I didn't need clichés dressed up as comfort.

The Art of Detachment

I didn’t need someone telling me to “heal,” “let it go,” or “be strong.”

I needed someone who actually saw me —
not the mask I’d perfected,
not the unshakeable façade,
not the man who always said “I’m good,”
but the man underneath all of that.
The one I didn’t show anyone because I thought it would cost me something I couldn’t afford to lose.

I needed someone who could stand next to me in the dark
long enough for me to realize I wasn’t dead,
just buried under years of pressure, pain, and pretending.

But no one came.
And when no one comes, you learn what kind of man you are by the way you crawl back to your own life.
One inch at a time.
One breath at a time.
One moment where you choose not to disappear.

This book isn’t written from a mountaintop.
It’s written from inside the fire and from beyond it —
from the man who almost didn’t make it back,
and from the man who finally did,
scarred, changed, but undeniably alive.

I’m not here to teach you how to fake strength.
I’m not here to tell you to numb it, outrun it, or bury it deeper.

I’m here to tell you that the storm you’re in
is not the end of you.
It’s the shaping of you —
the part no one talks about because it isn’t pretty
and it isn’t easy
and it feels nothing like the hero stories we were fed growing up.

And I’m not leaving you in it alone.

As you move through these pages,
read them like someone is standing beside you —
not pulling you,
not dragging you,
just refusing to walk away while you find your footing again.

You don’t have to be perfect.
You don’t have to be prepared.
You don’t even have to believe you’re salvageable yet.

You only have to keep turning pages.
I’ll meet you in every one,
right where you are,
not where you think you should be.

You may feel alone right now —
but you are not invisible anymore.

The climb begins here.

— Joe

PREFACE — THE RETURN FROM THE ASHES

This is not just a story about losing a woman; it is a story about losing the man I was when she was my world. The hardest part of losing her wasn't the loss itself; it was the slow, grinding realization that in the process, I had lost myself with her. That the man who once believed he could survive anything had vanished quietly, leaving only a stranger in his place.

People often think heartbreak is solely about missing someone. But what truly breaks a man is the moment he looks in the mirror and no longer recognizes the face staring back at him — the face that once had confidence, certainty, and a sense of direction, now hollowed out by absence, fatigue, and regret. I know this road intimately; I have walked it to the edges of despair, felt the way it erodes patience, humor, and even hope, until survival itself feels like a stubborn act of will.

The collapse doesn't happen all at once. It unfolds in increments — the day you stop trusting your instincts, the moment you begin to soften your voice and shrink your roar just to keep the peace, the quiet nights when loyalty twists into self-abandonment disguised as devotion. By the time the relationship ends, you're not just grieving her; you're grieving the man you thought you were, the man who believed he could hold everything together and still remain whole.

This book is about that resurrection. It's not about healing — it's about rebirth. It's not about recovery — it's about return. Not to who you were before the collapse, but to the man you could only become because of it; the man forged in the fire of loss, tempered by sleepless nights, doubt, and a relentless confrontation with your own inadequacies.

Most men never make that turn. They survive the loss but never reclaim themselves. They live half-alive, orbiting a wound that becomes their identity, a quiet ache they wear like armor. Sovereignty lies in choosing differently. Resurrection is not merely "coming back" — it is stepping fully into the man who could only emerge after fire and absence, the one who is made stronger precisely because the world tried to break him.

If you are here, you are already standing at the threshold of that awakening. This book will not drag you through the mire; it will initiate you into a new way of being. I will not teach you how to numb the pain, how to hide it, or how to pretend it isn't there. I will teach you how to become the man who can hold it, who can walk through it, who can emerge from it whole.

To walk this road, you don't need perfection; you need willingness. To rise again, you don't need certainty; you need direction. And if you don't yet believe you can become that man, borrow my belief until you do — let it be a lifeline until your own heart finds its strength.

The past is no longer your reference point. Only the fire remains. By the end of this journey, you will not be asking whether you can get her back; you will be deciding who is worthy of standing beside you, and more importantly, who is worthy of the man you are becoming.

The ashes were not your ending; they were simply the ground from which you will rise. The real break doesn't occur when she leaves; it happens when you confront the reality of living in your own skin without her. This is where true transformation begins, and this is the path we will explore together.

There are two kinds of pain a man can face in his lifetime.

The kind that wounds him —
and the kind that remakes him.

Heartbreak is the only wound that can do both.

A man can survive war, business failure, bankruptcy, exhaustion, betrayal, and still remain intact…
but losing the woman he built his future around —
that is the one collapse that leaves him face to face with himself.

Not the mask.
Not the role.
Not the reputation.

Himself.

The part of him no one else sees.
The part of him he has long avoided.
The part of him that remained unclaimed — until she left.

Every man who has ever loved deeply knows this truth but rarely speaks it:

The moment she leaves, a line appears in your life —
the man before the fire, and the man after.

This book is not about the woman.
It is about who you become because she is gone.

It is about the version of you that can only be born
after the ashes bury the one who could not remain.

Detachment is not forgetting her.
It is no longer abandoning yourself.

It is not indifference.
It is sovereignty.

It is the process of returning home
to the man you were before the world taught you to give your soul away
just to keep love in the room.

This book will not coddle you.
It will not tell you time will fix you.
It will not tell you to "move on."

It will show you how to rise clean from the wreckage,
to walk through fire and emerge as the man your pain was shaping you to become.

If you feel your chest tighten as you read this,
good — it means the part of you that refuses to die in the dark
just heard footsteps coming back for him.

Turn the page.

This begins the moment you choose
not just to survive what broke you —
but to rebuild with the steel it left behind.

The Art of Detachment

Opening: The Day She Left

This isn't about death.
It's about something crueler — watching someone you love disappear while she's still alive.

You wake up and she's everywhere: in your phone, in your chest, in the empty space on the passenger seat. You tell yourself you're fine, but your body knows you're lying. The nervous system doesn't negotiate — it responds. And yours is still reacting to the absence it hasn't accepted yet. Her laugh echoes through your head like a ghost looping on a broken record, reminding you she once lived inside your everyday rhythm.

Detachment isn't about pretending you don't care.
It's about surviving what caring did to you — learning how to stay upright while the emotional architecture you built around her collapses inward.

You can't think your way out of it. Logic doesn't touch the ache. You're dealing with biochemical withdrawal — dopamine, oxytocin, routine, the familiar tether of companionship. Your nervous system is still wired to her frequency, still expecting her voice, her presence, her patterns. Every memory hits like a dose you didn't ask for. Every silence exposes how much of your life you had unconsciously synced to hers.

You loved her. Maybe you still do.
But this book isn't about getting her back.
It's about getting *you* back — the parts of you that faded while you were trying to keep her close, the parts that now need you more than she ever did.

The Art of Detachment

PART I
THE FALLOUT

Chapter 1 — The Fallout

There's a moment after every breakup when the world goes quiet. You scroll, stare, drive, work, talk — but none of it lands. The background hum that once kept you anchored is gone. You're not just missing a person; you're missing a rhythm your body built itself around, a pattern that told your nervous system what "home" felt like.

The masculine instinct is to fix it — to send the message, make the call, explain what she misunderstood.
But the truth is brutal: she doesn't misunderstand.
She's simply gone. And until you let that reality hit you clean, you'll keep bleeding energy into a battle that ended long before you admitted it.

The first step is not strength.
It's surrender.

Sit in the wreckage.
Don't try to rebuild yet.
Don't seek closure. Closure is the story we invent when we can't handle the silence. She didn't leave because you failed — she left because her path demanded it.
And you're still here because you don't yet know who you are when you're not orbiting her.

That's the wound.

It's not the loss of love that hurts the most.
It's the collapse of identity. You built a world around her — her approval, her warmth, the way she made you feel solid without

having to try.
When she left, she took the mirror.
Now you're forced to look at the bare version of yourself you'd been hiding behind her reflection.

This is the beginning of detachment:
not coldness, not numbness, but truth.

You were addicted to the feeling of being chosen.
Now you'll learn the far heavier skill — choosing yourself even when no one's hands are reaching for you.

Every man who has ever risen from heartbreak has walked through this same fire — the sleepless nights that feel endless, the mornings that sting, the questions that echo like accusations: *Was I not enough? Was any of it real?*

The answers don't matter.
What matters is what you do with the silence that follows.

You can chase distraction, or you can build discipline.
You can scroll through her photos and reopen the wound, or you can rebuild the frame that held your masculinity.
You can drown in memories, or you can learn to breathe through the storm instead of begging it to stop.

The fallout isn't punishment.
It's purification.

When the smoke clears, you'll see what the relationship was trying to reveal the whole time:
that love without self-possession turns you into a hostage,
that obsession dressed as devotion steals your center,

and that sometimes losing her is the only doorway back to yourself.

So don't rush the process.
Let the silence bruise you clean.
Each day without her is a rep in the gym of detachment —
painful, necessary, strengthening.

You're not moving on yet.
You're moving through.

And somewhere on the other side of this ache, you'll meet the man you were meant to become — the one who can love fiercely without trading away his identity to keep love in the room.

The Aftermath

The first night alone is when the truth hits — not as a thought,
but as a presence that should be there and isn't.
Your body doesn't understand it yet.
It still expects her.

You lie there in the dark and it feels like the air itself is missing weight.
Her side of the bed is too cold, too flat, too untouched — like the world has been emptied of her outline.
Your chest feels caved in, as if something was ripped out from behind your ribs and left your frame sagging without support.
Your skin tightens, bracing for contact your body still believes is inevitable.

People think heartbreak is emotional.
It isn't.
It's neurological.

Your nervous system doesn't know she's gone.
It only knows she hasn't touched you yet.

My heart wasn't "sad."
It was starving — a hunger so physical it felt like it was happening in the bone marrow.

I kept shifting, turning, breathing wrong — my body trying to find a position where the ache might settle, where something inside me would stop rattling.
But nothing settled.
I wasn't lying in a bed — I was lying inside the hollow her absence carved out.

That's when the mind begins its assault.

Not memories — assault.
Sharp, intrusive thought-loops that rush forward as if they're trying to keep me alive:

Maybe she'll come back.
Maybe she'll text.
Maybe this isn't real.
Maybe if I just—

It's not hope.
Hope is gentle.
This is compulsion — the brain clawing for oxygen while drowning.

The Art of Detachment

Because when your body was with her, it wasn't romance you were feeling — it was regulation.
Your entire system learned to breathe through her.
She became the rhythm your body synched itself to.

Without her there, the mind starts looking for her like a missing limb.

You don't toss and turn because you're restless.
You toss and turn because the body is trying to find the doorway back into your own skin.

But there is no doorway.

There's only thought.

Thought becomes the cage.
Thought becomes the hand around your throat.
Thought becomes the punishment.

You don't fear the night because you're alone —
you fear it because you can't escape the version of your mind that wakes up when the world goes still.

So you get up.
You walk around.
You change rooms.
You stare at the floor, the wall, your phone, nothing.

It's not the silence you're trying to escape.

It's you.

The pacing isn't movement — it's survival.
Your feet are trying to outrun the noise in your head.
Your body is begging for a moment of quiet that never comes.

But there's nowhere to go.

There's no version of the night where she suddenly appears and your nervous system finally exhales.
There is only this:

the loop,
the ache,
the circling,
the hunger for contact
your body still believes is coming.

You don't miss her in concept.
You miss her body telling your body that you are not alone.

This is the part nobody warns men about.

You don't just lose her —
you lose the regulator built into her touch.

And when that disappears, you don't just ache —
you collapse internally, and you collapse alone.

The War in the Mind

The worst part isn't the bed.
It isn't the room.
It isn't even the loneliness.

The Art of Detachment

It's the mind that won't let you leave her.

When a bond like this breaks, the body aches —
but the mind begs.

It searches for her the way a drowning man searches for the surface:
not thoughtfully, instinctively.
It's a desperation that bypasses logic and goes straight to survival.

You don't think — you reach.
Not with your hands, but with obsession.

The thoughts don't arrive politely.
They slam through you like a door kicked open:

She has to feel this too.
There's no way she can sleep right now.
She'll break before I do.
She'll remember what we had.
She'll realize it was real.
She'll come back.

Your brain manufactures a thousand futures in which she returns
—
because the alternative feels like stepping off a cliff barefoot:

That she won't.

No one teaches men how to sit with that.
We're taught how to build, how to chase, how to fix —
not how to lose what refuses to be repaired.

And so the mind keeps bargaining:

If I had just…
If she would just…
If I can get one more chance…
If I can hold her again…

You don't want closure — you want contact.
You don't want clarity — you want her nervous system pressed against yours,
the way it used to quiet the riot inside your chest.

You'd take one night.
One hour.
One breath in her arms just to stop the shaking underneath your ribs.

This is the part men are ashamed to admit —
not that they loved her,
not that they miss her,
but that they still ache for her more than they respect their own sanity.

Detachment doesn't begin with letting go.
Detachment begins with realizing just how deeply attached you still are.

And that realization feels like a collapse —
a silent implosion somewhere beneath the sternum.

The pacing gets worse.
The rooms feel smaller.
Your lungs tighten because the body is waiting for a signal
that isn't coming.

The Art of Detachment

You tell yourself to stop thinking about her —
but you can't, because thinking of her is the only thing
that keeps the internal shaking from tearing you apart.

That's the trap.
The obsession feels like comfort even as it is killing you.

You're not replaying memories because you want to —
you're replaying them because your nervous system is scavenging
for scraps of her presence,
trying to recreate the regulation she once provided.

The body claws through the mind looking for her.

You don't want answers.
You want regulation.

This is why heartbreak feels like psychosis —
because the brain keeps insisting the solution is external,
and the body keeps demanding the hit,
and there is no hit coming.

So you spiral.

You pace until your chest burns.
You walk into one room and forget why you're there.
You sit down and stand right back up.
You check your phone even though you know nothing will be
there.

It isn't weakness.

It's withdrawal.

The kind of withdrawal only someone who has been bonded at the nervous system level can understand —
where losing her feels like losing a part of your internal wiring.

You're not losing your mind.
You're losing your oxygen supply.

And without her, every second is a suffocation you can't name.

The Breaking Point

There comes a moment in the night when exhaustion should force your body to shut down —
but it doesn't.

Your limbs are heavy.
Your eyes burn.
Your muscles tremble with fatigue.
But the mind refuses to dim, refuses to unclench, refuses to grant you even a moment of mercy.

Because sleep isn't rest right now —
sleep is agreement.
Sleep is surrender to the truth you've been outrunning:
she is gone.

And you're not ready for that truth.
Not tonight.
Maybe not for months.
Maybe not until something inside you finally breaks wide open.

The Art of Detachment

So you keep fighting a war that ended without your permission —
the war of keeping her alive inside your imagination.

Because admitting she's gone is one loss,
but confronting the version of yourself that died with her —
that's the second death.
The one no man wants to face.
The one that doesn't leave a mark on your skin,
but leaves cracks through your entire sense of self.

No one sees this part from the outside.
To them, you look tired, distracted, "going through it."
But inside, something fundamental is collapsing.

Because you didn't just lose her —
you lost the man you were when she loved you.

When she was here, you didn't have to question your worth.
You *felt* it through how she looked at you,
how she touched you,
how her body folded into yours like you were the only safe place
she had left in the world.

Her presence was proof that you belonged somewhere.

When she left, that proof evaporated.
And with it, the reflection of yourself you'd been leaning on.

Now you're standing in a room with no mirror —
no witness to your strength,
no confirmation that you matter,
no anchor holding you in place.

Just the echo chamber of your mind,
tightening around itself.

This is where despair stops being poetic
and starts becoming a physical creature inside your chest.
Where longing shifts into panic —
not *"I want her back."*
But
"Who the hell am I without the man she allowed me to be?"

That's the fracture.
That's the wound that actually bleeds.

Because you're not only craving her —
you're craving the version of yourself you could only access through her presence.
The man who breathed differently when she was in the room.
The man whose nervous system settled the moment she touched him.
The man who felt real.

And when that man vanishes, the breakdown doesn't happen dramatically.
There's no cinematic collapse.
No crying on the floor in perfect lighting.

It's quieter.
More frightening.
More human.

It's a man standing in a room that suddenly feels too big and too empty at the same time,
trying to outrun the gravitational pull of his own unraveling,

while every nerve-ending screams for contact it will never receive again.

Eventually the pacing stops —
not because your thoughts slow,
but because your body simply quits.
You sink onto the floor or onto the edge of the bed,
and the shaking moves from your hands
to somewhere deeper,
somewhere underneath thought.

Then comes the drop.
The crash.
The moment every man hits at least once in his lifetime:

the realization — undeniable, unsoftened —
that she is not coming back.

Not tonight.
Not tomorrow.
Not in the doorway you keep glancing at.
Not through your phone.
Not through hope.
Not through memory.

No cavalry.
No rescue.
No reversal.

Just you.
You and the void she left behind.
And the terrifying question that rises inside that void:

Who am I now?

No reversal.

Just you.
You and the void.

You can feel something in you starting to break — not cleanly,
but like a foundation collapsing in slow motion,
cracks spreading under pressure you can no longer hold.
A splintering.
A sinking.
A grief with teeth.

It isn't heartbreak.
Heartbreak is sorrow.

This is deconstruction —
the stripping away of the man you were with her,
until the question you've avoided your entire life stands in front of you
with no place left to hide:

Who am I without her?

And in that moment — that collapsing, breathless, shaking moment —
the truth lands with surgical precision:

I am not fighting to get her back.
I am fighting because I don't yet know how to survive myself without her.

That is the real beginning.

The Art of Detachment

Not the breakup.
Not the silence.
Not the tears.

The real beginning is the moment you recognize
that the enemy isn't her absence —
it's the emptiness inside your own skin
now that she's no longer there to occupy the space you never learned to fill.

That is where Chapter 1 ends.

Not with acceptance.
Not with clarity.

But with the bare, unfiltered admission:
the doorway every man must crawl through before rebuilding starts —

"I don't know how to breathe without her yet."

The first night alone doesn't announce itself like thunder.
It arrives quietly, almost politely —
slipping beneath the doorframe like fog.

It's quiet at first — almost deceptively quiet —
just me, the bed, and a room that looks the same
but feels wrong, like someone removed the gravity from the air.

I don't break immediately.
I just… notice.

Joe Manzello

Notice the space where her body used to warm the sheets.
Notice the weight that isn't there.
Notice that the stillness doesn't calm me —
it presses into me,
like the room knows something I'm still refusing to face.

There's a heaviness in my chest, not sharp,
but hollow —
like a support beam was pulled from inside my ribs
and everything is sagging inward.

My body is waiting for her long before my mind admits it.

It expects her warmth,
her familiar weight tilting the mattress,
the sound of her breathing,
the unconscious way my nervous system calibrated itself
around her presence without asking permission.

But nothing comes.

The body feels it first —
the absence.

Not missing her voice.
Not missing her humor.

Missing her physical existence —
the literal, tangible reality of her next to me.

This is the part nobody talks about —
that the nervous system doesn't end the relationship when she
walks out.

The Art of Detachment

It keeps searching for her.
It keeps reaching for her.
It keeps waiting for her touch
the way lungs wait for oxygen.

My heart wasn't grieving yet.
It was starving.
Pulling at the inside of my ribs with something feral,
instinctive,
ancient.

I shift in the bed.
Turn once.
Twice.
Nothing settles.

My skin feels tight,
like it's bracing for contact
that will never come again.

I'm not lying alone —
I'm lying inside the vacuum her absence carved out of my life.

And beneath that emptiness, something starts to shift —
a low electrical current rising under the skin,
a feeling without a name,
the first tremor before the collapse.

The mind hasn't begun its assault yet,
but I can feel it crouching in the dark,
waiting for the exact second my guard drops.

Because this is how the descent always begins —
not with a dramatic blow,
but with the quiet recognition
that she is gone
and my body still hasn't gotten the message.

Eventually the stillness becomes unbearable.
Not because of the room —
but because my mind begins to move,
slowly at first,
like an old hinge groaning open in the dark.

Then faster.
Closer.
Hungrier.

The body aches,
but the mind begs.

It starts reaching for her the way a drowning man kicks toward the surface —
not logically,
but violently, instinctively,
as if survival depends on it.

Memory transforms into a predator.

Not memories —
imprints.

The way her breathing shifted when she was falling asleep against me.
The way her body curved into mine so naturally it felt rehearsed by lifetimes.

The Art of Detachment

The way my chest would settle without permission the moment her warmth touched it.

My nervous system is still tuned to her frequency —
still convinced she will walk into the room
and flip off the pain like a switch.

But she doesn't.

And that's when the mind begins bargaining with reality.

Not through words —
through desperation.

She feels me right now.
She has to.
She's thinking about me.
Some part of her must still be connected.
This can't just disappear.
Not like this.

I'm not thinking **about** her.
I'm thinking **toward** her —
reaching through the dark with thought alone,
as if the right amount of longing
could drag her back into the doorway.

But she doesn't come.

And the reaching sharpens into panic.

This is when the pacing starts —
not to move,
but to outrun the mind.

I get up.
Sit down.
Stand again.
Walk into another room and instantly forget why I'm there.

I'm not avoiding the silence —
I'm trying to escape the thoughts that have locked onto me
like a shadow I cannot shake.

Every step becomes a negotiation with a ghost.

Maybe she'll text.
Maybe she's crying too.
Maybe tomorrow she'll break first.
Maybe this isn't the ending.

But under every maybe lies the truth my mind refuses to face:

What if she never does?

What if she never comes back?

The mind will do anything to avoid that question —
because the moment it lands,
the collapse begins.

So it bargains.
It rewrites.
It rewinds.
It replays.

The Art of Detachment

Not scenes —
sensations.

Her head tucked under my chin.
Her hand sliding across my chest.
The way my breath automatically steadied when I held her.

I am not missing her presence.

I am missing the version of myself
that only existed in her arms.

The man who breathed differently with her weight against him.
The man who could finally stop bracing.
The man who felt like he was allowed to rest.
The man who had a home.

People call this heartbreak.
But heartbreak is grief.

This is **withdrawal**.

And withdrawal is a war no one else can see.

There comes a moment in that pacing
where the room stops feeling like a room
and starts feeling like a cage.

Not because I'm trapped in it —
but because I'm trapped in myself.

My body wants her.
My mind hunts her.
But she is nowhere to receive the reaching.

That's when the panic stops being restless
and turns existential.

I am not afraid of the dark.
I am afraid of the version of myself
that exists without her.

The thoughts circle like vultures:

She should be here.
She was supposed to be here.
Her body against mine was the only place I made sense.

And then it hits —
not gently,
but with the blunt force of truth:

I didn't just lose comfort.
I lost orientation.

She wasn't my peace.
She was my north.

My nervous system didn't bond to a relationship —
it bonded to **her**.

To her eyes,
her voice,
her energy wrapping around me like gravity—
she didn't just hold me;

The Art of Detachment

she **aligned** me.
She pulled me into a version of myself I didn't know how to reach alone.

And now that gravity is gone.

The world hasn't gone dark—
it's gone directionless.
Every step forward feels like a step taken without a compass,
without a center of balance,
without the invisible force that once told me where "home" was.

This is the part that breaks me:
not the loneliness,
not the longing,
not even the missing—

but the collapse of meaning itself.

Without her touch,
my body doesn't know how to settle.
It keeps bracing, tightening, scanning for something it can no longer find.

Without her presence,
my identity doesn't know where it lives.
It wanders inside me like a displaced animal looking for the den it once had.

When she left,
it wasn't only her absence that hollowed me out—
it was the disappearance of the man I only knew how to be beneath her hands,

in her gaze,
inside the gravity of her acceptance.

I move through the house like I'm searching for something lost,
but what I'm actually looking for
is myself.

And I can't find him.

Because he lived there—
in that connection,
in that anchoring softness,
in that wordless certainty of being chosen
and wanted
and held.

She didn't just walk away with her future—
she walked away with my reflection.

And the truth begins to surface,
slowly,
horrifically,
like watching the floor give way beneath you in real time:

I don't know how to exist without the man I was when she was mine.

That realization doesn't hit like pain.
Pain is familiar.

This hits like erasure—
as if someone reached inside,
removed the center of me,
and left the outer shell standing upright.

The Art of Detachment

I am not grieving a breakup—
I am grieving a version of myself
I no longer know how to access.

And in the middle of that realization—
in the quiet,
in the pacing,
in the suffocating collapse beneath the ribs—
something inside me begins to break.

Not loudly.
Not dramatically.

But with the clean, silent violence
of a fault line giving way.

At some point the pacing stops—not because the thoughts slow down,
but because the body can't carry them anymore.

The legs give out before the mind does.

I sit.
Or fold.
Or collapse forward into myself.

It isn't weakness—
it's gravity finally asserting the truth:
the weight of everything she took with her
has finally announced itself.

Not her attention.
Not her affection.
Not her presence.

Joe Manzello

Me.

She took me.

The man who breathed easily in her arms.
The man who slept without bracing.
The man whose chest wasn't a battleground.
The man who didn't have to hold himself together by force.

People think heartbreak is about wanting her back.

But heartbreak is wanting **yourself** back
and realizing you don't know how to find him without her.

I don't cry because I miss her.
I cry because her absence erased the only version of me
that ever felt fully alive.

This is where the world narrows.
Where thought stops being noise
and sharpens into a blade.

Not *I want her.*

But:
Without her, I don't know where I exist.

This is the real loss—
the loss no one warns men about.

The moment not when the relationship ends—
but when *you* do.

The Art of Detachment

I am left alone inside a mind
that no longer feels like a place a person can live.

And that is when the final truth lands—
sharp, unwelcome, irreversible:

I am not fighting the fact that she is gone…
I am fighting the fact that meaning went with her.

The collapse isn't emotional—
it's existential.

It's realizing the body is starving,
the mind is spiraling,
and the self is missing—

and there is no one coming back
to return me to myself.

And so I sit there in the quiet,
not because peace arrived,
but because there is nowhere left to run.

This is where detachment truly begins:

Not in strength—
but in ruin.

Not in letting go—
but in being forced to face
who I am without the woman
who once made me feel alive.

And in that hollow, shaking stillness—
with nothing left to bargain with—
the truth finally settles with full, unforgiving weight:

She wasn't just someone I loved.

She was the last place
I knew who I was.

The Fracture of Identity

"The heartbreak is not the loss of her —
it is the loss of who you were when she was yours."

There is a moment in a man's life —
sometimes sudden, sometimes slow —
when the person he thinks he is
and the person he has actually become
split apart.

Not publicly.
Not in some dramatic collapse.
Internally —
quietly, privately, beneath the skin where no one is looking.

And here's the truth men rarely admit:

This fracture doesn't begin the day she leaves.
It starts long before that.

It begins the first time you silence your own truth just to keep the peace.
The first time you shrink your instincts so you don't lose connection.

The Art of Detachment

The first time you bend yourself into a shape that isn't yours,
not because she asked you to—
but because you didn't trust that you were enough as you were.

A man doesn't break when the relationship ends.

He breaks when the man he sees in the mirror
no longer resembles the man he feels in his spirit.

That is the first wound.
The quiet one.
The one that starts the erosion long before the goodbye ever happens.

Identity doesn't shatter at once.
It dissolves slowly —
left behind in the places where you try to hold her:

Piece by piece.
Concession by concession.
Boundary after boundary.
Unspoken "I'll let this go"
followed by unspoken "I'll shrink here too."

Until what remains is a man still standing—
but no longer rooted in himself.

The world still sees strength.
They still see stability.
But what they can't see is the hairline crack forming through your center,

the fault line that's been spreading quietly under the surface
for months or years.

This is the fracture of identity —
the exact moment a man loses his internal axis.

And once a man loses his center,
attachment stops being about love
and becomes about **survival**.

That is why heartbreak hits men with such violence:

We are not grieving what left us.
We are grieving the pieces of ourselves
we abandoned in order to keep it.

You don't miss her —
not in the way people imagine.

You miss **you**.
You miss the version of yourself
you stopped being in order to maintain the connection.

You miss the man who trusted himself.
The man who spoke without flinching.
The man whose fire burned clean.
The man who didn't hesitate,
who didn't second-guess his own instincts,
who didn't negotiate his own worth.

You miss the man before the fracture.

This is why heartbreak doesn't just ache —
it disorients.

The Art of Detachment

It is not emotional loss.
It is **dislocation from self**.

A woman can walk away from you and life still moves forward…
but when *you* walk away from yourself,
everything inside you halts.

Not forward.
Not backward.
Just suspended —
caught between the man you used to be
and the man you no longer know how to return to.

This is the beginning of the fall.

Not when love ends —

but when your self-sovereignty does.

Chapter 2
Addiction to Her Energy

The craving doesn't begin in the heart.
It begins lower, deeper — in the places thought can't reach.

The body is the first to panic.
It goes searching for her before the mind can even name the hunger, every nerve-ending scanning for the last source of calm it remembers.

I don't want a conversation.
I don't want meanings or explanations.
I don't want the neatness of closure.

I want contact.

Skin that quiets mine.
Breath that tells my lungs they can stand down.
Her weight against me — the only thing that ever muted the storm inside my chest.

People who've never been bonded like this think it's romance.
It isn't.
It's regulation.

You don't crave **her presence** first —
you crave the **chemical silence** she used to pulse into your nervous system.

She wasn't the woman who soothed me.
She was the switch that shut my alarms off.

The Art of Detachment

And without her, everything blares.

This is why men fall back into memories —
not out of softness,
but because the body is trying to recreate a hit
that no longer exists in the real world.

It's not nostalgia.
It's withdrawal.

The mind replays moments like it's trying to slip back inside them physically —
not replaying words or scenes,
but the *temperature* of her,
the way her presence made my heartbeat settle like a stone sinking into still water.

I walk the house not because I'm restless,
but because every room feels like it's holding the faint echo
of where she once quieted me.

The craving sharpens.
It grows teeth.
It becomes animal.

My nervous system starts screaming its bargain:

Bring her back
and the shaking stops.

Bring her back
and I'll breathe normally again.

Bring her back
and I'll feel like myself.

And this is where the shift happens —
where pure craving mutates into negotiation.

Not with her.
With reality itself.

If she comes back,
I'll undo every mistake.
If she comes back,
I'll remake myself in any shape she needs.
If she comes back,
I'll surrender whatever I have to —
just let her turn toward me again.

Let her choose me again.
Let me be the man she rests against.
Let me be the man she returns to.

It doesn't feel like ego in this moment.
It feels like survival —
like I'm bargaining for oxygen.

Because the mind has latched onto one truth with terrifying certainty:

She is the doorway back into myself.

If she returns,
I return.

If she reaches for me,
the man I lost inside her love rises from the wreckage.

This is the hook.
The tether.
The addiction.

Not to her body —
but to the version of myself that only came alive
when she wanted me.

PART II

The longer the craving goes unmet,
the more the mind turns inward and begins **reshaping the past into a place of refuge**.

Not to remember her—
to **retrieve the version of myself that only existed** when she was still choosing me.

I don't fantasize about conversations.
I don't replay apologies.

I fantasize about her choosing me again.

Because that single decision—
that single shift of her gaze back toward me—
feels like it would silence the entire storm.

The pacing.
The ache.

The collapse.
The war behind my ribs.

All of it feels like it would stop
if she just reached for me the way she once did—
not gently, but with certainty.

That's when the addiction shows its real teeth—
because it stops being about wanting her presence
and becomes about wanting *resurrection.*

I don't want any woman.
I don't want distraction.
I don't want a body that fills space but not meaning.

I want reinstatement.

I want the universe to reverse course,
to rewrite the scene,
to put me back in the position where her choice made me whole.

It feels like there's a locked door somewhere inside me,
and behind it is the man I lost
the night she stopped choosing me.

And the mind starts whispering—
quiet, desperate, convincing:

If she wanted me again,
I would stabilize.

If she chose me again,
my scattered pieces would fall back into place.

The Art of Detachment

If she returned,
I wouldn't feel like a ghost in my own life.

This is why "move on" feels impossible.

Because I'm not trying to get over her—
I'm trying to get *back to me*.

She wasn't just someone I loved—
she was the structure my identity leaned against.

Without that structure,
I feel like vapor—
dispersed,
uncontained,
unlocated.

And here is the truth most men will never speak aloud:

I don't want validation.
I don't want attention.
I don't want access.

I want to be claimed.

Claimed the way I once was—
with no hesitation,
no doubt,
no question of whether I belonged in her world.

Claimed in a way that told my nervous system,
"You are not drifting—you are rooted."

This is why rejection feels like death—
not because a woman walked away,
but because your place in existence went with her.

That's when jealousy rises—
not as comparison,
but as displacement.

Not "he has what I want,"
but "he stands where I once did."

Someone else stepping into the foundation
that once held the weight of my being.

It isn't anger—
it's dislocation.

It isn't envy—
it's existential eviction.

Jealousy isn't
"I wish I were him."
It's
"I used to be him—
and I don't know where to exist now that I'm not."

This is where confidence fractures—
not because I stopped believing in myself,
but because I no longer know where I fit
in the architecture of my own life.

It isn't pride.
It isn't weakness.
It isn't ego.

It is **identity withdrawal**.

The body screams for touch,
but the soul screams for **placement**.

And in the absence of both,
the mind becomes a battlefield
with no doorway out.

Because the truth I can barely whisper—
not to the world,
not even fully to myself—
is this:

I don't just want her back.

I want to be
the place she returns to.

PART III

There comes a point where the craving stops feeling physical
and starts feeling **existential**.

My skin is still starving for her,
but beneath that hunger is something more primal,
a kind of quiet terror that settles under the ribs:

The terror
of no longer belonging to her.

Because if I am not hers,
then who exactly am I supposed to be now?

The mind tries to solve it in the only way it knows how—
by reaching for the last coordinates
where I remember feeling like I existed.

It keeps dragging me back through memory,
not to revisit her smile,
but to slip back into the man I was
when her presence validated my being.

Those moments weren't nostalgia.
They were **identity anchors**—
small, sacred points that held my entire sense of self in place.

A forehead resting against hers.
A hand cupping the back of her neck.
Her exhale sinking into my chest like warm gravity.
Her body folding into mine
as if I were the only shelter she trusted.

I wasn't just holding her—
I was holding the version of myself
that made sense.

And now, without that frame around me,
everything inside feels uncontained.

Directionless.
Unwitnessed.
Unlocated.

This is why the thoughts won't stop.
Why the mind replays the same memories
like a needle carving deeper into a vinyl groove.

The Art of Detachment

Why I move through the world
like a structure whose foundation has quietly rotted away.

I am not craving her affection—
I am craving **reintegration**.

The nervous system keeps trying
to drag me back toward the last place
where I felt whole, steady, anchored.

Because something inside me still believes:

If she chooses me again,
I will re-form.

If she comes back,
the fractured pieces will find their shape.

If she returns,
I won't feel like I am disappearing from my own life.

This isn't reasoning.
It's imprint.

And imprint doesn't loosen its grip with time—
it loosens only when transformation forces it to.

Until then, it clamps down like metal.

It whispers:
I am not finished.
We are not finished.
This connection has to live somewhere.

The craving shifts into something darker—
a search for proof that I still exist in her internal world.

Because if she still feels me anywhere,
even faintly,
then the man I was in her arms
hasn't died completely.

And this is the moment where longing
crosses its invisible threshold
and hardens into obsession.

I am no longer looking for contact.
I am hunting for **evidence**—
evidence that I am still real to her,
still present in some corner of her memory,
still occupying even a shadow of space in her heart.

Because if she still feels me,
then I am still someone.
Then I haven't been erased.

And that is the wound most men never name:

I'm not afraid I lost her—
I'm afraid I no longer exist
in the place where I once mattered most.

PART IV

Eventually the hunger stops feeling like longing
and starts feeling like a **sentence** carried out against you.

She is not choosing me.

The Art of Detachment

Not now.
Not tonight.
Not in the exact moment where my whole being leans toward her
as if she were oxygen.

And there is a particular kind of hurt
that only appears when you finally understand
that the woman who used to reach for you without thought
no longer reaches at all.

That shift doesn't sting—
it **breaks** something inside a man.

Not because he lost affection,
but because he lost his **place in the world**.

The body doesn't understand logic.
It still screams:
Bring her back.
Bring her back.
Bring her back.

But beneath that desperate chant,
another voice rises—
quieter, emptier, almost childish in its fear:

What if she never does?

What if I am no longer the man she returns to?

What if the door back into myself
is now locked on her side forever?

That's where jealousy is born—
not as comparison,
but as **replacement terror**.

Not
someone else has her,
but
someone else now occupies the place
where my identity once rested.

Someone else is the ground beneath her feet.
Someone else is the presence she softens into.
Someone else is the home she returns to.

And in that moment,
the addiction is no longer about her body—

it becomes a fight for the survival of **my own identity**.

Because if she gives that belonging to someone else,
then the part of me that lived inside her love
has nowhere left to exist.

I can feel it happening—
not panic,
not heartbreak,
but a hollow internal collapse:

If I am not hers,
then who am I now?

This is where defeat starts to seep in,
because the mind still clings to the myth
that salvation sits in her hands.

The Art of Detachment

It still whispers:
If she chose me again,
this would stop.
If she chose me again,
I would come back to life.

And so the addiction twists itself into devotion—
not to her love,
but to a single defining outcome:

her choosing me
again.

Not so I can feel loved—
but so I can feel **restored**.

Because right now,
I don't want a future.

I want relief.
Relief from being unclaimed.
Relief from being unmirrored.
Relief from drifting without a center.

I want to be who I was
when she laid her head on my chest
and my entire being recognized itself in her breathing.

Not wanted.
Not desired.

Belonged to.

Because somewhere deep inside,
beneath pride, beneath logic, beneath the persona,
there is a belief that if she just turned toward me once more—
if she simply chose me—
the fracture would close
and I would reassemble in an instant.

That belief is what traps men.

Not love.
Not longing.
Not fear.

The conviction
that we cannot heal
unless she chooses us again.

And as long as that belief holds power,
detachment feels like a death—

because the self we are trying to detach from
is the **only version of us that ever felt like home**.

Withdrawal of The Soul

"When she leaves, the body remains — but the center vanishes."

A man can endure almost any external collapse —
money lost, status stripped, careers burned to ash, friendships dissolved,
even the slow erosion of reputation.

But when the center inside him disappears,
his **soul drops into freefall.**

This is why heartbreak isn't sadness —
sadness is soft, human, survivable.

Heartbreak feels like **withdrawal** —
the body registering absence
the way lungs register the sudden theft of air.

You don't just miss her —
you miss the *internal stability* her presence gave you,
the grounding you outsourced to her touch,
the sanctuary you built inside her softness
because you never built one inside your own skin.

You never noticed how much of your spiritual spine
was held upright by her
until she was gone
and your nervous system had nowhere left to land.

This is why your chest feels cored-out,
why sleep becomes impossible,
why your mind replays the past like a survival algorithm.

Your system is trying to get "home" —
and for too long, **home was her.**

A man doesn't withdraw from love —
he withdraws from losing the place
where his identity was housed.

That is why the first stage after the fracture
is not grief —
it is **disorientation.**

The question is never truly:
"Why did she leave me?"

The real question, buried beneath the ache, is:
"Where do I go now that I can no longer return to myself through her?"

When a woman leaves,
she doesn't just exit your life —
she strips away the emotional scaffolding
you unknowingly built your entire sense of "I'm okay" inside.

It is not the woman that shatters a man —
it is the eviction
from the version of himself
that only existed through the mirror she held.

That emptiness you feel?
That isn't heartbreak.

That is **soul displacement.**

And until a man re-roots his being inside his own body,
every memory feels like gasping for air.

This is why panic rises from nowhere,
why silence feels predatory,
why solitude tastes like death.

You're not lonely —
you're **disconnected from your center.**

And a man disconnected from his center
will do anything to climb back inside his own skin again —
even if it means crawling toward the very fire
that scorched him.

This is not weakness.

This is **spiritual starvation** —
the soul clawing for its own return.

And until a man understands
that the ache is not truly for *her*,
but for **himself**,
he will keep trying to extinguish the flames
by running back into the burning house.

Love as Oxygen

"What you called missing her was never about love — it was missing the place where your entire nervous system finally unclenched."

Men don't bond
by accident.
When a man truly attaches,
it doesn't happen in his mind —
it happens in his body.

She wasn't just a partner.
She became a **regulating field**,
a living environment your system recalibrated around.

Her presence eased the tension that lived in your ribs.
Her voice softened the armor you had worn for years.
Her body silenced the war behind your forehead.
Her touch dropped your pulse faster than anything you've ever used to cope.

You were never addicted to *her*.
You were addicted to the **version of yourself** you could only access
in the sanctuary of her arms.

This is why people who have never felt a masculine attachment at depth
cannot comprehend its gravity.

Men don't fall in love with a woman's face or her figure —
they fall in love with the **way they breathe** in her presence.

It feels spiritual because it is.
Your nervous system recognized safety in her
long before your mind understood what was happening.

And that is why the separation hits like death:
you didn't just lose connection —
you lost **regulation**.

For a man, love isn't romance.
Love is oxygen.

The Art of Detachment

This is why breakups hit men late,
and why they hit like a collapsing lung.
We don't register abandonment in the heart —
we register **deprivation in the body**.

She wasn't simply the love you lost —
she was the **homeostasis you outsourced**,
the balancing force that kept your interior world from tipping over.

Without her, the system crashes.

The panic.
The hollowness.
The subtle internal shaking.
The compulsive need to reach out
just to feel *normal* for five minutes.

Not out of love —
out of **desperation to recalibrate**.

Because somewhere during the relationship,
her nervous system became the place yours curled up and rested.

You didn't just love her —
you **located yourself** inside her.

That is why heartbreak doesn't feel like loss —
it feels like **suffocation**.

Not "she is gone,"
but
"my grounding is gone."

And until you learn how to regulate inside your own chest,
you will keep mistaking longing for love,
withdrawal for destiny,
and the ache for evidence that she was “the one.”

What you’re craving isn’t her…

It’s oxygen.

Chapter 3
The Obsession Loop

It hits like electricity under the skin.
Not a spark — a surge.

Not anger, not jealousy, not even fear.
Voltage.
A live current ripping through the chest, lighting every nerve like a fuse-line set too close to fire.

Heat crawls up the neck.
The skull tightens as if the bone itself is bracing, trying to contain a storm it already knows it can't hold.

I'm not thinking in sentences anymore.
I'm feeling a current with nowhere to go — pressure without direction, pain without language.

And then the image detonates:
her body in someone else's hands.

It doesn't matter if it's true.
The nervous system doesn't need evidence — only imagination.
And imagination is merciless.

Adrenaline spikes.
Breath fractures.
Vision narrows even with my eyes shut.

I'm not afraid of the image.
I'm afraid of what it awakens in me —
a version of myself carved out of instinct and threat, not reason.

Joe Manzello

There's a second — a single, unstable second —
where I feel the floor tilt inside me.
Where I feel capable of tearing the night itself just to stop the picture from playing.

It isn't violence toward anyone.

It's pressure in a sealed container,
a red heat with no release valve,
a reactor humming with the rods pulled out.

The body wants to launch.
The soul wants to collapse.
Both impulses crash into each other and cancel out.
My hands shake without moving.

If grief is water, I could drown.
This is fire — and it burns in place.

I tell myself to breathe.
My ribs refuse.
I tell myself to calm down.
The furnace snarls back.

Because this isn't a thought.
It's a signal.
The limbic system screaming *invasion.*
The deepest part of me insisting, *A sacred space has been breached.*

The worst part isn't the image itself.
It's the residue —
the scorch mark it leaves long after the picture fades.

A pulse behind the sternum.
A metallic buzz in the forearms.
A live wire humming inside the jaw.

The Art of Detachment

In that moment, I am not a man in a room.
I am a containment problem.

I fear the edge inside me more than anything outside of me.

Because I know what this feeling can turn a man into
if he lets the current run unchecked —
the kind of man who confuses reaction with strength,
impulse with action,
pain with purpose.

So I stay still.
Motionless.
While a war happens beneath the surface of my skin.

And the mind, trying to help, only throws fuel.

It starts running diagnostics at impossible speed:

Was I not enough?
Did I misread everything?
Did I build my identity on borrowed ground?
Is someone else now receiving what once held me together?

Each question is kerosene.
Each imagined answer a match.

The body doesn't care that none of it's real.
It only hears *threat*
and keeps flooding my system with heat.

I ground my tongue to the roof of my mouth.
Box-breathe.
Anchor my feet to the floor like I'm bracing a door
with a fire raging on the other side.

Except the fire is in here.

There's a point where the surge peaks
and a man faces two choices:

Let the current take him —
or learn to hold it without exploding.

One path turns you into your own cautionary tale.
The other turns you into a forge.

I don't feel noble.
I feel barely contained.

But containment is the first victory.
Not control — that's a myth.
Containment — that's survival.

I ride the breath like it's the only rope I have:
in through the nose,
down the spine,
hold,
out slow,
longer than the body wants.

The heat doesn't disappear.
It condenses.

It becomes a single white-hot core in the center of my chest,
and I stand there with it —
not because I'm strong,
but because every way I run makes me smaller.

This is how the obsession loop forms its shape:

**Image → Surge → Fear of myself → Containment →
Image again.**

The Art of Detachment

A centrifuge.
Spinning until something separates.

And finally, I understand:

The image isn't random.
It is the psyche pressing on the fracture line,
testing the exact place where I still believe
my existence depended on her body choosing mine.

Another man's hands aren't just contact.
They symbolize erasure —
spiritual displacement —
proof that the cathedral that once held me
now opens its doors to a stranger.

My nervous system doesn't comprehend heartbreak.
It only understands alarms.

And so, it alarms.

Again.
And again.
The cycle hits like a heartbeat with no pulse behind it—
an involuntary reflex, a voltage loop that won't let me out.

Each round feels the same at first:
the spike, the image, the heat that climbs the spine like a hand
with no mercy.
But underneath it—deeper than the adrenaline—
there's a quieter truth forming like sediment at the bottom of the
wave:

I am not afraid of losing her.
I am afraid of losing **myself** to what this feeling could sculpt me

into
if I stop holding the line.

That realization lands like a grim kind of clarity—
a boundary drawn in fire, not ink.
A place inside me that says,
You don't get to cross this and still recognize who you are on the other side.

But the image doesn't honor boundaries.
It doesn't negotiate.
It doesn't pause to let me gather myself.

It comes back with the precision of a blade striking the same wound:
Surge.
Heat.
Tunnel vision tightening like hands around the skull.
Jaw locking until it feels carved from metal.

My body tries to commit a kind of emotional time-travel,
dragging me backward—to when I was the familiar weight beside her,
when her body answered mine without hesitation,
when I didn't have to imagine myself there because I was.

But the present has no softness to return to.
No doors open.
No place to land.

So I do the only thing left:
I hold the current again.
I let it roar inside me without letting it claim the world outside me.

And in that violent stillness, I learn something no book,
no philosophy, no mentor ever prepared me for:

The Art of Detachment

A man becomes what he can survive **without unleashing**.

If I can sit inside this surge—this animal voltage—
and not turn it outward,
not shape it into anger, or action, or collapse,
then something in me hardens in the right way.
Not bitterness—
but backbone.

It isn't healing.
Healing is still miles inland.
This is **forging**—
metal under pressure choosing shape instead of shatter.

The obsession loop hasn't broken.
It still spins with the same brutal rhythm.
But something inside the rotation shifts—barely, but undeniably.

For the first time, the fire doesn't feel like it's devouring me.
It feels like something I'm learning to grip with both hands.

And in that tiny, stolen breath between pulses,
a thought rises that wasn't available before:

If I can survive this storm without losing my name,
maybe I don't need her body to remind me I belong in my own.

It's not peace—peace is a foreign language.
It's not relief—relief is still on the other side of the mountain.

It's a handhold in the rock.
A single grip of ground in the avalanche.

I take it.
I breathe into it.
I anchor myself there.

And I brace—quietly, steadily—for the next wave that's already forming.

PART II

The moment the surge dips, something else rises—
not calm, not clarity, but a kind of internal scrambling,
as if the mind is trying to gather itself after being hit by a wave
that never touched water.

It isn't curiosity.
It isn't even desire.
It's compulsion wearing the mask of urgency.

The same instinct that once reached for her waist in the dark
now reaches for evidence like a man feeling for a pulse on a
collapsing body.

My hands move before thought does—
phone unlocked,
screens lighting up the room,
thumb flicking,
apps opening one after another
like doors in a burning hallway.

None of this is about information.
It's about relief—
the smallest scrap of proof that I haven't been completely erased.

A sign I still exist somewhere in her orbit.
A fragment of her world that hasn't closed the door behind me.

Because if I still exist *there*,
even just as an aftertaste,
then maybe I still exist *here*
as something more than a man pacing the ruins of his own
meaning.

The Art of Detachment

The panic has shape now.
It has appetite.
It needs data the way a drowning body needs air—
not thoughtfully,
but violently.

Did she post?
Did she shift?
Did her silence change tone?
Is someone else's shadow beginning to appear where mine used to live?

Every scroll is a heartbeat muttering the same plea:
Please still see me.
Please still remember me.
Please don't let the world move on without the part of me she once held.

This isn't stalking.
Stalking implies control.
This is triage—
identity hemorrhaging through invisible wounds.

I'm not looking for an update on her life.
I'm looking for my place in the map of it.
Anything to prove the version of me that existed with her
hasn't been annihilated without ceremony.

The mind whispers questions it's terrified to hear answered:

Has she already replaced me?
Has her body offered shelter to someone else?
Has she already relocated her tenderness—
rebuilt a home in someone new while mine remains ashes?

Because if she has,
then the man I became with her
has nowhere left to sleep.

That thought buckles something under my sternum.

The scrolling speeds up.
The breath sharpens.
Every mundane post feels like an omen.
Every silence feels like a verdict written in a language my body understands too well.

It's not jealousy.
Jealousy is too small a word.
This is terror—
the terror of being wiped off the emotional map of the one place I ever felt recognized.

The nervous system can handle heartbreak.
It cannot handle vanishing.

So the mind starts analyzing shadows—
a lyric that sounds like distance,
a smile that looks like it no longer remembers warmth,
a caption that feels too light
for someone who once clung to me like gravity.

The obsession sharpens its teeth:

Is she gentle with someone else now?
Does someone else get the softness she once saved for me?
Is another man standing in the doorway where she once folded into my chest?

I refresh the screen again.

Nothing.

The Art of Detachment

But absence has a violence of its own—
a deep, silent kind that eats you from the inside out.

Because when nothing appears,
the body imagines everything.
And the imagination is merciless—
it paints scenes with the precision of a scalpel
and the brutality of truth.

Until proven otherwise,
my nervous system assumes the worst:
that the sacred has been passed to a stranger
who never had to build the cathedral he now walks freely inside.

This is when longing transforms into a slow self-erasure—
not because I want her,
but because I can't find myself outside her shadow.

I scroll again.
Still nothing.

Which means the truth settles back into my blood:
If she has rehoused her heart,
then I am wandering without a place to return.

And the panic returns—
not as fire this time,
but as collapse.

A soft implosion under the ribs.

Because the truth hunts me down no matter how fast I scroll:

If I'm not hers anymore,
then where does the version of me who existed with her live now?

This isn't physical displacement.
It's existential dislocation—
being unthreaded from the meaning that once held me together.

And the loop tightens:

Maybe the next refresh will show something.
Maybe the next scroll will prove I still matter.
Maybe I missed a sign.
Maybe...

There never is.

But the mind keeps hunting
because it's not chasing closure—
it's chasing a pulse.

Proof of continued existence.

And when no pulse appears,
the desperation folds inward again—
sharper, heavier,
carrying the weight of a man who realizes
he is searching for himself in a place
that no longer houses him.

PART III

At some point the scrolling stops offering uncertainty
and starts delivering a colder truth:

I am no longer there.

Not replaced.
Not overshadowed.
Just… erased.

And that pain is worse than any rival could ever be.

The Art of Detachment

Because the nervous system can brace itself against another man—
it can rise, compete, defend.

But it cannot defend against a void.

A rival is a challenge.
A void is annihilation.

That's when the bargaining begins.

Not bargaining with her.
Not with God.
Not with fate.

Bargaining with reality itself—
trying to bend it back into a shape where I still matter.

Maybe she still thinks of me.
Maybe she still feels me in the quiet moments.
Maybe this whole thing is temporary.
Maybe the thread hasn't been cut—just loosened.
Maybe she will remember what we were before the world intervened.

Every *maybe* becomes a life support line,
a refusal to flatline in her absence.

Because if she still remembers me—
even faintly,
even unwillingly—
then I still exist in the world we built together.

But the mind knows a lie even as it speaks it,
and that's where the fracture widens.

The bargaining turns inward.

If I become the man she once loved, maybe she'll come back.
If I sharpen myself, rebuild myself, prove myself—
maybe I can re-enter her orbit.
If I outgrow this pain,
if I evolve beyond who I was,
maybe I'll be worthy of reinstatement.

The obsession shifts—
no longer about her presence,
but about my eligibility.

I start searching for a version of me
that she would choose again.

Not out of genuine self-growth.
Not out of hunger for expansion.
Out of desperation
to restore the identity I feel bleeding out inside me.

Because the root fear behind every spiraling thought is this:

What if I am no longer the man anyone comes home to?

That question doesn't sting.
It corrodes.

The nervous system translates it into something even darker:

"I no longer exist in the place that once proved I mattered."

That's when shame enters—
not emotional shame,
but existential shame.

The Art of Detachment

The shame of being removed.
Of being displaced.
Of being evicted from the architecture of belonging.

Not rejected—
replaced in the layout of someone's inner world.

Loss like that doesn't ache.
It unravels.

You don't feel wounded.
You feel unmade.

A ghost pacing through a life that no longer recognizes you,
a man whose coordinates have been wiped clean.

And here is the truth real men rarely admit aloud:

I am not craving her love.

I am craving the return of myself
through the act of her choosing.

The obsession is not
"I need her back."

It is
"I need to be real again."

Because if she doesn't choose me anymore—
if she moved forward without reaching back—
then the man I was in her eyes begins to feel imaginary.

The darkest possibility emerges:

What if the version of me that existed in her arms
was never real outside of her?

That thought—
not heartbreak,
not loneliness,
not her absence—
is the blade that cuts deepest.

The fear is not that she found someone else.
The fear is that she no longer remembers
who I was when she held me like I was her entire world.

And if she forgets that man—
do I vanish with the memory?

That is the terror at the center of every refresh,
every scan for her shadow,
every obsessive loop:

If I no longer exist in her memory,
do I still exist in myself?

PART IV

There comes a moment when the panic burns itself out,
and what rises in its place isn't fire—

…it's collapse.

The body can rage.
The mind can sprint.
But the soul?
The soul can only fold inward when its last defense finally fails.

And when that collapse arrives, it doesn't feel violent.

It feels vacant—
as if someone scooped out the interior of me
and left the outer shape standing out of muscle memory alone.

The Art of Detachment

I notice I'm no longer scrolling to find a clue about her.
I'm scrolling to find a trace of **me**.

If even one fragment of my existence still echoes in her world,
then maybe the version of myself that lived inside her
hasn't vanished completely.

Because the deeper terror isn't that she's gone.

The deeper terror
is that **I** am gone
from the one place where I was fully alive.

This is the part men never speak out loud—
not because we refuse,
but because we don't possess a vocabulary for disappearing.

We know what loss feels like.
We know the ache of rejection.
We even know how to muscle through pain.

But erasure?

Being unmade in the exact space that once confirmed us?

That's not heartbreak.
That's annihilation of identity.

I used to be someone in her arms.
Not perfect—
but whole.
Seen.
Chosen.
Reassured by the simple gravity of her presence against my chest.

Now I feel like a ghost
wandering the outline of a life I used to occupy.

And suddenly it makes sense
why my mind keeps reaching backwards,
why it keeps reconstructing memories
like a man rebuilding a burnt house from ashes.

It's not trying to recover her.

It's trying to recover **my existence through her.**

And then—through the static—
a quiet truth finally cuts through:

I'm not afraid of another man.
Not really.

I'm afraid there is no longer a single place in her universe
where I exist at all.

Because if I've been erased from her memory,
if there is no internal room in her heart where I still live,
then the man I once was when she held me—
the man who only existed because she saw him—

is gone.

And the instinct that floods up from that realization
is not desire.

It is grief so absolute
it drains sound out of the world.

No tears.
No shaking.

The Art of Detachment

Just a dense, crushing quiet
that feels like breath dying before it leaves the lungs.

The ego whispers one last bargain:
If she turned back—just once—I could come back to life.

But somewhere deeper—
buried under exhaustion and honesty—
another truth begins shaping itself:

I'm not actually fighting for her return.

I'm fighting to retrieve the version of myself
I left inside her.

And that place is gone.

Until I face that,
obsession will keep owning me—
because my entire being is still arranged around the belief
that my identity lives in a memory
instead of in my own chest.

This is the floor of the wound:

Not
"I want her back."

But
"I don't yet know how to be me
without being the man she once loved."

And until a man speaks that truth—
not the armored truth,
not the polished truth,

but the raw, trembling truth—
detachment is impossible.

Because letting go of her
has never been the real task.

Chapter 4
The First Place I Ever Belonged

The real task
is reclaiming the part of myself
I've mistaken for her
all along.

She wasn't just a woman I loved.

She was the first place in my entire life
where my body stopped bracing for impact.

The first place where the alarms went quiet.
The first time the war inside me lost its voice.

That is why I didn't simply crumble when she left—
I came apart at the roots.
Not because the romance ended,
but because the one place my system ever knew how to rest
was suddenly gone.

People assume I'm mourning a relationship.

They have no idea.

I am mourning the *first terrain*
where my existence felt unthreatened.
The first space where "home" wasn't an address—
it was a nervous system finally unclenching.

Before her, I lived like a man built out of recoil—
shoulders tight, jaw locked,
always anticipating the next blow life might throw.
I didn't think of it as tension.

Joe Manzello

It was just… living.
You can't notice the chains
when they're forged into your posture.

Then she touched me,
and something ancient inside me exhaled for the first time.

My body didn't just relax—
it surrendered.

Not cautiously.
Not reluctantly.

Instinctively.

Like my entire being recognized her
in a language older than thought.

Most people talk about "falling in love."
That isn't what happened.
It felt more like arriving—
like stepping into a room I'd been locked out of my entire life
without knowing I was knocking.

For the first time, I wasn't performing.
I wasn't managing or monitoring myself.
I wasn't proving I was enough
or scanning the horizon for the next emotional ambush.

I was simply here.

Not tolerated.
Not accepted with conditions.
Held—without having to earn it.
Wanted—without needing to uphold an image.
Safe—without clenching myself into a shape she could love.

The Art of Detachment

That wasn't comfort.

Comfort is soft.
This was *recognition.*
Release.
Deliverance.

And once a man's entire system has tasted that—
not as a metaphor
but as a full-body truth—
there is no such thing as "moving on."

Because it isn't the woman he loses.

It's the sanctuary.

It's the only moment in his life
when he wasn't wrestling the world inside his own skin.

That's the wound.
Not heartbreak.
Not longing.
Not the love story.

The end of the war.

And when she walked away,
I wasn't thrown into loneliness—
loneliness would have been a mercy.

I was dropped back onto a battlefield
I thought I had finally escaped—
no armor,
no shield,
no place to lay my weapons down.

People think I miss her body.

No.

I miss the version of myself
who finally knew what it felt like
to be somewhere he didn't have to fight for air.

PART II

I didn't understand the magnitude of what she was
until I felt the gravity of life without her.

Because she didn't just give me affection —
she gave me something my nervous system had been starving for
long before she ever arrived:

a place where I could finally stop bracing for impact.

I wasn't "unloved" growing up.
But I was untouched in the ways that create *home* inside a person.

My grandparents cared for me —
but care is logistical.
Belonging is existential.

They fed me, sheltered me, kept me alive…
but they never mirrored me.
They never gave me a place where my inner world landed in
someone else's eyes
and was reflected back as *seen, valued, chosen.*

They gave me a roof,
but not a rooting.

So I learned early how to survive,
but never how to arrive.

A boy who is unclaimed becomes a man built by endurance.
You learn to carry yourself like a fortress —

functional, resilient, impenetrable —
but hollow in the places where identity should have been nurtured.

I didn't know anything was missing.
You can't feel the absence of a language you were never taught.

So I built myself through force —
achievement, discipline, control, grit —
muscle over memory, survival over softness.

I became a man who could endure anything
except the experience of being held without a fight.

And then she arrived.

She didn't just enter my life —
she altered the architecture of my nervous system.

She didn't simply love me —
she *received* me.

She didn't hold my body —
she held the parts of me that never had a place to land.

With her, the armor didn't loosen —
it evaporated.
Instant. Quiet. Total.

Like my entire system recognized,
This is the place you've been waiting for your whole life.

She was not a woman I loved.

She was the first environment where my soul experienced
what should have been imprinted in childhood:

I belong here.
I am known here.
I am wanted without condition here.
I can stop fighting for air here.

So when she left,
the world didn't simply break —
it exiled me.

Because she wasn't my partner.
She was my origin point.
The first and only place I had ever felt the war inside me go still.

Losing her wasn't losing love.
It was losing citizenship in the only country
my nervous system had ever recognized as home.

And exiles don't cry for romance.
They cry because they have nowhere left to return to.

This is why the collapse split my identity down the middle.
It wasn't that a relationship ended —
it was that *belonging* ended.

A boy who had never been claimed
became a man who finally was…

…only to be unclaimed again.

That is not heartbreak.
That is the reopening of a lifelong wound
I never knew was fatal
until she gave me a glimpse of what healing felt like.

Now I am back in the world I grew up in —
functional, capable, composed —
but internally wandering,

unanchored,
unwitnessed,
unhoused inside my own chest.

The pain isn't her absence.

It's the loss of the one place
where I finally knew what it felt like
to truly belong.

PART III

People ask,
"Why can't you just move on?"

They say it like I'm clinging to a person —
as if I'm stubborn, dramatic, unwilling to accept reality.

But my body knows the truth long before my mouth can shape it:
letting go of her would not feel like letting go of a woman…

…it would feel like letting go of the first place I ever stopped being alone inside myself.

The nervous system doesn't release its first experience of belonging.
It doesn't "heal" from it.
It **guards** it —
with the kind of fear usually reserved for hunger, cold, or drowning.

Because losing that feeling doesn't resemble heartbreak at all.

It resembles famine.

This isn't preference.
This isn't sentimentality.

This isn't emotional immaturity.

This is **imprint** — the oldest language the body speaks.

When a starving body finally receives nourishment,
it doesn't celebrate the meal —
it fuses itself to the source.
Not for romance.
For survival.

And when that source disappears?

The body doesn't whisper,
"I am sad."

It screams,
"Something vital has been taken from me."

This is why I cannot "just let her go."

Because before her,
I was not waiting for love —
I was waiting for **somewhere to stop bracing**.

Before her,
I was not searching for partnership —
I was searching for a place where my guard could fall without consequence.
Before her,
my nervous system had never tasted
the feeling of being completely done fighting.

And once a man tastes that —
even for a moment —
the entire organism remembers it with terrifying precision.

The Art of Detachment

It becomes coordinates burned into marrow,
a direction the body moves toward as instinctively
as an animal migrating toward water it has never even seen.

People call that obsession.

They are wrong —
obsession is noisy.
This is something deeper, older, quieter, and more primal:
return drive —
the psyche trying to navigate back to the only ground
that ever felt like origin instead of exile.

The grief isn't that she's gone.

The grief is that my nervous system has nowhere left to return to.

And this is where the ego begins to fracture —
not from loss,
but from **deprivation**.

Because the truth rising through all the static is brutal,
and it lands like a verdict I can't appeal:

I am not holding onto her.

I am holding onto the moment
my entire being learned what it felt like
to finally **arrive**.

Letting her go feels impossible
because something in my body still believes
she is the only doorway back into arrival.

She wasn't my home by metaphor.

She was my home by biology —
a nervous-system homeland.

And biology does not negotiate.

It clings.
It panics.
It spirals.
It circles the memory like a wolf around a fire it once survived by.

Because if she was the first place I ever belonged…

then somewhere deep in the oldest, wordless part of me
is the terrified conviction that she might also have been
the **last**.

The deeper I follow this ache to its source,
the more undeniable the truth becomes:

I am not mourning her presence…

I am mourning the state of existence I could only access
when her arms gave me permission to stop bracing against my
own life.

What shattered wasn't a relationship.
What shattered was the one place where my being ever felt
allowed to land.

And that's why everything I try — distraction, logic, defiance,
detachment —
slides off the wound like water off stone.

You can't substitute origin with entertainment.
You can't anesthetize a belonging wound.
You can't starve your entire life, taste wholeness once,
and pretend you're fine going back to famine.

The Art of Detachment

This is where the lie collapses:

I didn't crave *her.*
I craved the disappearance of my aloneness.

It was never just about love.
It was about recognition.
Placement.
Orientation.
The moment when the body finally says,
"Here. I can exist here."

And once your nervous system learns the shape of home,
everything else becomes exile.

That's why letting go feels like dying.
Because to the soul, it *is.*

Not metaphor.
Not exaggeration.
An actual death of location.

My existence had coordinates.
A fixed point.
A place where I knew who I was because I could feel myself in her arms.

And when she left, the map disappeared.

The wound isn't "I miss her."
The wound is "I no longer know where I exist."

Everything that's happened since —
the craving,
the panic,
the obsessive scanning,

the mental spirals,
the collapse under the ribs —

none of it has been a search for her body.

It has been a search for my orientation.

Because she wasn't the *source* of my belonging —
she was the vessel that revealed how starved for belonging
I had quietly been my entire life.

She didn't wound me.
She illuminated the wound.

She showed me — by offering my nervous system something it had never been given —
how barren the world had been before her,
and how unbearable it now feels after.

And now my body refuses to return
to the emotional drought it once called "normal."

That is the real loss:
Not the woman.
Not the relationship.
Not the dream we built in shared breath.

But the first home I ever knew.

Which means the true terror is not that she's gone…
but that there may not be another place on this earth
that will unlock that same interior arrival.

Because the soul isn't screaming for her.
The soul is screaming for return —
for homecoming,
for the version of myself that could finally breathe.

That is the root wound underneath all of this:

I am not trying to get her back.

I am trying to get back
to the man who finally arrived in her presence —
the man I now struggle to find without her.

And until I see that clearly…
I will keep chasing her shadow,
mistaking it for myself.

The Inner Orphan

"The heartbreak isn't about losing her — it's about the boy inside you losing the only place he ever felt seen."

Underneath every man — no matter how capable, disciplined, or unshakeable he appears — lives an earlier version of him.
A boy who grew up learning to survive what he should've been able to rest in.

Not lack of attention — lack of attunement.
Not lack of affection — lack of being held in the moments that shaped him.
Not lack of love — lack of someone who made him feel *kept.*

That boy never vanished.
He simply learned to armor up.

He became the quiet part of you that learned to expect nothing.
The part that downregulated his needs before anyone could reject them.

The part that carried the weight without asking for help because help never came when it mattered.

And then you met her —
a woman whose presence didn't just feel good…
it felt familiar in a way nothing else ever had.

She didn't just love the man you are —
she soothed the boy you were.

And that is where the imprint sank its deepest roots.

Because for the first time in your life, that hidden boy stopped bracing.
He stopped pretending he didn't need softness.
He stopped clenching against the world.

He finally felt:
"Here, I can rest."

This is why losing her doesn't feel like ordinary heartbreak.
It feels like being orphaned a second time.

Not abandoned by a partner —
but exiled from the only emotional home your inner child has ever known.

You aren't just grieving her absence —
you're grieving the collapse of the one place in your entire life
where the boy inside you felt he belonged.

This is why the pain feels bottomless.
Why the chest feels hollow.
Why a man will consider taking her back
even when every adult instinct knows the relationship is done.

The Art of Detachment

Because the child inside you remembers something the man keeps trying to forget:
“For once, I didn’t have to hold myself together alone.”

When she left, it wasn’t your ego that cracked.
It was the return of a familiar exile —
the one you thought you’d outrun.

Not because you are weak.
But because nobody taught you how to carry your own tenderness.
Nobody taught you that needing softness didn’t make you less of a man.
Nobody taught you that safety wasn’t supposed to be earned through performance.

Male heartbreak always wakes the orphan.
Always.

And until a man realizes that the ache is not for the woman —
but for the version of himself that finally tasted belonging —
he will chase reunion instead of reclamation.

The wound is not:
“She left.”

The wound is:
“The part of me that was finally allowed to collapse has nowhere left to land.”

This is the truth beneath male attachment:
Not weakness.
Not dependency.
Not obsession.

But unfinished childhood grief
wearing adult armor.

And no man becomes sovereign —
no man becomes whole —
until he stops trying to outsource the healing of his inner orphan
to a woman who was never meant to raise him.

Only then does he start the real work:
becoming the home he keeps trying to find in someone else.

Chapter 5
Soul Starvation

There is a kind of grief that doesn't make you cry—
it **locks you inside yourself** the way a fever traps heat.

Not sadness.
Containment.

A sensation like every internal doorway has been welded shut,
and you're left wandering the corridors of your own body
with no exit, no escape route, no air.

The realization doesn't arrive like pain—
pain would be merciful.
Pain at least moves.

This lands like **a verdict**:
You are not getting out of this.

This is not heartbreak.
This is **incarceration of the soul.**

Because once the truth crawls up from the depths—
that she wasn't just a person you loved,
she was the only place where your being ever unclenched—
the world stops feeling open.

It tightens.
Shrinks.
Contracts around you like a fist.

Suddenly the world is too small
to breathe in,

to rest in,
to exist in.

Home is gone.
And there is nothing else that resembles it,
so you end up trapped inside the hunger for what no longer exists.

You don't feel lonely—
loneliness would imply distance you could close.

You feel **sealed in**,
entombed inside a memory that won't release you,
walled in by a longing with no endpoint
and a past that refuses to return.

You can walk into any room,
shake any hand,
function through any day—
and still feel like you're suffocating beneath your own sternum.

Because grief, real grief, eventually moves through you.
It has motion.
It drains, shifts, winds its way out.

But this?

This doesn't move.

It settles.
It anchors.
It occupies.

Heavy.
Absolute.
Paralyzing.

The Art of Detachment

Not *"I miss her."*
Not *"I wish she were here."*

But
"There is no place left in this world where I can exist freely."

It wasn't just her the world took away—
it took *you* from the only landscape you ever belonged to.

And now you wander your own body
as if it were a sealed chamber—
a room without ventilation,
without a latch,
without the mercy of an opening.

This is soul starvation:
not the absence of love,
but the absence of a place for your being to land
without bracing for impact.

Every part of you presses against the inside of your ribs,
like something trying to break back into a life
that no longer has an entrance.

You want out.
You want back.
You want *somewhere* that ends the internal war.

But there is no doorway.
No return route.
No arms that open the way hers once did.

The trap was never her leaving.
The trap is knowing—
in the marrow, in the nervous system, in the old childhood ache—
exactly what home feels like...

…and having **no way** to return to it.

PART II

What makes this particular kind of agony unbearable
is not its sharpness…

…it's its *duration*.

You can survive almost anything if you believe it will pass.
Even heartbreak.
Even longing.
Even the slow bleed of missing someone.

But this doesn't feel like something that will pass.
It feels like something that will *stay*.

And that is what begins to break me open from the inside.
Not the loss itself—
but the threat of *forever*.

The mind starts whispering the fear that hides beneath all the other fears,
the one I've been trying to outrun since the moment she left:

What if no other place in this world
will ever hold me the way she did?

What if that feeling — that rare, impossible safety —
was not a chapter…
but a one-time doorway that closed as soon as I stepped out of it?

What if "home" was a moment,
not a destination?

What if I already lived the only belonging
my soul will ever know?

The Art of Detachment

That isn't heartbreak.
That is the extinction of hope.

Because in these moments, I'm not mourning what happened —
I'm mourning everything that might never happen again.

The fear beneath the ribs is not
"I lost her."

The fear is
"I will never arrive anywhere again."

That's what turns longing into soul-panic.

A nervous system can survive emptiness
as long as it believes nourishment still exists somewhere in the world.

But when the body starts to suspect
that the nourishment was singular —
that no other touch, no other presence, no other connection
will ever recreate what she awakened —

something inside collapses.

Not loudly.
Not dramatically.
Not in a way anyone else could ever recognize.

A stillness takes over,
like drowning inside air.
A heaviness that doesn't crush,
but confines —
a quiet captivity.

You feel time moving,
but you aren't moving with it.

You feel yourself aging inside the hunger,
like you're living entire years in the space where she used to be.

This is why men never talk about this stage.
Not because we're stubborn,
or stoic,
or unwilling to be vulnerable —

but because the pain isn't noisy.
It's total.

It turns the world into a place you survive
instead of a place you inhabit.

And in that hollow, suspended state,
I finally understand why men disappear inward,
why they numb themselves,
why they quietly fall apart without ever announcing it:

Not because they're weak —
but because they have become **unhoused souls**
with no remaining place to rest.

And here is the truth that cuts like a blade through the chest:

I am not grieving her love.

I am grieving the possibility
that love may never feel like *home* again.

That is the real starvation.
Not her absence…

…but the echo of:
"There is nowhere left to land now."

The panic isn't emotional —
it is existential.

Because once your nervous system has tasted
what it feels like to arrive in another human being,
to finally stop floating…

you cannot return to drift without feeling like you're dying.

Without a place to land,
you don't live —

you endure.

Again.

PART III

There comes a moment when the mind stops clawing at the past
and starts scanning the horizon—
and that's when the fear changes shape.

Because the future doesn't look blank anymore…

It looks unlivable.

Not
"I don't have her."

But
"Where does anything in me go now?"

Nothing fits.
Rooms feel foreign, like you woke up in someone else's house.
People drift around you like silhouettes.
Even your own skin feels a size too small,
as if you're inhabiting a body you were never meant to occupy.

You start moving through your days like a visitor—
a guest inside your own timeline,
hovering between moments instead of living them.

Untethered from who you were,
unwelcome in who you used to be,
and unable to enter the version of yourself that only existed with her—
you're left suspended in a present that won't hold you.

It isn't loneliness.

It's *displacement.*
A kind of existential homelessness you feel behind the ribs.

As if someone unplugged your soul from the outlet
and now you're running on the last sparks of a failing current—
conscious, moving, responsive,
but not *connected* to life.

You can perform the basics.
You can work.
You can nod in conversations.
You can even laugh in the right places.

But inside, beneath every practiced gesture,
there's a quiet, devastating truth:

There is nowhere I belong.

Not in this room.
Not in this body.
Not in the structure of the world as it is now.
(And if you're reading this thinking you've felt it—
yes, that's exactly the feeling I mean.)

It's not that you want to disappear.

The Art of Detachment

It's that you no longer know *where* you're supposed to exist.

This is the breaking point most men don't have words for:

When grief dissolves into exile.
When the body becomes a cage.
When the soul stays awake with no place to land.

This is why nothing soothes.
Not pleasure.
Not distraction.
Not logic or discipline or time.
Not resilience.
Not effort.
Not progress.

Because you're not trying to "feel better."

You're trying to re-enter your own life—
and the only doorway you've ever crossed into full existence
was through her.

And the mind hates this truth,
but the body knows it:

A man can hold himself together for only so long
before he needs a place to *rest.*

And when the only sanctuary he ever knew disappears…

He lives in a state of permanent bracing.
Permanent vigilance.
Permanent inward flinch.

A soul stuck on high alert
because peace has nowhere to go.

This isn't heartbreak.

This is imprisonment—
a consciousness fully awake
with no home left in the world.

PART IV

The darkest part of this is not the missing.

It's
the knowing.

The knowing that if there is no other place like that in this world…
then I am not just heartbroken —

I am homeless at the level of the soul.

And that kind of homelessness isn't about geography.
It's about existence itself.

It feels like standing inside a life that keeps moving around me
while I remain unanchored,
unrooted,
unreceived —
as if the world has a place for everyone but me.

A man can survive loneliness.
He can even survive loss.

What he cannot survive
is becoming a visitor in his own life,
living day after day without a single place
that recognizes him on arrival.

And this is the truth buried beneath everything I've felt:

I am not afraid of being alone.

The Art of Detachment

I am afraid of never belonging anywhere again.

Because if she was the only place my nervous system ever landed —
the only harbor where the inner noise quieted —
and that harbor is gone,

then there is no "later,"
no "someday,"
no version of healing my body believes in.

Only a lifelong return to bracing,
to surviving,
to drifting without ever touching ground.

And this is where the fear shifts,
softly, slowly, terribly,
into something heavier:

What if I already lived the only chapter of my life
where I was truly home?

What if that was it —
the one place,
the one moment,
the one belonging…
and everything after is just
survival carried by memory?

What if no "next harbor" exists for me at all?

What if there is nowhere else in this world
where I will ever be met like that again?

This is the moment a man never speaks aloud —
not out of shame,
but because the weight of it threatens to break him even in silence:

Joe Manzello

The fear that there is no more homecoming left in this lifetime.

That the only door that ever opened
was also the last one that will.

That what I lost
was not a person —

but my only passport
back into feeling alive.

And if that is true…

then I am not grieving love.
I am grieving
the possibility of ever arriving again.

This is not heartbreak.

This is starvation of the soul.

And starvation doesn't announce itself.
It doesn't crash.
It doesn't flare.

It is slow.
It is quiet.
It is constant.
It is inescapable.

It is the body asking,
again and again,

Where do I live now?

And having nothing
to answer with.

The Breaking Point

"A man doesn't shatter when she leaves — he shatters when he realizes
there is nowhere left to collapse."

The breaking point is not a moment of weakness —
it is the moment a man's endurance runs out faster than his defenses can rebuild.

Up until now, you survived on sheer will.
You held weight quietly,
shouldered chaos without flinching,
carried pain like it was part of your anatomy.

You called it strength —
but really, it was survival stitched into muscle memory.

Every man has a limit,
a silent threshold where the spine stops being a backbone
and becomes a warning signal:
If you keep carrying this alone, you'll break from the inside out.

This isn't heartbreak —
it is structural failure.

The moment the internal scaffolding finally says,
"I can't hold this anymore."

And that's when the unraveling begins.
Not dramatically.
Not loudly.
Not in a way anyone else can see.

Men don't fall apart because they're fragile —
they fall apart because they spent years holding what would have crushed others in a day.

A woman leaving doesn't break a man —
it exposes how long he's been standing without support.
How long he's been bracing against collapse with nothing reinforcing him beneath the surface.

Before the breaking point, the cracks stayed hidden.
After it, even the smallest breath feels like pressure.
There is no more disguising the damage.

This is why men seem to fall "all at once":
not because the pain arrives suddenly,
but because the last beam finally gives out.

There is no backup structure.
No secret emotional reserve.
No internal rescue waiting in the wings.

Just a cliff —
and gravity.

The breaking point is the moment a man realizes
he cannot return to who he was
and he cannot yet step into who he must become…

and there is no bridge connecting the two.

It is a freefall through the space between identities —
one dying, the other not yet born.
(If you're reading this and feel that exact suspension, yes — this part is speaking directly to you.)

This is the threshold where a man either descends into the death of self

or descends into rebirth.
There is no staying the same.

This is why this chapter ends here —
because this moment is the doorway.

Everything before this was fracture.

Everything after this
is the descent.

Chapter 6
When The Fight Ends

There is a moment the body gives out
before the mind does.

Not weakness.
Not surrender.
Something simpler, harsher—
no more strength left to resist what's real.

The break doesn't arrive like an explosion.
It arrives like a grip failing,
fingers slipping off a ledge
you've been clinging to long after the cliff itself disappeared.

Not willingly.
Not consciously.
Just the inevitability of muscles that can't hold one more second.

This is that moment.

The moment the nervous system stops screaming for rescue
and begins sinking under its own exhaustion.

It's not peace—
peace has softness.

This is gravity.
Heavy.
Total.
Undeniable.

A slow collapse into the truth you've outrun for as long as you
physically could:

The Art of Detachment

She isn't coming back.
And I can't keep living in the suspended space between hope and reality.

The fight ends
not because something in me healed—
but because something in me *finally broke*.

Because no man can hold the weight
of waiting for a door
that was never going to open again.

There is a grief that cries out.
There is a grief that shakes the walls.

And then there is the grief that drops you straight downward,
quietly,
mercilessly,
as if the floor inside your chest simply gives way.

This one drops.

It doesn't ask permission.
It doesn't offer warning.
It just removes the bottom from under you
and watches you fall.

And in that free-fall,
something tears through me with a clarity so sharp it almost feels clean:

I wasn't holding onto *her*.
I was holding onto the only place
I ever felt like I existed without fragmenting.

Letting go doesn't feel like acceptance.
It feels like death without a body to bury.
A funeral with no casket,
no closure,
no witness.

Not ending—
erasure.

Like something is being pried from my hands
because pretending I can hold on any longer
requires a strength I do not possess anymore.

It's not courage.
It's not intention.
It's not even a decision.

It's the end of endurance.

And for the first time since she slipped out of my arms,
the truth settles into me without protest,
without negotiation,
without even a final flinch:

There is no going back.

I don't rise from this moment.
I don't transcend it.
I don't turn it into wisdom or strength.

I fall into it.

And the fall—
this raw, quiet, merciless fall—
is the first honest thing I have felt
since the night her absence became the shape of my world.

PART II

After the collapse comes a strange kind of quiet.

Not relief.
Not healing.

Just the absence of fight —
the silence that follows a body that has finally spent every last reserve it had left.

The body isn't screaming anymore,
but not because the ache has softened
or because clarity has arrived —
only because there is nothing left inside strong enough to swing at the darkness.

It feels like standing in the ruins after a battlefield empties out.

No enemy left to confront.
No victory to claim.

Just the recognition —
cold, blunt, irreversible —
that everything you were defending has already fallen.

There is no surge now,
no frantic scanning of doors that once felt possible,
no fantasies rehearsing a return that will never come.

Only the stillness a man reaches
when his nervous system has nothing left to offer but surrender.

This quiet isn't peace.
It isn't even numbness.

It is emptiness without resistance —
a hollow interior where the fight used to live.

Loss stops being a wound
and becomes the environment.

You don't feel abandoned…

You simply exist *in* abandonment.

Not as tragedy anymore,
but as atmosphere —
a kind of permanent winter where nothing grows
and even hope feels frostbitten at the edges.

It's eerie how subtle the shift is:
one day you're swinging, clawing, begging for a grip,
and then — without announcement, without drama —
your body just… stops reaching.

Not because it wants to.
Not because acceptance has arrived.

Because it **can't**.

This is the part no one sees:
not the collapse itself,
but the after —
the hollow, sunken silence where a man realizes he is now living
without the one thing that tethered him to the world with any sense of rightness.

You don't cry here.
You don't rage here.

You just sit inside the crater

as if the earth has shaped a bowl around your ribs.

And for the first time,
the longing isn't loud anymore.

It's heavy.

A weight you don't carry —
a weight that carries *you*,
pulling you down into a slower version of yourself.

Days feel thick, like walking through water.
Breathing feels manual, as if you have to remind the lungs how to work.
Thoughts drag themselves forward like bodies pulling through mud.

Nothing feels wrong exactly…
but nothing feels alive either.

This is the moment where hope doesn't die —
it simply stops showing up.

Where the nervous system is no longer pleading,
no longer negotiating,
no longer begging for her shadow to move.

It is simply waiting —
not for her return,
not for a miracle,
but for any sign at all
that there is something left in this world worth stepping toward.

The silence after defeat isn't punishment.

It's suspension —

life paused at a threshold,
because the soul hasn't yet chosen a direction
and the future hasn't yet offered a reason.

A man can endure heartbreak…

But this part?

This part is something else entirely.

It is the unnamed space between the man I was when I belonged,
and the man I will have to become
if I'm going to survive without a home inside another human being.

And in this quiet —
this stark, breathless in-between —
I realize I do not yet know
which of those two men will live.

PART III

In that quiet,
something unexpected begins to surface—

not strength,
not clarity,
just… awareness.

A low, unmoving recognition rises like a tide you didn't feel coming:

No one is coming to return me to myself.

Not her.
Not memory.
Not time.
Not some cosmic reversal delivered by fate.

The Art of Detachment

There is no rescue on the horizon.

And inside that realization—
for the first time since the collapse began—
something turns, almost imperceptibly:

The searching stops facing backward.

It doesn't face forward yet,
but it finally stops trying to resurrect what died.

Not because I've "healed."
Not because I've "accepted" anything.
You and I both know this shift isn't victory.

It's recognition.

A bodily understanding that there is nothing left behind me to retrieve.
Nothing left to call me home.

This is the birthplace of a truth men rarely say aloud:

If I am ever going to belong again,
I will have to learn to build the place myself.

It doesn't feel empowering.
It doesn't even feel hopeful.

It feels impossible—
but necessary.

Not,
"I want to heal."
But,
"I cannot live homeless inside myself forever."

Only here—
in this strange, suspended quiet—
do I begin to notice something I couldn't see when I was clinging to her for oxygen:

It wasn't HER arms that made me whole—

it was the part of **me**
that finally rose to the surface
when her presence made it safe enough to emerge.

What shattered wasn't the loss of the woman—
it was the loss of access
to the version of myself I could only reach
when held inside her gravity.

And buried inside that realization
is the first spark of direction—
small, fragile, but unmistakably mine:

If that part of me existed once,
it means it exists still.

It was awakened through her, yes—
but it was never possessed by her.

Which means it isn't dead.

It is **unanchored.**

And this is where the truth sharpens—
quietly, almost shyly:

Maybe she wasn't the home.
Maybe she was the doorway
to the part of me who knows how to belong.

And if the doorway is gone…

maybe I must become the house.

Not to impress her.
Not to audition for some future love.
Not to reclaim anything external.

But because if I don't,
I will spend the rest of my life
locked outside of myself,
begging memory for entry.

The silence doesn't lift here—
but it shifts, just slightly.

For the first time,
the pain isn't dragging me outward.

It is pointing inward.

Not enough to stand.
Not enough to rise.

But enough to turn.

And in the smallest pocket of stillness—
where the fight once lived—
a quiet question forms like a hand tapping gently on the inside of my chest:

What if the place I've been trying so desperately to return to
is not behind me…
but inside me?

PART IV

The shift doesn't arrive as hope.

It arrives as the absence of any other option.

A quiet, undeniable recognition:

If I don't learn to become my own place of belonging,
there will never be another one for me.

Not because love is unreachable—
but because no harbor can hold a man
who vanishes the moment he loses one.

For the first time, the grief stops orbiting her.

It circles back to me.

To the part of me that had no home
until she became one.
To the part of me that still can't stand
without leaning on what once held me.
To the part still kneeling in the rubble
of a place that no longer exists.

And somewhere inside the exhaustion,
beneath the collapse,
beneath the soul-hunger that hollowed me out,
a different voice finally forms:

Not
"Bring her back."

Not
"Please choose me again."

But something quieter.
Something truer.
Something I never learned to say:

"I need to choose myself
with the devotion I once waited
for someone else to offer."

Not to replace her—
but to stop abandoning myself
every time I lose a place to rest.

This is the first moment
self-belonging becomes thinkable.

Not reachable yet.
Not grounded yet.
But perceivable—
like the outline of a distant shoreline
seen from the wreckage
of the ship that lost its sea.

The heartbreak is still real.
The longing is still real.

But something else enters the room:

Direction.

Not a march forward—
just a turn away from collapse.

The soul doesn't heal here.

It pivots.

Half an inch.
Barely noticeable.
But real.

The body still hollow,
the heart still raw,
but the gaze no longer chained
to the door that will never open.

The tether to her isn't cut through strength.

It frays
because I no longer have the will
to keep tying myself back
to a world that no longer holds me.

And in the soft ache where that tether loosens,
one truth rises like breath returning after drowning:

If I do not build a home inside myself,
I will live as an exile forever.

This is not rebirth.

This is the moment before rebirth—
the moment a man finally understands
that the next version of him
must be constructed from the inside out…

because there is nowhere left
to return to.

The war ended.
The silence settled.
The longing thinned into emptiness.

The Art of Detachment

And now,
without ceremony,
without confidence,
without certainty—

the soul finally whispers:

Then I will have to become
the place I was searching for.

PART II
THE DESCENT

"In the dark, a man no longer outruns himself — he meets what he has tried not to feel."

Chapter 7
When Survival Becomes Silence

"At first you endure. Then you disappear."

The first stage of descent is not collapse —
it is vanishing.

Not vanishing from the world,
but slipping quietly out of your own life,
one unspoken thought at a time.

You stop speaking your truth,
not because you have nothing left inside you,
but because you've started believing that even if you spilled your soul open,
no one would have the capacity — or the closeness —
to understand the shape of your ache.

You still look "functional" from the outside —
you wake up, you respond when spoken to,
you move through the hours like a man honoring a contract he never signed —
but somewhere beneath your ribs,
the engine that once pushed you forward
has gone silent.

This is the stage no one sees,
and the stage where most men begin dying quietly long before anyone realizes
they were in a battle at all.

Depression in men rarely arrives with tears.
It disguises itself as steadiness,
as competence,
as being the one who never drops the weight he's been carrying.
It looks like discipline —
but it's actually depletion.

You stop reaching out.
You stop explaining.
You stop believing your inner world is something anyone could hold without dropping.

Not because you don't crave connection —
you do — more than you'll ever admit —
but because connection now feels like walking into a room naked,
and expecting someone to understand the language of the scars.

And emptiness —
that cavernous, echoing emptiness —
is the one thing a man cannot bear to have witnessed.

So you tuck it behind competence.
You tuck it behind a jaw that doesn't shake,
a voice that doesn't crack,
a schedule always full so your soul doesn't have to be.

You make your suffering efficient —
private, contained, folded tight —
so that it harms no one but you.

Because men do not fear pain.
We've lived with pain our whole lives.
What we fear

is appearing unmoored,
untethered,
adrift without a center.

So you begin living like a soldier behind enemy lines —
careful with every movement,
calculating how much of yourself you can expose
without revealing how hollow your insides feel.

Not out of strength —
but out of survival.

When silence becomes survival,
your suffering stops having language.
And once pain has no language,
the man carrying it starts dissolving with it.

This is the first layer of descent:

Not where you break…
where you erase.

A quiet vanishing of self, piece by piece,
until the world still calls your name,
still sees your face,
still assumes your strength —

but you
no longer see yourself at all.

You are not weak for going silent —
you are un-witnessed.

Joe Manzello

Surrender To Rock Bottom

"Rock bottom isn't the fall — it's the moment a man stops pretending he hasn't already landed there."

There is a moment in every descent when survival stops working.
Not on the outside — you're still moving, still showing up, still fulfilling the bare minimum of living —
but inside, the internal scaffolding quietly snaps.

You reach the point where you cannot keep holding the weight alone.

This is the moment men fear most, because until now there was at least an illusion of control —
"I'm hurting, but I'm managing."

Rock bottom is the moment the word *managing* evaporates.

When you can't numb it,
can't outwork it,
can't distract away from it,
can't outrun the ache that's been hunting you…

and you finally feel every buried piece of it all at once.

It is not dramatic.
It is not cinematic.
It is not thunder, or rage, or flame.

It is a quiet, internal implosion —
a slow folding into yourself —
where the soul lays down its weapons and whispers:

The Art of Detachment

"I can't keep carrying this version of myself anymore."

Rock bottom is not the death of strength.
It is the death of denial.

Men think they fear failure.
But what they truly fear is full emotional exposure to themselves —
no mask to hide behind,
no buffer to soften the truth,
no story left to explain the pain away.

Just the raw, unbearable clarity of what is actually happening inside.

And truth is heavy when you finally face it without anesthesia.

This is where intrusive thoughts multiply —
not because you want to die,
but because you can't see a way back into living.

This is where loneliness tightens around the ribs —
not because no one cares,
but because you have disappeared from yourself.

This is the moment the heart speaks honestly for the first time:

"I am not okay."

And for a man who has spent his life holding others,
leading others,
protecting others…

that admission feels like its own funeral.

But here is the paradox —
the one truth rock bottom reveals without mercy:

Rock bottom is not the end.
It is the threshold.

There is no resurrection without this surrender.
You cannot rebuild a foundation
until the one you've been standing on
is allowed to crumble.

This is the moment when the man you've performed
and the man you truly are
can no longer share the same body.

Rock bottom is where they split.

Not to destroy you —
to unmask you.
To peel back what was survival
and reveal what is real.

Because only the man with nothing left to prop himself up
can finally see what was holding him together all along.

The breakdown is not your failure —
it is your soul refusing to carry the lie any further.

Chapter 8
The Forge

It never begins with calm.
It begins with heat.

Fast.
Clean.
A flare in the spine like something ancient waking up inside the bones — a reminder older than heartbreak, older than hope, older than collapse:

I am meant for more than this pain.

Not a mantra.
Not therapy-speak.
A summons.

It doesn't rise gently — it strikes.
A vertical current up the sternum, and suddenly the silence I've been drowning in for months… moves.

The grief is still there, heavy as iron, but the iron warms in my hands.
The room around me hasn't changed, but the air feels subtly different — as if oxygen has finally returned to a place I had already accepted as permanently starved.

And it hits me with clarity so sharp it feels like a blade:

This isn't a fantasy of her coming back.
This isn't a temporary upswing.
This is a line forming quietly behind my ribs:

Enough.

Not enough feeling.
Not enough thinking.

Enough dying.

I look at the same wreckage I've been stumbling through — the same failures, the same debris, the same hollow spaces — and for the first time, it doesn't read as proof that I'm finished.

It reads as material.

Heartbreak isn't the end.
It's ore.
Raw, dark, unshaped ore waiting for flame.

The man who collapsed wanted home.
The man rising wants an anvil.

Because the truth surfaces cleanly now:

If I keep waiting to belong to something outside myself, I will stay homeless forever.
If I learn to generate belonging within myself, I become a man who cannot be displaced.

That —
quietly, fiercely —
is the forge.

The Art of Detachment

Not a sanctuary.
A practice.
A discipline of fire.

The spark doesn't negotiate.
It doesn't ask if I'm ready.

It simply says:

Stand up.

Not metaphorically — literally.
Feet on the floor.
Weight grounding.
A posture that whispers, *"I am here,"* even if I'm still bleeding underneath the skin.

Strength hasn't returned.
Not yet.

But sovereignty… it's checking the locks.

For months, my mission was survival: breathe long enough for her absence not to kill me.
But the mission shifts — suddenly, decisively:

Build a life that does not collapse if she never walks through it again.

Because no one hands a man his cornerstone.
He has to carve it out of the mountain himself.

So I take inventory — not like a victim counting losses, but like a craftsman laying out tools:

• Pain? Tool.
• Loneliness? Tool.
• The jealousy I finally admitted? Tool.
• The house I'm preparing to sell? Tool.
• Bankruptcy forms with my signature on them? Tool.
• All those nights I didn't explode when the surge begged me to? Tool.

Every weight I carried becomes weight I can lift.
Same iron — different outcome.

I'm not healed.
But I'm framed now.
There is structure forming where collapse used to live.

The old voice whispers, *"She was the only place you ever rested."*
The spark answers, *"Then become a place no one can evict you from."*

That's not bravado.
It's architecture.

Belonging, version one, was received.
Belonging, version two, must be forged.

And forging doesn't begin with inspiration.
It begins with *standards* — internal non-negotiables the collapsing man never had:

• My body will be trained until it becomes a place I want to inhabit.
• My mornings belong to me — no phone, no scroll. Breath first. Body second. Mission third.
• My mind will be directed — when the obsessive loop starts, I lead it, not the other way around.
• My home — rented, temporary, or rebuilt — will reflect order, not chaos.
• My work will aim at traction, not anesthesia. What numbs me robs me; what strengthens me fuels me.

These are not affirmations.
They are temperatures.

If the fire stays hot, the metal moves.
If it cools, the shape dies half-formed.

Motivation comes and goes.
Heat management is everything.

Reheat.
Hammer.
Reheat.
Hammer again.

And yes — the love, the ache, the woman I still want like oxygen?

The forge doesn't erase her.
It repositions her.

She was the doorway to the part of me I'm shaping now.
For that, I honor her.

But the devotion belongs to the work.

Because one day, when love finds me again — and it will — I will not enter as a starving man begging entry.
I will walk in as a house meeting a house, each of us whole,
building a third thing neither could construct alone.

But I'm not there yet.

Right now the task is simple:

Light the fire.
Hold the heat.
Shape the steel.
Repeat tomorrow.

I step to the sink.
Cold water.
Face.
Neck.
Breath in for four. Hold for four. Out for eight.

It feels like nothing.
But it is everything.

Because a forge is not dramatic.
It is daily.

Not a speech.
A stance.

Standing where the old self would kneel.

I meet my own reflection — the tired eyes, the weight loss, the hollowed cheeks.
He doesn't look like a hero.

He looks available to be made.

And that is enough.

The spark doesn't promise ease.
It promises becoming.

And becoming is the only thing more powerful than belonging — because once you become, you carry your belonging with you.

I towel off, clear the desk, open the window.
Cold air hits warm blood and the line inside me steadies:

I am meant for more than this pain.

Not because I deserve it.
Because I'm willing to forge it.

Today won't be perfect.
Tonight might hurt.

But the fire is lit.

And I am done pretending I am a man who cannot be made.

PART II

The spark is the ignition.

But the forge is the discipline.

Nothing mystical.
Nothing dramatic.
Just the truth every man eventually confronts:

If I do not turn this into a process, the fire dies.

Fire without containment burns out.
Fire with direction becomes force.

So the first thing a man builds in himself
isn't confidence…

…it's **order**.

Not for presentation.
Not for revenge.
Not to "show her."

But to create a foundation strong enough
to hold the weight of the man he's becoming.

Because the version of me who belonged in her arms
was real—
but he was standing on borrowed flooring.

This version will be built
on bedrock I lay myself.

And that starts small.
Brutally small.
Almost insultingly small—
the kind of small that makes you wonder if it even matters.

(It does. More than anything that came before.)

Because sovereignty doesn’t begin with a breakthrough.
It begins with **reclaiming one square inch of reality at a time.**

The first inch is the body.

Not for aesthetics—
but for residence.

If I’m going to inhabit myself again,
this body can’t feel like foreign territory.

A man cannot feel like home
if he feels like a stranger in his own form.

Training stops being cosmetic here.
It becomes citizenship.

You don’t lift to sculpt—
you lift to **return**.

Next comes breath.

Not spiritual fluff.
Not performance.

Nervous system sovereignty.

Breath is how you tell the body,
“We live here now. Not in memory. Not in fantasy. Here.”

When the loop starts,
when the ache spikes,
when the mind tries to drag me backward—

breath is the first hammer strike.

Not to erase the pain—
but to hold steady **inside** it.

Because I'm not training to feel better.
I'm training to become inhabitable again.

Then comes **order**.

Not pretty spaces.
Not Instagram minimalism.

Proof.

A man who commands his space
re-teaches his nervous system
to experience himself as the ground
instead of the exile.

Every surface I reclaim outside
is a surface I reclaim inside.

Clean desk = clarity.
Cold shower = control.
Early morning = sovereignty.
No scrolling before breath = my mind belongs to me.

This is not routine.
This is reconstruction.

The Art of Detachment

You rebuild belonging
the way a blacksmith rebuilds steel:

heat, repetition,
and refusal to collapse back into softness.

The old self waited to be chosen.
The forged self wakes up and chooses himself first.

Not sentimentally—
operationally.

Before women.
Before validation.
Before nostalgia.

Body first.
Breath second.
Order third.
Mission fourth.

Not because doing these things makes life easy.
But because NOT doing them
makes collapse inevitable.

This is the first law of becoming:

When a man stops abandoning himself,
the world loses the power to orphan him.

And for the first time since losing her,
a new truth begins to root itself beneath the ribs—

I am not only someone who once belonged.
I am someone learning
to become the place of belonging
itself.

Not ready.
Not finished.

But forging.

PART III

Something shifts the moment the work stops being a reaction and starts becoming a declaration.

At first, every rep, every breath, every small act of order
was just a tourniquet —
something to keep the break from widening.

But repetition has its own alchemy.
It doesn't just strengthen muscle;
it rewrites identity.

When the body starts moving before the mind negotiates,
when breath arrives before panic can rise,
when structure exists before chaos wakes —
a quiet transformation begins:

I stop seeing myself as the man who shattered…
and begin seeing myself as the man who is reconstructing.

The nervous system notices before the mind does.
It sends a different signal now:

The Art of Detachment

We aren't prey anymore.
Not hunted by memory.
Not cornered by longing.
Not defined by what left.

The forged man doesn't wake up asking,
"Will today be gentle with me?"
He plants his feet on the floor
as if re-entry itself is a victory.
Not ego —
reclamation.

I'm no longer wandering through my life
like someone temporarily visiting.
I'm beginning to move like someone who has a key to his own door.

And the discipline —
the early mornings,
the breathwork,
the cold water,
the order —
it's no longer about controlling pain.

It's about proving, again and again,
that I can hold myself
without splintering.

That I am not something fragile.
That I am no longer waiting for a harbor —
I am learning to *become* one.

For the first time since she left,
my body doesn't feel like a cage
I'm trying to escape.

It feels like a forge.

Heat with direction.
Constraint with purpose.
Pressure that shapes instead of suffocates.

The mirror changes too.
I no longer see a man emptied by loss —
I see a man capable of building
what grief tried to convince him he would never have again.

Not replacing her.
Not erasing her.
Becoming a man who cannot be undone
by the absence of another.

And the craving —
it doesn't disappear.
But it stops commanding the room.
It narrows, refines, instructs.

It becomes a teacher instead of a tether.

Before, I wanted her to grant me back to myself.
Now I want to become the kind of man
who doesn't vanish when someone walks away.

The old version waited for belonging
like weather.

The Art of Detachment

Unpredictable, external,
a thing he hoped might arrive.

This version earns it
from the inside out.

And the body responds:
the spine settles higher,
the breath reaches deeper,
the world expands inside the chest
instead of crushing it.

This is no longer survival.

This is becoming.

Not for her.
Not for vindication.
Not to prove anything to anyone watching.

For me.

Because beneath the collapse,
below the hunger,
beneath the old ache that once defined me,
something steadier is speaking:

I was never meant to be a man
held together by someone else's hands.

I was meant to be a man
who cannot be undone.

PART IV (Final)

There is a moment—
quiet, understated, almost shy in its arrival—
when I realize I am no longer simply enduring my life…

…I am beginning to re-enter it.

Not in a triumphant surge.
Not in a cinematic return.
Just a subtle tilt, an internal click,
a shift of gravity I can feel more than name.

The axis has turned.

Before, every day felt like terrain I had to drag myself across.
A field of hours to survive, nothing more.

But now—
every day feels like ground I can *build* on.

That is the difference between survival and forging:

Survival whispers,
"How do I outlast this?"

Forging asks,
"What can I create from this?"

The shift begins inside,
but it shows itself in small, almost invisible ways —
the kind only a man coming back to himself would notice:

The Art of Detachment

I stand a moment longer before sitting.
I breathe before reacting.
I straighten the room before collapsing into it.
I choose my direction before drifting into default.

And in these tiny, unremarkable decisions,
something sacred rises:

I begin to trust myself again.

Trust that I won't abandon my own center.
Trust that I won't fold back into hunger.
Trust that I'll never hand the keys to my existence
to someone else's embrace again.

The tether to her thins—
not from force, not from anger,
but from growth.

I'm not trying to let go anymore.

I'm simply moving forward far enough
that I no longer need something behind me to hold.

This is the part people misunderstand about men who transform:

We don't heal when the pain disappears.
We heal when the past stops being the source of who we are.

The old identity whispered,
"I am the man she made whole."

But the new identity begins to root as:

Joe Manzello

"I am the man who makes myself whole."

It isn't complete yet—
but it's assembling itself piece by piece,
like bones remembering their shape after a long collapse.

This is the quiet birth of masculine sovereignty:

When belonging moves
from outside the ribs
to inside them.

I don't know the destination yet.
I don't know the full shape of the man I'm becoming.

But for the first time,
the road beneath my feet feels like mine.

Not hers.
Not memory's.
Not the echo of the life I lost.

Mine.

And something deep in my bones recognizes it—
a sensation like light forged into armor,
or a spine supported by a truth older than grief.

The man I am becoming
is not born from her absence.

He is born from the moment I chose
to build a home inside myself

rather than beg for a doorway
back into one that vanished.

The grief is still here—
but now it burns cleaner,
like fuel.

The longing remains—
but now it points forward,
not backward.

And the dependence
—the old gravitational pull—
is gone.

In its place stands the first law
of the forged masculine:

No one will ever again be the reason I exist.

But someone—someday—
will meet the man who already does.

Brotherhood Vs Isolation

"A man doesn't need a crowd — he needs one place where his armor can come off without costing him his dignity."

When the fall becomes descent,
a man reaches the first true crossroads of the underworld:

Isolation
or
Brotherhood.

Most men choose isolation—
not because solitude feels noble,
but because vulnerability now feels fatal.

A man who has been betrayed by intimacy learns a quiet, brutal equation:
"If someone sees me without my armor, they will leave."

So he withdraws.

Not to punish anyone.
Not to spite the world.
But to avoid the unbearable wound of being abandoned while exposed.

Isolation feels like safety
because only the self can't leave.

Brotherhood feels like risk
because it requires letting someone see the damage.

And when you're already in the dark,
risk feels like annihilation.

But isolation has a cost no one warns you about:

You become both the wounded and the medic—
the man bleeding
and the only witness to the bleeding.

That is how despair roots itself.
Not from the pain itself,
but from pain that goes unwitnessed so long it becomes your identity.

A man can survive almost anything
as long as someone sees him.
But unseen pain becomes a personality.

Brotherhood is not "friendship."
Brotherhood is the resurrection of witness.

It is another man meeting your gaze and wordlessly communicating:

"You are not crazy for hurting.
You are not weak for collapsing.
You are not the only one who has walked this valley."

A woman can love a man fiercely, deeply, wholly—
but she cannot hold the masculine psyche at its rawest.
Not because she lacks compassion,
but because she cannot decode the weight a man carries when his soul goes silent.

Only another man knows the cost of staying upright
while wanting to disappear.
Only another man recognizes the fracture behind the still face.
Only another man understands the heaviness of waking up
when your soul hasn't risen with you.

Brotherhood is not a luxury.
It is structural reinforcement.

Not men drinking.
Not men venting.
Not proximity.

Witness.
A stable pair of eyes that says:

"You're not broken.
You're becoming."

When another man sits with you without flinching,
the nervous system receives proof it forgot it needed:

"I can come back online."
"I am not the only one who has been here."
"I am not beyond repair."

No man climbs out of the underworld alone.
Some walk most of the distance bloodied and silent,
but the upward turn—the real one—
begins the moment another man's presence interrupts the lie that you are alone in your suffering.

And if you're reading this and it hits a little too close,
that's not an accident.
It's recognition.

Even in the dark,
even right now—

you are still moving.
You are still becoming.

And you are not the only one who has ever stood at this crossroads.

Pillar Quote (chapter seal):

"Isolation turns pain into identity.
Brotherhood turns pain into initiation."

Chapter 9
The Return To Wholeness

Integration never begins with strength.
It begins with a quieter, sharper recognition:

I was never missing power —
I was missing a place inside myself capable of holding it.

The collapse didn't take anything from me.
It only exposed that I had nowhere stable to set the parts of myself I had been carrying.

And now the fire inside doesn't feel like defiance anymore —
it feels like the gathering of scattered pieces.

Not a comeback.
A completion that had been waiting for years.

Because the truth that surfaces here is simple and devastating:

I was never too weak.
I was never too lost.
I was never "not enough."

I was unfinished — living as a draft of myself.

Strength was there — the world respected it.
Depth was there — she felt it instantly.

But no one ever saw both at the same time…
because I had never learned to let them occupy the same room within me.

To men, I played the warrior.
To her, I revealed the soul.

To myself, I was a divided man —
splitting open depending on who stood across from me.

Not because anyone failed me,
but because I had built my life on compartments instead of wholeness.

And fragmentation is fertile ground for starvation.
You cannot feel rooted when you only allow half your truth to breathe at once.
You cannot belong when your own internal world is split into sectors.

Wholeness is not "being strong."
Wholeness is becoming indivisible.

The man emerging now is not "stronger" than before —
he is singular, gathered, aligned.

Not one version for the world
and another for intimacy…

but *one unified presence*
that no longer fractures under environment, pressure, or attachment.

This is the moment a deeper understanding hits:

She was never meant to be the destination.
She was the mirror that revealed the unfinished architecture within me.

Her loss became the doorway
into the rooms of myself I had never entered.

The grief became the fire
that burned off everything too fragile to continue with me.

And the forge I have been building inside myself
is not creating someone new —

it is letting the full weight of who I already am
finally take its shape without apology.

Before, belonging required her nearness.
Now, belonging begins inside my own ribcage.

Before, my identity was defined by contrast to what I lost.
Now, identity begins to rise in possession of itself.

This chapter is not about becoming "stronger."

It is about becoming so integrated
that I cannot be torn from myself again.

Because once a man returns to wholeness —
no relationship can complete him,
and no heartbreak can hollow him out.

He doesn't go searching for home.

He moves as a man who carries home within him.

PART II

When a man lives divided,
his nervous system spends its entire life doing work his mind never names.

Strength, when it stands alone, becomes a kind of armoring—
a body braced for conflict, even in moments meant for rest.

And depth, when it isn't partnered with structure,
turns into raw exposure—
a soul wide open with no shield to stand behind.

Integration ends that constant compensation.

The body stops running defense
and begins to set down roots.

For the first time in years—maybe for the first time in my life—
my nervous system isn't scanning for incoming threats
or waiting for someone to show up and stabilize me.

It is inhabiting me.

This is a different kind of masculine quiet.
Not softness.
Not surrender.
But ownership—
the kind that rises when the self is finally occupied from within.

The shift is unmistakable:

hypervigilance → grounded presence.

And this grounded presence feels nothing like the "steady" I faked for years.
That was management.
Control.
A rehearsed calm I held like a mask.

This is different.
This is an inner weight that comes from actually being here,
not hovering outside myself hoping someone will open the door and let me in.

There is no bracing anymore—
because for the first time,
there is nowhere I expect to be pushed from.

This may be the first moment since childhood—
no, deeper than childhood—
that I feel I belong inside my own skin.

Women can feel this without needing language.
Men can sense it without explanation.

Because it's the unmistakable energy of a man who has become:
unshaken, not rigid...
still, not stuck...
anchored, not attached.

It is the nervous system of a man who has finally returned to himself.

The Art of Detachment

Nothing outside determines my center now—
not who stays,
not who leaves,
not whether I'm wanted,
not whether I'm remembered.

For the first time, my body isn't searching for a home.

It is learning to be one.

When the muscle of strength and the marrow of depth finally unify,
the charge that used to explode outward
turns inward
and becomes gravity.

And that gravity is not hardness—
it is substance.
A grounded weight that quietly tells the world:

"I exist whether I am chosen or not."

This is what women point to when they say a man feels "safe," though most men never reach the architecture required to become it.

Because real masculine safety isn't a man who can guard her body—
it's a man who no longer abandons his own soul.

When that happens, stillness turns into power.

Not passivity.
Not numbness.
But a center that cannot be yanked off-course
by longing,
or fear,
or memory,
or desire,
or any outcome he cannot control.

Because once a man learns to live at home in himself,
nothing the world takes
and nothing it gives
has the ability to exile him again.

PART III

Presence is not confidence.
It is not posture, not tone, not the absence of fear.

Presence is undivided existence—
the moment a man stops bleeding pieces of himself into places that cannot hold him.

For years, my energy leaked everywhere but here:
outward into longing,
into panic,
into fantasies of what could return,
into memories of who I once was in someone else's arms.

Every direction except inward.

Back then, my presence was conditional—
I could stand tall among men,

soften around her,
brace around my past,
and disintegrate the moment I was alone.

There wasn't one version of me—
there were four,
and none of them were the whole man.

Now the line is clean.
Sharp.
Unmistakable:

I am the same man in every room.

Not a warrior in one space and a wounded child in another.
Not open only to the woman who felt safe.
Not armored in the face of memory.
Not restless inside my own skin.

One man.
One frame.
One center.

This is what real masculine presence feels like:

I do not contract for approval.
I do not stretch myself to be chosen.
I do not fold my instincts to keep the peace.
I do not dilute myself to fit the moment.

I occupy.

Occupy my stance.
Occupy my breath.
Occupy the square foot of earth beneath my feet like I have a right to be here—
because I do.

When a man finally integrates,
he doesn't wait to be welcomed into a room…

he arrives.

Not through volume.
Not through power plays.
Through *weight*—
the quiet gravity of someone whose worth is not borrowed anymore.

People feel the difference before I speak.

Because before, without realizing it,
I was always asking a silent question:
"Is there space for me here?"

A man can't rise when he's negotiating his existence.

But now, there's no negotiation.
No permission-seeking.
No shrinking myself to avoid being too much,
and no expanding myself to avoid being too little.

I belong because I'm here.
Because I'm anchored.

The Art of Detachment

Because I carry my own coordinates now.
Because I am not searching for ground—

I am ground.

Others sense it instantly.
Not charisma.
Not charm.

Gravity.

And gravity is forged only by men who have known weight—
men who have lived the exile,
who have walked without a home inside themselves,
who have starved for a belonging they thought only another person could give them.

Only after you've known that kind of starvation
can you learn to generate your own nourishment.

Only after you've been unrooted
can you learn how to become your own soil.

This is the presence that draws respect,
that softens fear,
that steadies a room without effort:

Not dominance.
Not control.

Sovereignty.

Not a man standing against the world—
a man standing within himself.

And once presence becomes sovereignty,
relationships stop being about hunger,
stop being about filling a void,
stop being about being chosen just to feel whole.

They become about alignment—
two complete structures meeting,
not two incomplete souls reaching for shelter.

Because when you carry this kind of presence…

you stop seeking shelter.
You become it.

PART IV

Integration doesn't arrive with a miracle or a climax…

…it *recognizes itself* in you before you consciously notice the shift.

There is a moment — subtle, almost eerily quiet —
when I look at the man I'm standing as
and something inside me exhales with certainty:

This is who I was always building toward.

Not the fighter stripped of tenderness.
Not the heart without armor.
Not the productive machine who forgot how to breathe.
Not the lover who needed someone else to steady him.

The Art of Detachment

But the *whole man* —
the one who existed in outline form for years,
waiting for a catalyst sharp enough, honest enough,
to finish the carving.

The collapse didn't destroy me.
It revealed where I was unfinished.

The grief didn't empty me.
It carved the interior space
I am finally strong enough to occupy.

And I don't need applause or external acknowledgment to confirm it —
I can feel the shift down in the marrow.

There is weight in the posture —
not a burden,
a gravity that wasn't there before.

There is clarity in the gaze —
not the intensity of a man surviving,
but the presence of a man *returned.*

There is calm in the chest —
not numbness,
but a steady residence
that comes from finally having a place to live inside myself.

For the first time,
there are no scattered pieces of me hiding in old versions, old rooms, old memories.

I'm not outsourcing myself.
I'm not waiting to be mirrored into existence.
I'm not asking another human being to hold the parts of me I can now hold.

I am held —
by my own hands,
in my own frame,
in my own name.

And it's not the way she once held me —
not as rescue,
not as refuge…

but as *rooted belonging*.

This is the quiet victory no one sees from the outside:

I'm no longer trying to resurrect the man I was in her presence.

I am becoming
the man whose outline I only glimpsed *through* her —
a man I didn't yet have the structure to inhabit.

The warrior and the witness.
The backbone and the breath.
The flame and the stillness.

Strength + depth = wholeness.
Wholeness = sovereignty.

I don't need a harbor
to know where I live.

The Art of Detachment

Because I am becoming the place
no loss,
no absence,
no leaving
can exile me from.

And this realization doesn't inflate me —
it steadies me.

Because for the first time in my entire life,
I don't feel like I am trying to return
to some former version of myself.

I feel like I am finally arriving.

Chapter 10
The Sacred Grief

"Grief does not destroy a man — it baptizes him into honesty."

There comes a point in the descent
where resisting the pain costs more energy than surrendering to it.

And that is where masculine grief truly begins—
not the cinematic grief people romanticize,
not the poetic ache described in love songs,
not the heartbreak others assume you're drowning in…

but the *other* grief.
The ancient one.
The one that feels older than your body
and deeper than your lifetime.

The sacred grief.

The grief that shreds pretense,
pulls truth out of hiding,
and forces you to face what you should have mourned decades before.

A man doesn't break by crying for her.

He breaks because he is finally crying for:

• every version of himself that lived unwitnessed,
• the boy who learned to fall silently because no one came,
• the teenager who hardened instead of asking for help,

• the man who swallowed pain so convincingly he forgot it was inside him.

This grief isn't about what left.

It is about what was never allowed to surface.

You are not grieving *her*.
You are grieving:

• the self you exiled to survive,
• the home you waited a lifetime to feel,
• the illusion of safety you mistook for permanence,
• the identity that collapsed when your anchor disappeared.

This is why masculine grief feels primordial—
because it isn't born when she walks away.

It is *awakened* by the echo her absence exposes.

Most men never reach this part.
They outrun it.
They sedate it.
They bury it under new bodies, new distractions, new noise.

Not because they don't feel—
but because feeling *this* is like standing uncovered
in front of a truth big enough to unmake them.

There is no armor here.
No posture.
No persona to hide inside.

Just a man and his unprocessed life.
Just a man realizing he never learned how to hold himself
because he was always holding everyone else.

This grief is sacred because it purifies without humiliating.
It softens without dissolving.
It empties without erasing.

It burns away every counterfeit layer
until only the real man remains—
the one who has carried a lifetime of unresolved pain
without a single witness.

You cannot resurrect
while clutching the ghosts of what you never allowed yourself to mourn.

This is not the grief of losing someone you loved.
This is the grief of recognizing
just how much of yourself you carried alone
because you believed you had no other option.

And here is the truth beneath all truths:

Grief is not weakness.
Grief is the pulse that proves something inside you
is still alive enough
to rise again.

The Sacred Grief Protocol

Grief stops owning a man the moment he stops running from it and turns to face it as something he now commands.

Not an intruder.
Not a punishment.
A territory.

A landscape he walks not as victim…
but as sovereign.

Because the truth is this:

Grief is not something that happens *to* a man —
it becomes something that belongs *with* him.

A province of his inner world
that he learns to inhabit without losing himself inside it.

The world trains men to avoid this place at all costs.
Numb it.
Work through it.
Refuse it.
Drown it.
Outperform it.
Spiritualize it until it loses its teeth.

Anything but stand still
and feel the full temperature of what is burning inside.

But reclamation begins the first moment a man says:

"This pain is mine.
It shaped me.
And I will not exile it."

Because grief — when stripped of story, stripped of sentiment — is not a wound.

It is a record.

A record of where the soul once rooted itself deeply enough to be changed forever by the experience.

Only men capable of profound love
are capable of this magnitude of grief.

Only men with real depth
can be cracked open and still remain standing.

A smaller man would've drowned in distraction.
A shallower man would've numbed it into silence.
A man without root would've mistaken this ache
for something to replace instead of something to honor.

But *you* feel this because you are built for more.

This level of grief is not proof you are damaged —
it is proof you are capable.

Capable of bond.
Capable of devotion.
Capable of presence.
Capable of becoming someone who lives with depth instead of fear.

The Art of Detachment

The warrior stance is never:

"Oh God, this hurts."

The warrior stance is:

"Of course it hurts.
I loved with everything I had —
which means something in me is still alive."

Sacred grief does not reject the fire.
It steps into it.

It lets the flames climb the ribs,
burn through the illusions,
consume the old stories,
and leave behind nothing but the raw metal
that can be shaped into a new form.

Because grief — when claimed instead of escaped —
becomes both weapon and wisdom.

Not a scar.
A brandmark.
A sign of initiation into a version of manhood
that cannot be taught through ease.

A man who can carry his grief
without letting it hollow him out
is not softened by the experience…

He becomes untouchable.

Not because he healed "perfectly,"
but because nothing the world can take from him
is greater than what he has already survived within himself.

This is the turn —
the moment grief stops being about longing
and becomes about sovereignty.

No longer:

"I miss her."

But:

"This fire is mine.
And it will fuel my becoming."

This is the threshold of Sacred Grief:

When you stop begging the pain to leave…

and begin asking, quietly, with reverence:

"What is this pain here to make of me?"

There is a difference between feeling grief
and holding grief.

Feeling grief is collapse—
a drowning, a plunge, a surrender where the pain decides the terms.

The Art of Detachment

Holding grief is sovereignty—
the pain still burns, still presses, still tries to speak…
but it speaks inside your walls, not over them.

One turns you into a trembling body.
The other turns you into a container that does not leak.

This is the masculine threshold most never reach—
the moment when grief stops behaving like an intruder
and begins to behave like a force you can house
without losing the structure of yourself.

And the shift is subtle, almost imperceptible:
not heroic, not cinematic—
just a quiet inner alignment where something in the chest says:

This isn't here to break me.
This is here to be carried.

For the first time, the nervous system doesn't panic:
no command to run,
no instinct to numb,
no frantic reaching for rescue.

It just… steadies.

Not because the grief has softened—
but because I have hardened where it matters.

Before, the grief felt like being swept under a tide
that didn't care if I surfaced again.

Now it feels like weight placed across my shoulders—
heavy, yes,
but resting on a spine that finally knows how to bear it.

This is the turning point where the masculine stops being shaped by pain
and starts shaping pain into something worthy.

Because the moment I stand with it—truly stand—
the grief no longer threatens to erase me.

It becomes density.
Substance.
A deeper gravity in the bones.

This is why warriors throughout history
treated grief not as torment but as initiation—
because a man becomes real
when he learns to hold what once collapsed him.

I don't numb it.
I don't reinterpret it.
I don't try to make it spiritual or poetic or reasonable.

I face it.
Unhidden.
Unmasked.
With full consciousness of its weight.

And in that confrontation, the same energy that once shattered me
begins to gather itself—
thickening in the chest, solidifying in the abdomen—
like molten iron cooling into something that can cut and protect.

The Art of Detachment

This is when grief becomes power:
not the power to dominate the world,
but the deeper power to never vanish from myself again.

Because once I can stand inside the fire
without contracting,
without pleading,
without narrating myself as a victim of fate—

the pain transforms from wound
to resource.

A currency earned in blood and memory.

A man who has been to that depth
and still stands upright
becomes untouchable—not by armor,
but by truth.

There is no therapy that can replace this moment.
No philosophy.
No "letting go."

Only one passage leads here:
choosing to remain in contact with my own suffering
until it stops speaking in threats
and begins speaking in allegiance.

Where I once whispered,
"Please release me,"

I now speak with quiet authority:

You are mine.
You live inside my frame.
You do not command me.
You fortify me.

This is not overcoming grief.

This is dominion—
the reclamation of territory within myself
that I once abandoned.

From this point forward, grief is no longer an event
that happens *to* me.

It is evidence of where I have been,
and proof of the man I am becoming.

PART III

When a man first collapses, grief feels like loss.

When a man begins to rise, grief becomes weight.

But when a man finally *claims* his grief…

…it becomes direction.

There is a moment — subtle, almost reluctant — when I stop treating the pain like an intruder and start treating it like a companion with something to teach me.

And the second I stop fleeing it
and start *holding* it,

something unfamiliar stirs beneath the ache:

movement.

Not comfort.
Not clarity.
Not "healing."

A pulse.
A forward tilt.
A sense that the pain isn't dragging me backward anymore…
— it's beginning to *push me forward.*

Because grief, when witnessed consciously instead of survived blindly, forces a different question than the old one:

"If this much love once lived in me…
what architecture am I now meant to build from that kind of capacity?"

The world tells men that grief is an unraveling.
But grief isn't proof of weakness —

grief is proof of depth.

And the moment depth meets strength,
it starts transforming into purpose.

Every sovereign man eventually hits the same line in the sand — a line he doesn't speak, but feels in the marrow:

"This pain is not here to crush me.
It is here to measure the weight I am capable of carrying."

That's the moment grief becomes sacred:
when it stops being the debris of loss
and becomes the forge-level heat
that hardens the steel of a man's identity.

Because the pain reveals something crucial:

- I was capable of loving to my full depth.
- I was capable of surrender without shrinking.
- I was capable of opening beyond my defenses.

Most men never even arrive at that threshold.
They never access the parts of themselves deep enough
to generate grief of this magnitude.

The ache is evidence that I was alive in a way many men never touch.

And now, that same ache becomes raw fuel —
fuel for the version of me who will not fold, fracture, or vanish
the next time love calls his name.

This is reclamation.

Not "healing the wound."
Not pretending it didn't break me open.

The Art of Detachment

Reclamation is owning the *energy* inside the wound
and redirecting it into becoming.

And once the pain stops dominating me
and starts *answering* to me…

another voice rises from deep within the ache:

Use me.

Use the hollow spaces to build discipline.
Use the longing to sculpt purpose.
Use the memory to create meaning.
Use what once emptied you
to architect the man you are stepping into now.

This is the breakthrough most men never reach:

Grief is not something you "move past."
It is something you grow beyond.

Not by shrinking it —
but by expanding the man who carries it.

This is the moment the wound stops feeling like a void
and starts feeling like a blueprint.

The pain doesn't disappear —
I become larger than it.

And for the first time, I understand with full-body certainty:

This grief is not the end of my story.

It is the template
for the scale and magnitude
of the man I am meant to become.

PART IV

There comes a moment when grief is no longer a weight strapped to my back—

it becomes the ground beneath my feet.

Not heaviness,
not ache,
but territory.

Land I didn't choose,
but land I now command.

The world keeps telling men to "move on," to outgrow their wounds like they're stepping out of an old coat.
But a sovereign man doesn't move past pain—

he builds upward from it.

This is the final stage of reclamation:

The wound becomes landscape.

The Art of Detachment

Once, grief felt like an open pit—
a drop,
a dark,
a place I kept falling through.

Now it feels like something else entirely—

bedrock.
Stone with my name carved into it.
A frontier I bled for.

I don't wish it away.
I don't fantasize about undoing it.

It stands as a boundary line between the man I used to be
and the man who refused to die inside the fracture.

It's the marker of every mile I crawled when walking wasn't possible,
every breath I took when breathing felt undeserved.

It's the scar that whispers,
"You will never shrink back into the shape you held before this."

Because this is the moment grief stops being emotional
and becomes structural—
a beam in the architecture of who I am now.

Not evidence of damage,
but evidence of depth.

Not proof of abandonment,
but proof of root.
Not the sign of a breaking—
the sign of a becoming.

A man who has never been shattered
cannot fathom the true dimensions of his soul.

A man who has never grieved with his entire chest
never learns the true capacity of his heart.

But a man who has stood inside grief—
not flailing,
not bargaining,
not running—
who inhaled even when the air cut like glass,
who held his ground even when everything in him begged to go numb,
who carried the hunger without disappearing…

that man doesn't merely survive.

He ascends.

This is where reclamation ends—
and sovereignty begins:

Not with,
"I wish it hadn't happened,"
but with:

"This is part of my kingdom now."

The wound doesn't close.
It is anointed.

And from that anointing comes a sentence very few men earn the right to speak without flinching:

"Nothing that comes after this can unmake me."

Not because life will ease its tests,
but because I no longer stand outside myself
hoping for permission to exist.

I belong here.
In my ribs.
In my truth.
In my entirety.

No fragments left behind.
No exile.
No begging for a place to land.

Inside this belonging, a new stillness takes shape—
not the stillness of numbness,
but the stillness of a man who has finally returned to himself.

The grief is no longer a prison cell.

It is soil.

Claimed.
Forged.
Inherited.

The ground upon which the rest of my life will rise.

Releasing What Will Not Return

"Letting go is not moving on — it is stopping the
spiritual hemorrhage of trying to hold what has already left."

There comes a point in the descent
when a man realizes he is no longer grieving *her* —
he is grieving the bond.
The sanctuary.
The mirror.
The version of himself that once had a place to land inside her presence.

This is why letting go feels like pulling the spine out of your own chest:
you are not releasing a woman —
you are releasing the last coordinates your nervous system called *home.*

But no man rises while gripping the ghost of belonging.

Letting go is not dismissal.
It is not coldness.
It is not pretending the love meant nothing.

The Art of Detachment

Letting go is recognizing the truth the body always knew:
you cannot breathe through lungs that left with her.
You cannot live inside memories that require your absence to stay alive.
You cannot resurrect a world that demands your burial to exist.

Letting go is the moment a man turns toward his own life again and admits:

"If I keep reaching backward, I will never return to myself."

Releasing her is not a betrayal of the love you felt —
it is the first act of loyalty to the man you are becoming.

Not the man who revolved around her.
Not the man who waited for her.
Not the man whose identity was shaped by her gaze.

You.

Because the version of you that clings is the version still starving to be chosen.
The version who releases is the one who begins choosing himself.

You do not let go because she was unworthy.
You let go because your soul cannot evolve while kneeling at an altar that no longer opens its doors.

Your future cannot enter a room still occupied by a shrine to your past.
Your breath cannot expand inside a cage built from yesterday's longing.

And the man you are now becoming —
the man forged in collapse and rebuilt in fire —
cannot survive if you continue breathing through a memory
instead of lungs.

Letting go is not surrender.
It is the first permission you grant yourself to live again.

To stand.
To inhale.
To return.

Not to her —
but to the life waiting on the other side of release.

PART III — THE RECLAMATION

"Resurrection never waits for relief — it begins the moment a man decides to rise with the ache still burning under his ribs."

This is the turning of the axis.

Not because the burden has lifted,
but because you finally stop abandoning yourself beneath it.

The fall exposed the fracture.
The descent exposed the wound.
But reclamation exposes something else entirely —
the part of you that refuses to stay underground.

This is not the rebuilding of a life.
This is the rebuilding of an interior world:
the return of spine, of direction,
of a man reclaiming the ground of his own existence.

We are no longer addressing the shattered man,
the man wandering through hunger,
the man curled beneath the weight of what he lost.

We are addressing the one who is rising.

The tone shifts here —
not toward comfort,
but toward consecration.

Something in you stands up

not because it is healed,
but because it is done living on its knees.

You are no longer bowed over the grave of what ended…
you are standing in front of the forge
where the man you are becoming
will be made.

This is reclamation:
not a return to who you were,
but the emergence of who you were always meant to be
once the version built on longing finally burned away.

Chapter 11
Rebuilding The Frame

"Before a man becomes unshakable, he must first remember what he stands on."

The first step in reclamation is not confidence,
not discipline,
not mission—

it is rebuilding the *internal architecture* that those things rest on.

A shattered frame makes even a powerful man crumble.
A fortified frame allows even a wounded man to rise with intention.

This is where most men misunderstand healing:
they chase relief, distraction, or emotional anesthetic…
instead of becoming the kind of man whose structure can *hold* a life worth living.

Pain was never the enemy.
A hollow frame was.

Your frame is built from four pillars—
not theoretical, not inspirational—
but structural:

1. Truth — not preference, not narrative, but unfiltered reality.
2. Responsibility — authorship of your becoming, not spectatorship.
3. Standards — identity expressed through action, not aspiration.

4. Self-respect — the return of non-negotiables that shape the man.

Without these pillars, a man clings to whatever temporarily feels like ground.
That is how a man dissolves into a woman—
not out of love,
but because she becomes the scaffolding he never built in himself.

Rebuilding the frame means one thing:

Your life becomes the place you root into—
not a person.

Before the breakup, you leaned your identity against her reflection.
In reclamation, you fasten that identity into your own spine.

This is the turning point where the question changes from

"What did I lose?"
to
"What am I building with what remains?"

Pain still moves through you here,
but for the first time since the collapse—
pain is not the architect.

You are.

Identity Before Execution

Most men try to fix their life by fixing their behavior.
They hustle.

They grind.
They "get their shit together,"

yet underneath it all, they remain fractured.

That's why nothing sticks.

You cannot outwork the version of yourself you still believe you are.

Before discipline can take root,
identity must return—
not as memory,
but as orientation.

When you were strongest in life, it wasn't because of motivation.
It was because you moved in alignment with a man whose values were immovable.
That man wasn't performing strength—
he was embodying it.

He didn't need hacks.
He didn't need hype.
He didn't need external push.

He had identity—
and identity naturally produced discipline.

The reverse is also true:

When identity shatters,
discipline collapses with it.

This heartbreak didn't just cost you a relationship—
it cost you the axis your entire internal ecosystem revolved around.

You didn't lose "love."
You lost the self your discipline depended on.

Reclamation begins with a single question:

"Who am I when no one is choosing me?"

Until that question is answered,
you will keep shaping yourself for others
instead of shaping yourself from within.

Identity first.
Discipline next.
Power last.

This is the masculine sequence of resurrection.

You don't rebuild the life—
you rebuild the man who will build the life.

Identity as a Threshold, Not a Memory

Rebuilding identity is not a return to who you were before her.
That man is gone—
and he deserves to be.

The goal is not restoration.
The goal is ascension.

You are becoming the man who could *only* emerge after everything you built yourself around was stripped away.

The old identity was dependent on reflection.
This one must anchor itself in self-recognition.

So the question evolves:

Not:
"Who was I before?"

But:
"Who must I now become—
that no one and nothing can take from me?"

This is where a man distinguishes ego identity from soul identity.

Ego identity says:
• "I am who she saw in me."
• "I am who the world recognizes."
• "I am who I am when I am successful."

Soul identity says:
• "I am who remains when nothing external validates me."

Most men never reach this level
because they've never been stripped down far enough to discover it.

You have.

This is why your resurrection won't be a return—
it will be an unveiling.

Not the man the world remembers,
but the man who does not disappear
when love does.

This frame—soul over ego—
is your first true sovereignty.

Because once identity is internal:

- Approval becomes optional
- Validation becomes irrelevant
- Proving becomes obsolete
- Begging ends on contact
- Peace returns without negotiation

The deepest truth of reclamation is this:

You are not becoming "more."
You are removing everything you became to be kept.

Beneath the ache, beneath the hunger, beneath the longing—
there was always a man who never left,
only a man you silenced to survive.

Reclamation is his return.

Not the mask.
Not the performer.
Not the survivor.

The sovereign.

And sovereignty is not dominance—
it is possession of self so complete
that nothing external can ever unseat you.

Identity is not what rises last.
Identity is what rises first.
Everything else rises because of it.

Embodiment: The Man Who Returns to Himself

Identity is not a set of words.
Identity is an internal gravity.

You know a man's identity
not by what he says,
but by what he refuses to betray.

Before heartbreak, you lived outward-in:
the world → reflection → ego → behavior.

After reclamation, you move inward-out:
identity → conviction → alignment → embodiment.

You rebuild the frame
not by adding anything new—
but by stripping away everything that diluted you.

This is the moment a man stops negotiating with himself.

He no longer edits his standards to match his emotions.
He shapes his emotions to match his standards.

He no longer asks,
"Will this cost me her?"

He asks,
"Will this cost me *me*?"

This is the turning point:

You stop trying to *feel* like the man—
and you begin *acting* as the man,
long before the feeling arrives.

Sovereignty is not emotion-first.
It is identity-first.

And when you act in alignment with your true identity long enough,
your nervous system eventually whispers:

"I recognize this place.
I am home."

Not reaching outward.
Not starving inward.
Rooted.

And once a man roots into himself,
no woman becomes his oxygen ever again.

He may choose her.
He may build with her.
He may love her with depth, devotion, fire, and presence.
He may kneel to God beside her.

But he never collapses into her.

This is the foundation of becoming unshakeable:

A man cannot lose himself
once he knows where he returns to.

Pillar Quote (Chapter Seal**):**

"Identity is not what rises last —
it is what rises first,
and everything else rises because of it."

The Return Of Direction

"A man does not heal when he feels better —
he heals when he starts moving with purpose again."

There comes a moment in every resurrection
when the fog doesn't clear,
doesn't part,
doesn't offer mercy—
but something inside the chest shifts anyway.

Not hope.
Not clarity.
Not motivation.

Something quieter.
Something older.
A pull.

The faint, steady gravity of a man remembering
that he is not designed to drift.

Direction never returns like a sunrise—
bright, obvious, undeniable.
It returns like a coal buried beneath ash—
dull at first, barely warm to the touch,
yet somehow refusing to die.

You feel it before you can name it:
your energy stops bleeding backward
into what you lost,
and begins inching—almost imperceptibly—
toward what must be built next.

This is the first sign a man is coming back online:
his suffering stops repeating
and starts moving.

Not in leaps.
Not in revelations.
In inches.

And for a man who has been living inside disorientation,
an inch of motion feels like oxygen.

Because heartbreak does not take a man's strength—
it takes his orientation.
It scrambles his inner compass,
turns him into a fighter swinging in the dark
at things that no longer exist.

But when direction returns—
even before confidence,
even before certainty—
there is a hum beneath the ribs,
a low, dangerous vibration
that signals the engine is waking.

This danger isn't outward.
It isn't aggression.
It's the internal kind—
the kind that tells you:
"I am beginning to remember myself."

Direction is not "the plan."
Direction is the memory that you are a man who moves.

Until now, every motion you made
was a reaction to loss.
Every thought ricocheted inside grief.
Every breath was stolen by what you couldn't restore.

But from this point forward,
the axis tilts.

Not because the pain is gone—
but because you are no longer abandoning yourself beneath it.

The eyes stop searching backward for closure
and begin scanning forward for construction.

This is the birth of momentum—
and momentum is the first symptom of rebirth.

You do not need certainty.
You do not need a blueprint.
You do not need a single promise from the future.

You only need this:

movement.

The smallest forward step
breaks the gravitational pull of despair.

Grief was the descent.
Direction is the turn.

And a man who has turned—
even slightly,
even shakily—
has already begun to rise.

(Part II — The Stirring of Mission)

When direction first returns to a man's chest,
it doesn't reappear as a plan,
or a strategy,
or some clean motivational surge.

It arrives as recognition—
an ancient remembering beneath thought.

Not of *where* he is,
but of who he refuses to die as.

The Art of Detachment

This is where resurrection pivots from the external to the internal:
the man begins to feel drawn forward by identity,
not dragged forward by circumstances.

Long before anything in the world shifts,
something deep inside the ribs exhales and whispers:

"There is more of me I haven't lived yet."

This is not motivation.
Motivation is fickle, emotional, dependent on weather and mood.

This…
is summoning.

It is the soul tapping the shoulder of the wounded body,
reminding it that burial was never the final instruction.

You don't know the path yet,
you don't even know the first three feet of the road—
but you can suddenly feel the possibility of walking again.

A man does not rise because he feels ready.
A man rises because something primordial in him refuses extinction.

This shift is subtle, nearly invisible from the outside:
no epiphany,
no emotional crescendo,
no triumphant music building in the background.

Just a quiet, undeniable inner knowing:

“The life I am meant to build did not die with her.”

That is the first light—
not brightness,
but orientation.

Not answers,
but North.

And this is why vision must come before structure:

A man cannot architect a future
until he remembers he *still has* one.

The moment that spark returns—
even faintly,
even as a flicker in a cave—
the nervous system begins reorganizing around becoming.

You stop asking:

“Why did this happen to me?”

and begin asking:

“Who does this pain now require me to become?”

That right there—
is the pivot out of grief
and into destiny.

Choosing Life Again

The Art of Detachment

The true turning point isn't when the pain fades.
It's when you stop waiting to feel okay before you move.

There is a moment—small but seismic—
when a man chooses forward
even while his heart is still leaking through the seams of his chest.

That moment
is resurrection.

Not ease.
Not closure.
Not confidence.

Choice.

Until now, everything has been happening *to* you:
the breakup,
the collapse,
the shattering,
the paralysis of disbelief.

But here—right here—something reverses:
you stop reacting to what broke you
and begin *becoming* the man who outgrows the version of you who shattered.

You stop asking:

"Will this pain ever end?"

and begin asking:

"Who will I be when it does?"

Direction doesn't return through clarity—
direction returns through alignment.

The spine stiffens.
The jaw hardens.
The eyes rise—not out of anger,
but out of reclamation.

Not because the grief is gone,
but because you finally refuse to let the grief define the parameters of your life.

This is the return of masculine will—
quiet, steady, threaded through the bones like tempered steel.

There is still ache.
Still absence.
Still memory that burns when touched.

But beneath all of it, a new voice emerges:

"Get up.
We're not done."

A man who hears that voice—no matter how softly—
is already rising.

The world will not recognize the shift,
but *you* will,
because for the first time in a long time…

the future doesn't feel closed.

It feels waiting.

Not for her—
for *you.*

Ignition: The Refusal to Stay Broken

The first true spark of post-heartbreak power is not peace.

It is defiance.

A moment comes where the pain stops being the force that crushes you—
and becomes the very force you press your palms into as you stand.

You haven't transcended it yet.
You're still bleeding.
But you are no longer kneeling.

This is the masculine instinct that always precedes sovereignty:
not serenity,
but refusal.

Not refusal of her—
refusal of the version of yourself who stayed collapsed.

The inner voice shifts from:

"Please let this stop hurting…"

to:

"No. More."

Not whispered.
Declared internally like a judgment from the throne of your own bones.

This is the moment the nervous system pivots
from prey back to predator—
from victim of circumstance
to architect of rebirth.

Masculine will always returns before serenity.

A man becomes unshakeable only after he becomes unyielding.

Before sovereignty comes refusal.
Before rebirth comes revolt.
Before peace comes power.

The first form of direction after the fall is not clarity—
it is a vow:

"I will not die here."

Even if your ribs still burn,
even if memory still claws at the insides,
even if longing still pulses beneath every inhale—

something deeper has taken command.

Once that verdict is made,
your past no longer governs your axis.

You may still hurt—
but you are no longer conquered.

That is the shift no one else can see yet,
but you can—
because for the first time since everything broke…

you're standing.

And once a man stands,
the world begins to move around him differently.

Pillar Quote **(chapter seal):**

"A man doesn't rise when the pain ends — he rises when he refuses to remain on his knees."

Chapter 12
Becoming The Mountain

The Ascent Begins

A man becomes the mountain the moment he stops begging life to return him to where he fell…

…and instead begins rising toward the altitude his soul was cut to inhabit.

Not unshakeable through hardness,
but unshakeable through root.

There is a strange dignity that enters the body when grief is no longer treated as the site of collapse,
but the birthplace of ascent.
When pain stops functioning as residue
and becomes origin.

Because once a man claims his suffering as his own,
something ancient and immovable awakens inside him:

He no longer leans on the world —
the world begins to lean on *him*.

This is the genesis of the mountain:

Not "I hope I can stand."
Not "I will try to be strong."
But a vow so quiet it almost feels like memory:

"I will rise to the height I was carved for."

The Art of Detachment

Not to be admired —
to be anchored.

Not to tower above —
to hold above.

A mountain is not a refuge because it is soft.
It is a refuge because it does not move.

And a man becomes a summit the moment he stops descending
to meet others where they are…

…and becomes the place others must ascend
if they wish to stand beside him.

Not from withholding —
from self-respect.

Not from pride —
from refusal to shrink.

This is where reclamation becomes embodiment:
the grief no longer presses against me —
it rises beneath me,
lifting the frame it once crushed.

What once hollowed me
now becomes the altitude I stand on.

A weaker man would have shattered.
A fearful man would have sealed himself shut.
A numbed man would have vanished into distraction.

But a forged man performs a rarer act:

He rises through the wound,
not away from it.

The grief that kept me on the floor
is now the ground I push upward from.

Not healed —
ascended.

This is where I stop scanning for someone to gather me,
and become the one who witnesses my own ascent.

Before, home was something I stepped into.
Now, home is something built into my ribs.

The first truth of the mountain man emerges:

"I do not need to be chosen to be solid."

The spine stops asking for permission —
it claims height.

Before, I was asking the world where I fit,
hoping to be seen,
to be named,
to be held in place.

Mountains do not "fit."
Mountains define the landscape.

That is the shift.

The Art of Detachment

When a man becomes the mountain,
he stops waiting for the world to locate him —
and becomes the location.

He stops asking,
"Where do I stand?"

And begins declaring:

"Where I stand becomes the ground."

This is not dominance —
it is rooted identity.

A man who is still searching for his anchor
is a man the world can sway.

A man who *is* the anchor
is a man the world must adjust around.

This is why the mountain needs no guard:
it does not defend itself —
it simply does not move.

Nothing external can relocate a structure
that stands from its core.

Before, I used strength as armor —
a shield protecting a wound I had not yet claimed.

Now the wound itself has become the bedrock.

And when a wound becomes foundation,
nothing outside of you has leverage.

There is nothing left to expose.
Nothing left to destabilize.
Nothing left to threaten.

A man is only fragile where he is still split.

Once he is whole,
there is no fracture for the world to enter through.

People feel this before they understand it:
their tone shifts,
their energy organizes,
their posture recalibrates around your presence.

Not because you intimidate…

but because you have become a fixed point
in a world full of moving ones.

And fixed points reshape entire rooms.

The man I used to be begged for a harbor.
The man I am becoming is a landmark.

That is the meaning of "Becoming the Mountain":

Not stone.
Not coldness.
But reference.

A man who no longer reacts to life…

but stands as something life must react to.

Grief gave me depth.
Integration gave me center.
Reclamation gives me mass.

Now the world must move around me —
not the other way around.

This is where the masculine stops defending itself
and begins inhabiting itself.

Not unfeeling —
unshakable.

Not impenetrable —
impossible to uproot.

Because the pain that once knocked me off center
is now part of the center.

Nothing can exile me from myself anymore —

because I have become
the place I stand.

The Summit Masculine

When a man becomes the mountain,
he no longer moves toward the world…

…the world begins to orient itself around him.

Not because he withholds,
not because he postures,
but because he rises so fully into himself
that everything around him must adjust to the altitude.

People don't feel your strength first —
they feel your standard.

They don't feel invited downward;
they feel pulled upward,
as if the mere fact of your presence reveals
a height inside themselves they have been avoiding.

This is the energy of a summit:

"You may stand beside me —
but only by ascending."

Weak men collapse under that gravity.
Men addicted to comfort drift back into the valley.
Men who *think* they are ready but haven't built the spine for altitude
stall halfway up, choking on thin air.

But the men with density?
The ones with discipline in their blood
and marrow that remembers purpose?
They climb.

Not because you drag them —
but because your existence exposes
how small they have allowed themselves to live.

The Art of Detachment

This is why true masculine presence does not seduce.
It awakens.

And the shape of brotherhood shifts:

You are no longer looking for men to stand with.
Men rise to stand with you.

Your presence becomes a filter long before you speak:

The comfortable retreat

The uncertain disqualify themselves

The hungry sharpen their edges

You don't need to judge men.
The mountain judges them.

A summit does not chase.
A summit does not descend.
A summit does not negotiate altitude.

It waits at elevation
and lets gravity separate those who can stand in rare air
from those who cannot.

And a woman feels this too —
not as intimidation,
not as distance,
but as something ancient inside her settling:

The knowing, deep in her nervous system,
that this man does not seek a place to belong…

…he *is* a place to belong.

This is the difference between desire and ascent:

Desire says,
"I want you."

Ascent says,
"If you want this, you must rise to meet me."

The men who reach you
are not followers.
They are those who chose to transform themselves
in order to stand where you stand.

Not because you carried them —
but because the altitude itself demanded they evolve.

This is how your presence becomes legacy
even before your mission fully emerges:

You do not forge men by telling them who to be.
You forge men by standing somewhere
they can no longer pretend
they were not born to reach.

And the ones who climb that far?

Those become your tribe —
not because you lifted them…

…but because you proved the summit
was survivable.

The Unmovable Man

There comes a point in a man's evolution
where he no longer tries to *signal* strength…

because anyone standing near him can already feel
that nothing on earth can move him.

Not through force.
Not through fear.
Through presence—
that deep, unmistakable current in the air:

"I will not descend from my altitude for anyone."

At this stage, holding firm is no longer an act.
It's a nature.
A state of being.

This is the difference between a man who is protecting his heart
and a man who is governing his ground.

A guarded man fears intrusion.
An unmovable man
is simply unreachable at low altitude.

You do not drag a mountain downward—
you either ascend to meet it
or remain below.

And in this state of embodiment, I don't "avoid" collapse…
there is simply nowhere left inside me that collapses anymore.

The valley that once swallowed me
has been quarried into foundation.
There is no depth beneath me to return to.

This is the essence of integration:

The wound is not hidden.
The wound is not patched.
The wound becomes architecture—
woven into the steel of the structure itself.

Once a man reaches this form, two truths settle in the marrow:

1. **"I belong to myself** before I belong anywhere else**."**

No rejection can exile him.
No affection can destabilize him.

2. **"Anyone who** walks **beside me must rise** to meet my elevation**."**

Not a test.
An atmospheric requirement.

Because when identity is rooted—not performed—
the need for validation dissolves quietly.
The hunger for being understood disappears with it.
The ache for rescue died long before that.

In its place stands a rarer creature:

The Art of Detachment

A man who trusts the weight of his own gravity.

Not chasing.
Not pleading.
Not reaching.

Simply existing as a summit
others must climb to stand beside.

This is not hardness.
This is sovereignty.

Not resistance.
Root.

Not detachment.
Altitude.

Once I was a man searching for a home.
Now I am becoming the man
who is a place of arrival—

for himself first,
then for those strong enough
to breathe at this height.

The ascent is not complete…
but I no longer rise to escape a wound—

I rise
because the summit was always my elemental shape.

The Rise from Resistance to Resolve

There is a vast difference between a man who refuses to fall
and a man who refuses to turn back.

The first is survival.
The second is sovereignty.

A mountain is not defined by stillness—
but by its refusal to be rewritten by the storms around it.

Rain does not negotiate its slope.
Wind does not argue its posture.
Time does not persuade it to move.

It does not hold its place by effort.
It holds its place by essence.

This is the phase where a man stops "holding on"
and begins holding course.

He is no longer fighting collapse—
he is advancing through what once would have undone him.

Strength no longer erupts from crisis.
It radiates from identity.

A man becomes the mountain when:

- Pain no longer dictates his direction
- Fear no longer bargains for his future
- Longing no longer pulls him backward
- Doubt no longer stains his momentum

He stops checking if he can continue.
He simply continues.

The Art of Detachment

Not recklessly—
with quiet, deliberate certainty.

Not out of rage—
out of self-possession.

This is not where the heart stops hurting.
This is where the hurt stops steering the man.

The mountain does not resist the storm—
it simply refuses to bow to it.

This is masculine steadiness:
Not numb.
Not distant.
Not frozen.

But a direction stronger than disruption.

He no longer strives to be unbreakable…

he simply becomes unmoveable.

Steadiness vs Stillness

Most men misunderstand power.

They think "being the mountain" means
emotionless, expressionless, unresponsive—

a statue carved out of unprocessed tension.

That is stillness.
And stillness without soul is paralysis wearing armor.

Steadiness is different.

Steadiness isn't the absence of movement—
it is the refusal to be redirected by anything
smaller than your purpose.

A still man holds himself together.
A steady man carries himself forward.

A still man is bracing.
A steady man is becoming.

Stillness is fear disguised as discipline.
Steadiness is direction with roots.

A man who clings to stiffness cracks under pressure.
A man who stands steady bends without breaking.

That is why mountains are not revered for silence—
but for presence.

They exist as themselves
regardless of the emotional weather around them.

This is where your ascent shifts again—
your strength is no longer measured by how tightly you hold…

but by how deeply you stay aligned
while continuing to move.

The Art of Detachment

Steadiness says:
"I don't need certainty. I need identity."

Stillness whispers:
"I hope I don't break."

Steadiness declares:
"Even if I break,
I am still the one who rises."

Survival clings to foothold.
Sovereignty walks forward on its own ground.

The Weight of Integrity

When a man becomes steady instead of still,
his strength does not defend—it emanates.

People feel him before they understand him.
Not because he is loud—
but because he is *one piece*.

There is gravity in a man
who no longer lies to himself.

He doesn't justify.
He doesn't posture.
He doesn't ask for permission.

He stands in truth—
and truth carries mass.

Integrity is not "doing the right thing."
Integrity is remaining yourself
when doing so costs something.

And this is where your presence begins to transform rooms:

You do not convince—
you embody.

You do not posture strength—
you are strength, even in silence.

Respect is no longer demanded—
your existence sets the terms
in which disrespect cannot breathe.

This is the authority earned only by men
who rebuilt from the ruins inward:

• He does not need to be chosen
because he has already chosen himself
• He no longer hunts belonging
because he belongs to his own life
• He no longer fears loss
because nothing essential lives outside his chest

Men who have never died and come back
will not understand this presence.

Men who have will recognize it instantly.

It is the look in the eyes that says:

"I have already survived the bottom.
There is nothing you can take from me now."

This is not hardness.
This is wholeness.

Honor stops being a virtue—
it becomes a posture.

The Man Who Cannot Be Moved

A man becomes truly unshakeable
when he is no longer defending his identity—
he is inhabiting it.

External turbulence stops dictating internal reality.

Sun or storm—
he remains himself.

Chosen or rejected—
he remains himself.

Loved or left—
he remains himself.

This is sovereignty:

identity sealed against outcome.

When you reach this depth,
you stop fearing heartbreak—
not because you avoid connection…

but because you know
no loss can cost you your own existence again.

This is why kings do not chase.
They do not plead.
They do not grip.

They choose—
and what they choose must be worthy
of the man they had to become
to stand here.

A mountain does not return to lowlands.
Lowlands cannot sustain the altitude
of what he has become.

He no longer asks:
"What if I lose her?"

He asks:
"Can she breathe at this height?"

This is the shift from recovery
into ascension.

The storm is no longer the adversary.
Losing footing is no longer the fear.
You have become the ground beneath your own life.

From this elevation, a new peace forms—
not the peace of ease…

but the peace of unshakeable ownership.

You are not unfeeling.
You are unclaimable by collapse.

This is what makes a man immovable—

not armor,
but axis.

"The unmoving man is not the one who avoids the storm—
but the one whose identity remains untouched inside it."

Chapter 13
Rebuilding From The Ashes

Part I — The Cremation Of The Old Self

(Inferno → Revelation)

The death of the old self does not arrive as collapse—
it arrives as combustion.

Not a burial beneath soil,
but a burning away of every part of me that was never built to survive the climb.

All the lowering,
the shrinking,
the silent betrayals of my own spirit disguised as loyalty…

They don't fade gently.
They ignite.

Because nothing small can follow a man into altitude.

And as these old versions burn,
I finally understand something I never had language for:

I am not witnessing my death.
I am witnessing the death of the weight.

The armor I once thought kept me safe
was the same armor that kept my expansion caged.

The Art of Detachment

It wasn't weakness that held me down—
it was outdated protection masquerading as identity.

The fire exposes this truth with surgical clarity:

I never needed to create a new man…
I needed to incinerate everything that kept the real one buried.

And when the metal softens,
when the old shell melts off my ribs,
what rises first is not triumph—
it is relief.

Relief that my spine is no longer compensating.
Relief that my heart is no longer dragging a history behind it.
Relief that my nervous system finally stops bracing for abandonment.

For the first time since she walked away,
my body is not clutching.

It is releasing.

Not releasing her—
releasing the version of me who believed he had to descend to be loved.

That man is ash now.

Not annihilated—
integrated into the stone I now stand on.

The fire does not steal from me.
It reveals me.

And underneath the charred armor, something ancient stands upright:

Not the boy aching for belonging,
not the man starving for shelter,
but the sovereign who finally understands:

I was never meant to be chosen in the valley—
I was meant to be met on the ridge.

As the fire finishes its sanctification,
the relief shifts into something deeper:

Emergence.

A lifting beneath the sternum.
A subtle but unmistakable pull forward.
A sensation like my spine remembering its original height.

This is no longer survival.

This is arrival.

The grief that once hollowed me
is now the ground I push upward from.

And as I step beyond the flames,
I do not feel diminished.

I feel witnessed—
by myself.

Not as a shattered man piecing together a new shape—

but as a forged man
finally stepping into the height he carried all along.

What Does Not Follow Me Forward

Rebirth is never just the unveiling of a new self—
it is the refusal to drag the old world up the mountain with you.

The fire doesn't merely melt the armor.
It becomes the border.
A living threshold inside the soul that declares:

"That version of me will never walk this altitude again."

Not out of bitterness.
Not out of shame.
But because that man was engineered for survival…

…and the man emerging now is engineered for sovereignty.

Some parts of me simply cannot breathe where I'm going.

What Burns Forever

1. The man who descended to be loved

The self who shrank to be chosen—
extinguished.

Love must now meet me at elevation,
not in the hollows where I once hid myself to be kept.

2. The man who traded altitude for belonging

The one who lowered his height to maintain connection—
gone.

If someone wants to remain,
their feet must rise.
I will not descend to spare their climb.

3. The man who carried others before he carried himself

What I once labeled "strength"
was depletion.
What I called "leadership"
was self-erasure wearing a noble mask.

4. The man who confused devotion with self-sacrifice

The version of me who believed love was earned
by draining himself dry—
he is smoke now.

I don't hate these men.
I don't resent them.
They were prototypes—
early drafts carved from hunger and hope.
They taught me what I was capable of…
but they were never built to carry the weight of who I must become.

The Art of Detachment

You don't curse the scaffolding
when the structure finally stands.
You simply no longer need it.

The cremation is not fury.
It is final release.
A quiet, sovereign certainty:

They cannot survive in the air I now breathe.

Letting them fall away is not loss—
it is oxygen.
It is the lungs expanding again,
the ribcage reclaiming space,
the spirit standing upright without apology.

Now:

Instead of needing to be chosen,
I become a man who is only choosable at elevation.

Instead of stepping downward to meet,
I remain where I belong
and witness who is willing to rise.

Instead of proving devotion through depletion,
I give from a source that no longer leaks.

Instead of carrying others at the expense of myself,
I carry myself first—
so that when I lift,
it's from power, not absence.

This is the spiritual dividing line:

What once defined me now fuels me.
What once weakened me now builds me.

The man who knelt to be received
has returned to ash.

And the man who rises from that ash
is the one finally ready
to build at altitude.

What Survives The Fire

Fire does not erase a man.

It erases only what was never meant to stand with him in the first place.

Fire is not destruction —

it is revelation.

It shows you, with brutal honesty, what in you was temporary…

and what in you is eternal.

The pieces that cracked,
the identities that dissolved,
the versions of me that curled inward in fear —

those were never the core.

What remained glowing beneath the ruin
were the elements that refused to die.

Not the parts shaped by her,
or by longing,
or by hunger…

but the parts forged long before any collapse.

These are not ashes.

They are ore.

The raw metals a man rebuilds his life from.

What Rose Through the Flames

1. My capacity for devotion

Not the grasping kind,
not the anxious attachment disguised as loyalty —

but devotion that comes from the marrow.

The kind that endures,
not because it clings,
but because it was born clean.

It was never my weakness.
It was my inheritance.

2. My ability to walk through **hell and** keep moving

Pain did not undo me.

It clarified me.

There is a resilience woven into my bones
that didn't need to be learned —
only rediscovered.

Even when everything else collapsed,
my stance, somehow, did not.

3. My instinct to protect and provide

Not the version built on self-abandonment,
not the version that over-gave to feel worthy…

but the steady masculine instinct to create safety,
to build structure,
to lead with quiet certainty.

When a man leads himself,
that instinct becomes a gift —
not a leak.

4. My hunger for meaning

I have never been able to hide inside numbness.

Even in the darkest hour,
I kept searching for purpose inside the pain.

That hunger is proof:
I was built for ascent,
not escape.

5. My depth

Depth I once hid.
Depth I once diluted to stay palatable.
Depth I once offered only in fragments.

Grief did not create that depth —
it revealed it.

This depth is not something I pick up again.
It is something I finally claim.

These Are the Traits That Survived

They did not shatter.

They did not disappear.

They were only misused —
poured into places that could not hold them.

So now they shift:

From serving validation
→ to serving destiny.

From trying to be seen
→ to seeing myself first.

From belonging to someone else
→ to belonging to my own sovereignty.

These aren't the qualities I "get back."

These are the qualities I finally stand on.

Because rebuilding is not about retrieving what was lost…

It is about asserting what endured.

The world loves the story of heartbreak ruining men.

But heartbreak doesn't ruin a man.

It only ruins the parts of him that were never rooted.

And what stays standing after the fire—

those are the bones of the man who will never collapse again.

The pieces that survived the inferno
are the pieces worthy of building a life around.

And once I know what survived…
once I know what refused to die…

direction no longer feels like possibility.
It feels like inevitability.

Rebuilding does not begin the day a man "moves on."

It begins in the far quieter moment
when he looks toward the future
without bracing for impact.

Not because the grief has disappeared—
but because it finally has a place to rest
that is not inside his throat.

The Art of Detachment

This is the actual turning point:

Before, I lived *toward* what I lost—
haunted by it, orbiting it,
using it as the reference point for my suffering.

Now, I live *from* what survived—
from the parts of me that refused to break,
from the truth that endured the collapse.

The difference is total.
Irreversible.
A rebirth disguised as a subtle shift of gaze.

I am no longer attempting to resurrect who I was.

I am here.
Whole. Present. Held by my own frame.

And the question that once stalked me—

"How do I get through this?"

—no longer applies.

The new question rises with more weight:

"What will I build now
that nothing in this world can unmake me again?"

This is how masculine direction truly ignites:
Not through urgency,

not through desperation,
not through trying to outrun the wound…

…but through the quiet gravity of a man
who has reclaimed himself.

I am no longer climbing because I hurt.
I am climbing because the man I was
is too small for the man I am becoming.

This is why the old life had to burn—
not as punishment,
but as preparation.

Its ashes are not remnants of tragedy.
They are space—
sacred, earned, cleared for sovereignty.

And the ground beneath me now
doesn't feel fragile or temporary.

It feels mine.

Not borrowed from a relationship.
Not dependent on validation.
Not permitted by circumstance.

Mine by right of survival.
Mine by right of reclamation.
Mine because I finally stand on it
with both feet and my full name.

The first step forward does not feel like hope—
hope is soft, uncertain, childlike.

The Art of Detachment

This feels like claiming territory.
Like pressing my heel into soil
that recognizes me as its architect.

For the first time, the future does not resemble recovery.

It resembles construction.

I am not waiting for destiny to choose me.

I am choosing the life
that matches the man I've become at this altitude.

Not out of longing…
but out of authorship.

Because when a man survives his own fire
and emerges not burned,
but *revealed*,
he stops asking:

"What will happen next?"

And begins declaring:

"What I build next will rise to meet my height."

The rebuilding is already in motion—
not in the world around me,
but in the man who will shape it.

From here forward, everything becomes architecture.

Chapter 14
Rebuilding The Frame – Part II

Part I — The Return Of Direction

Rebuilding never begins with discipline.

It begins with a horizon.

A subtle shift —
quiet, unannounced —
like the faintest thinning of fog after months of walking through darkness.

A single line appears in the distance.

Not behind me —
not in memory, not in longing, not in the ruins I kept trying to resurrect —
but ahead.

For a long time, I believed I was stuck.

But I wasn't stuck —
I was aimless.

A man can endure agony.
A man can shoulder unbearable weight.
A man can survive collapse, loneliness, and the slow ache beneath the ribs.

But no man can move without a where.

The collapse took that first —
not my strength,

not my masculinity,
not my will to live…

It stole my *orientation.*

Because when a man loses his direction, he stops being defeated by pain
and starts being dissolved by drift.

Without a horizon, even the strongest man becomes idle.

So when the horizon returns —
not brightly, not triumphantly —
but as a thin, undeniable line breaking through the distance…

what rises inside is not excitement,
and not confidence.

It is alignment.

A quiet recalibration of the spine.
A somatic remembering:
I am not meant to stay here.

It is not motion yet —
but the reappearance of the possibility of motion.

That is resurrection.
Not force.
Not momentum.
Not motivation.

Aim.

The masculine does not awaken because it feels powerful.
It awakens because it finally has somewhere to go.

And for the first time since the collapse, the direction before me is
not blurred by hope,
not distorted by longing,
not stitched together from fragments of the past.

It is clean.
It is forward.
It is mine.

A future built, not from who I lost,
but from who I am becoming.

A horizon rising from the ashes —
upward, not backward.

And the moment I see it, something ancient re-enters my chest:

Trajectory.

The quiet, unshakeable knowing:
I know where I'm headed again.

And when a man knows where he is going,
he does not search for motivation.

He moves.

Direction is the masculine's ignition point.
Not intensity.
Not speed.
Not discipline.

Orientation.

Before this moment, I believed I needed more strength to rebuild.
More healing.
More clarity.
More closure.

But the truth is simpler and far more sacred:

I didn’t need more strength.
I needed a horizon.

And now that it has returned —
even faint, even forming —

the rebuild is already underway.

Building A Life At Altitude

Once direction returns,
the question is no longer:

“What do I rebuild?”

but something far more consequential:

“What is worthy of existing at this height?”

A man who rebuilds from the valley
can only recreate the life he lost—
the familiar, the comfortable,
the architecture built for a smaller version of himself.

But a man who rebuilds from a summit
doesn’t reconstruct…

He redefines.

Up here, the air is different.
So is the view.
So is the man.

And when the altitude changes,
the ecosystem must change with it.
The old habits, old agreements, old emotional postures—
they don't need to be resisted anymore.
They simply suffocate.
They cannot breathe in the thinner air of sovereignty.

You don't force yourself to stop lowering.
You don't lecture yourself into self-respect.
You don't discipline yourself into higher ground.

Your body refuses to descend
because it can now feel the treachery of that descent.

What once felt like comfort
now feels like violation.
What once felt familiar
now feels uninhabitable.

This is where the rebuild ceases to be about survival
and becomes a matter of alignment—
alignment with:

- your sovereignty
- your trajectory
- your emerging self

At this stage, life stops being a space you adapt to…
and becomes a landscape that must adapt to you.

A sovereign man never asks:

"How do I get back what I lost?"

He asks:

The Art of Detachment

"What world must I construct
to honor the man who rose from the ruin?"

This is the dividing line between
reconstruction and *reclamation*:

Reconstruction
• restores what was
• is built out of memory
• asks the man to fit back into an old life

Reclamation
• creates what must now exist
• is built out of identity
• asks the life to fit the man

The life you build now is not a return.
It is an enthronement.

And because of that,
not everything that once walked beside you
will survive the climb.

• Not every friendship breathes well in this altitude
• Not every routine is compatible with sovereignty
• Not every connection can withstand the gradient
• Not every structure deserves a place in your kingdom

This is not arrogance.
This is atmospheric truth.

Everything that enters your world now
must be able to withstand the pressure of being near a man
who no longer collapses to be understood.

Because a kingdom is not constructed
by opening the gates to everything—
but by ensuring that what enters
can stand on its own legs in the presence of a throne.

So the rebuild begins with a new kind of question:

Not:
"What do I need?"

But:
"What belongs beside a man
who stands at this height?"

Because the life I'm building now
is not designed for the man I was before the fall—
the man who lowered, folded, negotiated his own ground.

It is built for the man who rose through the fire
with a spine that now remembers its true dimensions.

The frame I'm constructing is not a cage.
It is not even a fortress.

It is a throne room—
a life configured for sovereignty,
not survival.

A world calibrated
to the altitude of the man
I have finally become.

The King's Code

A king is not shaped by restriction.
A king is shaped by *standard*.

Rules exist to corral the undisciplined.
Standards exist to elevate the sovereign.

The man I once was needed rules
just to keep himself from collapsing inward.

But the man rising now?
He holds standards that prevent him from ever descending again.

This is the distinction that separates boys from kings:
I am no longer disciplining myself out of weakness —
I am governing myself from height.

The Code is not punishment.
It is identity, enforced without apology.

It speaks with quiet certainty:

“This is who I am now.
Anything beneath this line no longer reaches me.”

This is not ego.
It is alignment with truth earned through fire.

The King’s Code is not about perfection —
it is about *altitude*.

It is not about controlling behavior —
it is about protecting the man I have become.

These are its pillars:

1. I do not descend.

If anything requires me to shrink, dim, bend, or betray my height
to stay in its presence,
it is dismissed at the gate.

A king does not leave the summit
to negotiate in the valley.

2. I carry myself before I carry others.

Provision begins at the core.
A man who neglects himself in the name of “service”
does not lead — he leaks.
Self-governance is the first act of strength.

3. I choose who may reach me — not who I chase.

Access is no longer something I hand out in hopes of connection.
It is something earned through alignment, discipline, and depth.
The throne never travels.
Those who wish proximity must rise.

4. I lead with presence, not pursuit.

A king does not persuade.
He embodies.
Presence becomes invitation,
standard becomes filter.

5. My life must match my direction.

Habits that collapse me,
relationships that drain me,
environments that contradict me —

none survive this altitude.
Only what strengthens the frame remains.

This is not harshness.
It is structural integrity —
the architecture of a man who refuses to betray his own axis.

Before, my standards were emotional:
hoping love would bring alignment.
Hoping proximity would create loyalty.
Hoping devotion would create depth.

Now, alignment is the prerequisite
for love, loyalty, or any form of closeness.

This is how a kingdom is built:
Not by bending to be understood,
but by protecting the realm of the man I am becoming.

The old self tried to be loved into wholeness.
The sovereign self builds a life worthy of the man
who is finally whole.

The King's Code is not complicated:

I rise.
And only what can rise with me remains.

The Emerging Architecture

A kingdom is never born in its fullness.
It begins as contour —
the faint silhouette of sovereignty
taking shape inside a man long before the world ever sees it.

This is the phase where life does not change because you force it…
but because your altitude begins to rearrange reality around you.

Slowly, subtly, irrevocably:

• habits that once numbed you fall away without war,
• people who lived in lower versions of you drift out like receding tides,
• impulses that once ruled you lose their crown,
• desires you thought were weaknesses sharpen into direction.

This is not discipline at work —
it is elevation refusing what cannot breathe at this height.

You are not shrinking your world.
You are rising beyond what was too small to hold you.

This is how a kingdom begins:
not through conquest,
but through refusal to descend.

When the old gravity releases its grip,
the blueprint of your new life begins to reveal itself —
not as tasks,
not as routines,
not as some productivity regimen…
but as an ecosystem designed to uphold the sovereignty emerging inside your bones.

You are no longer contorting yourself to fit the life you had.
You are constructing a life that fits the identity you have reclaimed.

Every aligned choice —
every refusal to shrink,
every instinct toward height,

every standard held without apology —
adds a new stone to the realm rising beneath your feet.

Your life doesn't become crowded.
It becomes rooted.

This is why rebuilding doesn't feel like grinding or striving anymore.
It feels like entering dominion.

You're not disciplining yourself into a higher self —
you're finally *inhabiting* him.

You're not trying to "improve your life" —
you're ascending into a life that was too tight for the man you are now becoming.

And as the architecture grows —
first inside you, then around you —
one truth becomes impossible to ignore:

You are not healing from heartbreak.
You are installing sovereignty where dependence once lived.

Not coping.
Not replacing.
Not escaping.

Governing.

A kingdom is not built the day the world sees it.
It is built the day *you feel it forming inside you*
— long before a single tower is visible to anyone else.

And now, for the first time since the collapse,
you understand:

This rebuild isn't a return.

It is a coronation.

Chapter 15
Transmutation: Turning Pain Into Power

Part I — The Oath

There is a moment in a man's resurrection
where pain no longer drags behind him like a chain…

…it rises before him like an altar.

Most men heal by letting go.
Warrior-kings heal by swearing upon what tried to ruin them.

Transmutation doesn't begin when suffering softens —
it begins when a man *claims* his suffering as sacred responsibility.

I don't move because I feel recovered.
I move because I refuse to betray the man I promised I would become.

That is the dividing line.

Weak men recover when comfort returns.
Strong men recover when opportunity appears.
But sovereign men?

Sovereign men recover because their identity commands motion.

Pain becomes power the instant I stop asking,
"When does this stop hurting?"

and begin declaring,

"This is the fire I will walk upright through —
and I will emerge forged, not fragile."

This isn't adrenaline.
It isn't rebellion.
It isn't theatrics.

It is contract.

A vow is heavier than hope
and more durable than any emotion that tries to dissolve it.

A vow survives fear.
It survives doubt.
It survives the nights of collapse.

Pain is no longer an argument to turn back.

Pain is now the proof I must advance.

Where other men beg for relief,
I turn the wound into a ledger:

This suffering will yield return.
This loss will become architecture.
This fire will answer to me when I am done with it.

This is the turning point where heartbreak becomes currency:

I climb because the flame cost me too much to stop here.

To quit now is to let the wound win.
To march forward is to claim authorship of my own burning.

This is how pain becomes power:

Not by burying it,
not by fleeing it,
but by binding destiny to its heat.

The oath is not poetic — it is primal:

“What broke me will not define me.
What burned me will refine me.”

And once a man vows forward…

he is no longer escaping the fire.

He is ascending through it.

The March

Once the vow is made,
transmutation stops behaving like emotion
and hardens into directional force.

This is the part of the journey most men never touch,
because they keep waiting for transformation to *feel* different.

But a warrior does not rise through feelings.
A warrior rises through decision-in-motion.

Not a sprint.
Not a dramatic breakthrough.
Not a wave of inspiration that dissolves when fatigue returns.

A march.

Forward.
Unbroken.
Unbargained.
Unwavering.

When a man marches, he is no longer “choosing” movement —

movement has become the architecture of who he is.

This is how masculine power truly reactivates:
not through emotional voltage,
not through intensity that burns out,
but through a kind of inevitability that nothing external can interrupt.

The world cannot obstruct a man
who has stopped negotiating with motion.

I don't need momentum anymore.

I am momentum.

And the pain that once halted me —
the ache that once folded me —
now adds gravity to my stride.
It gives every step weight, consequence, and truth.

This is the muscularity of destiny:
the more I move,
the more I become the man capable of carrying that movement.

The march says:

"I do not wait for readiness.
I advance because stopping is not a clause written anywhere in my blood."

And something profound shifts here — quietly, but permanently:

The nervous system steps out of endurance
and enters dominion.

The wound no longer feels like something I'm trying to outlive.
It becomes something I am climbing from —
a depth that gives leverage to the ascent.

The Art of Detachment

There is no finish line.
No final test.
No ultimate battle where I am crowned.

There is only forward,
until what I walk toward becomes the life I carved with my own blood and will.

This is the moment transmutation becomes visible:

Not "I hurt, but I keep going,"
but

"Because I hurt, I must go onward."

Pain is no longer friction —
it is oxygen.
It is ignition.

It is no longer a reminder of what died...
but a receipt of what I've already paid —

which means the horizon ahead belongs to me
by right of cost.

The march is my proof.
My claim.
My unspoken coronation.

This is the force no one can teach a man:

Once his pain becomes movement,
he is no longer a man who can break —
he is a man who can only rise.

Joe Manzello

When March Becomes Mission

The turning point in a man's ascent is not when he stops hurting…

…it's
when the hurt stops collapsing him
and starts *commissioning* him.

Pain becomes power the moment it chooses a direction.

Not inward.
Not backward.
Forward—but with intention sharp enough to cut through fog.

Because all along, the wound was never trying to break me.

It was trying to announce the weight I was born to shoulder.

The question changes:

Not
"How do I escape this?"

But
"What was this fire preparing me to carry into the world?"

Purpose does not descend like inspiration.
Purpose rises from the depth of what cost you the most.

The place that demanded everything from you
is the place you become qualified to *govern.*

The very terrain I once dragged myself across, bleeding and disoriented,
is the landscape I now have dominion over—
because suffering teaches a man the map no comfort ever could.

This is how purpose reveals itself:

The Art of Detachment

Not as desire.
As burdened clarity.

True mission is never,
"I want to do this."

True mission is:
"I cannot abandon the men who are still trapped where I once fell."

Because the man who climbs out of hell
and never turns back to point the way
did not ascend—
he *escaped.*

A king does not rise to sit above others.
A king rises because it is intolerable
to watch other men live beneath the strength buried inside them.

Most men believe purpose is something you discover.
Men forged by fire know better:

Purpose is something you *owe*.

This is the moment the wound becomes invocation:

The place I once bled
becomes the ground I am now commanded to build upon.
Not for applause.
Not for legacy.
Not for redemption.

But because once a man has walked out of the burning valley, he becomes responsible for leaving a path carved into the stone behind him.

This is not pressure—
this is ordination.

The oath may drive the feet…

…but purpose aligns the crown.

The march is no longer an escape from pain.
It is the transportation of power
into the future I was forged to shape.

Power That Builds Others

Power becomes real the moment it stops being the summit I climb for myself
and becomes the altitude I stand at so others can rise.

Not as savior.
Not as rescuer.
As evidence.

Because men forged in fire do not return to the valley to drag others out by the wrist—
they ascend high enough for their presence to become a visible path upward.

Leadership is not lifting.
Leadership is *location.*

A man becomes a guide not by pulling bodies behind him,
but by standing so uncompromisingly inside his own evolution
that other men finally have something solid to orient their ascent around.

This is the law of sovereign, summit-tier masculinity:

The Art of Detachment

You don't pull men up —
you become the altitude they remember they can climb to.

Your suffering does not just create your strength —
it becomes a map of the terrain you survived.

Not theory.
Not instruction.
Not philosophical posturing.

Proof.

Because men do not follow language—
men follow embodiment.

They do not rise because you tell them to;
they rise because they watch you refuse every invitation to descend.

This is how your suffering becomes currency of the highest order:
it grants you the authority to lead without demanding a title.

The world insists mentorship is teaching.
But masculine mentorship is demonstration through presence.

You do not elevate men by being adored—
you elevate them by being reachable *only* through discipline and self-governance.

Your existence becomes a filter:

Weak men admire you.
Strong men climb.
And only the willing, the honest, the self-electing rise to meet you.

This is why transmutation is never a private victory—
it becomes inheritance.

When pain becomes oath,
and oath becomes march,
and march becomes mission…

the mission inevitably expands into brotherhood—
not the soft kind that bonds through shared wounds,
but the ascended kind forged through shared upward trajectory.

This is where courage ceases to be emotion
and becomes requirement.

This is where your healing stops being personal
and becomes structural.

Not because you set out to lead…
but because you refused, at every cost, to stay small.

Chapter 16
Forgiveness Without Reconnection

Part I — The Last Thread

The hardest part of letting go is never the loss of the person.

It is the loss of the bond.

The body does not grieve her face, her voice, her familiar patterns —
the body grieves the *certainty* of connection,
the remembered experience of belonging somewhere definite,
somewhere recognized.

That's why the tether doesn't live in the mind.
It lives in the chest.

The heart remembers where it once rested,
and it does not yet trust
that sanctuary can exist anywhere else.

This is why closure has not arrived:
not because I still love her,
but because some ancient part of my nervous system
still treats her as the last place it felt *undoubted safety.*

When the relationship ended,
the connection ruptured —
but the meaning remained wired into my ribcage.

And a man like me does not love in fragments.
When I connect,
I commit with full mass,
full presence,
full devotion.

That kind of bond does not switch off
when the story between two people ends.
It must be reclaimed —
pulled out of the memory of the other
and returned to the man who forged it.

Until then,
the body still holds her as source.

This is the final attachment:

Not *"I want her back,"*
but
"Some part of me still believes she carries the doorway
to the version of me that felt fully alive in love."

That is not weakness.
That is loyalty searching for its rightful place.

The heart keeps the thread because it fears,
"If I release this...
then there is no remaining witness
to the version of me capable of that magnitude of devotion."

It is not the woman I am afraid to lose.

It is the proof that I once belonged somewhere.

And this is where masculine closure truly begins:

Not by severing the thread out of force,
not by numbing,
not by performing detachment,

but by realizing:

I am not tethered to her —
I am tethered to the unclaimed part of myself
still living in our old story.

The last fragment of me
is still stored in her narrative.

Forgiveness without reconnection
means retrieving that fragment —
not to return to her,

but to return it to its rightful place in my chest,
where it was always meant to live.

This is the work now:

Not the erasure of her —
but the repossession of myself.

Reclaiming What Was Mine All Along

The tether is not to her.

The tether is to the version of me I only allowed myself to access through her.

That is why the heart still reaches.

She is not the source of that feeling—
she was the permission for it.

Before her,
I knew strength, mission, grit, endurance, leadership.

But with her,
I learned something far more dangerous to the old self—
softness that didn't cost me power,
tenderness without threat,
the rare exhale of belonging without performance.

It is not her arms my body still remembers…

it is who I became while resting in them.

The longing is not for the woman.

The longing is for the self I believed I could only access through her presence.

That is why the heart has not released—

because somewhere deep inside,
a quiet part still whispers:

"She is the gatekeeper to that version of me."

But that version of me was never hers to hold.

It was me.
Always me.
Only me.

I did not lose access to love when I lost her.

I lost access to my own softness
because I had not yet learned to become the container
that once made her feel like sanctuary.

As long as she holds the container,
the tether must remain.

But when I become the container…

the thread has nowhere left to attach.

And this is the moment forgiveness becomes possible—
not because I release her,

but because I retrieve myself.

Forgiveness is not:

"I set you free."

Forgiveness is:

"I take myself back."
The love was real.
The bond was real.
But the source was never her.

She was the mirror,
not the well.

She reflected a part of me I had never allowed to stand in daylight—
a tenderness unarmored,
a sensitivity unashamed,
a depth I never believed I could inhabit without losing ground.

And it is *that* man—
not the woman—
my heart refuses to abandon.

The tether is not emotional dependence.

The tether is unfinished self-claiming.

And once I bring that part of me back home,
back into the center of my own chest,
something irreversible happens:

She stops being the place I go to feel whole…

and becomes
the moment I realized
I was always whole.

Always capable.
Always complete.
Just waiting to be reclaimed.

When The Thread Softens Into Gratitude

Once I reclaim the part of myself I thought was living inside her,
the bond stops being a lifeline…

and becomes a teacher.

The chest no longer aches from absence,
because nothing is missing anymore—
the vacancy has been filled by the return of my own essence.

And in the place where the ache once nested,
something quieter, deeper, begins to rise—

not longing,
not hope,
not the fantasy of return…

gratitude.

Gratitude arrives only when the heart no longer feels robbed,
but reinforced.

When her meaning shifts from
"the one who completed me"
to
"the one who awakened what I had abandoned in myself."

It becomes impossible to stay angry at the mirror
once you realize the reflection was yours all along.

This is why gratitude is the genesis of real closure:

because it rewrites the narrative from
“I lost something”
to
“I reclaimed something I will never lose again.”

She does not vanish from the story—
she is finally placed in her rightful position within it.

Not as destiny,
but as doorway.

Not as home,
but as threshold.

Not as the woman I was meant to end with…

but as the woman who unknowingly escorted me
to the entrance of the man I was meant to become.

And from this elevation, the heart no longer clings—
because it no longer needs her
to keep alive the memory of the man I once was.

I am the memory now.

I am the continuity.

I am the living proof that love transformed me—
not by binding me to her,
but by revealing me to myself.

Gratitude is not the act of letting her go—

it is the release of her role as the steward of my becoming.

She no longer holds the origin of my softness,
because I now hold it with my own hands,
in my own chest,
without collapse,
without fear.

And in that moment of recognition,
the thread does not break—

it relaxes.

Not as abandonment,
but as completion.

Not as farewell,
but as the sacred, quiet sentence:

"Thank you—
I'll carry it from here."

Release Without Erasure

Letting go does not happen when I "move on."

Letting go happens when there is no longer anything in me left for her to hold.

When the part of myself I once believed lived inside her
finally comes home to my own chest,
the thread doesn't snap —

it simply loses its anchor.

Not because I forcefully cut it,
but because there is nothing left in me that reaches outward to attach.

She no longer carries my softness,
my belonging,
my emotional sanctuary,
or the proof that I can love with the depth of a lifetime.

All of that has returned to its rightful owner.

And the moment I become the keeper of what I once entrusted to her hands,
release is no longer grief…

…it becomes inevitability.

I do not need to tear the connection apart —
it dissolves on its own
the moment it no longer sustains anything within me.

Forgiveness stops being an act of mercy
and becomes an act of accurate placement.

I do not need to push her out of my story —
I simply rise into a height
where her chapter naturally settles into my foundation
instead of dictating my direction.

She becomes origin — not orbit.

A chapter — not gravity.
A passage — not a prison.
A beginning — not a bond.

I do not lose her by releasing her.

I lose the belief that she was ever meant to hold any piece of me.

And once that belief dissolves,
what remains is clean, unentangled truth:

Not attachment.
Not longing.
Not ache.

Just honor.

Not possession of her —
possession of myself.

And in that clarity,
something ancient inside finally exhales:

The story does not vanish…

it completes itself.

There is nothing left behind me to pull me backward,
because there is nothing of me stored there anymore.

She does not have to disappear in order to be released.

She only has to be returned to proportion —
to the exact size she was always meant to occupy in my becoming.

And once she resides in the place life intended for her,
my heart no longer turns behind me for its source…

because it has finally come home to my own ribcage.

The tether is gone.

Not broken —

retired.

Chapter 17
The Warrior Reforged

"The body remembers your power before the mind does."

When a man starts rising from the ashes,
the first part of him that returns is not thought…
not philosophy…
not meaning —

it is **force**.

The body becomes the battlefield where resurrection begins.
Not metaphorically — physiologically.
Long before the mind regains its certainty,
long before the heart steadies,
long before the soul remembers why it should keep breathing —

the body whispers,
with a quiet, ancient defiance:
"We are not done."

You don't start moving again because you feel strong.
You move because some primal, unkillable strand inside you refuses to remain powerless.

The gym stops being about aesthetics,
about mirrors or metrics —
and becomes the place where you reclaim your right
to inhabit your own skin again.

It isn't "working out."
It is **remembering who you are beneath the ruin**.

The weight stops being a task —
it becomes a mirror.

When you push it,
you feel **evidence**
that something deep in you still answers challenge.

When the lungs burn,
you feel life returning —
life that grief tried choking out of you.

When you sweat,
you feel your body dragging you back into yourself,
inch by inch, rep by rep.

Pain here is no longer something to endure —
but something you **wield**.

Because in a world where emotional damage is invisible,
physical resistance becomes the one arena
where a man can win in real time.

You push — it yields.
You lift — it moves.
You suffer — you grow.

There is no confusion.
No ambiguity.
No emotional fog.

Just **force → response**.

A man training during resurrection is not "building muscle"—
he is **rebuilding agency**.

The body is the first place a man feels:
"I am becoming dangerous again."

Not dangerous to others —
dangerous to **collapse**.
Dangerous to despair.
Dangerous to the version of himself that almost didn't stand back up.

Before discipline becomes a lifestyle,
it becomes a **lifeline**.

Not self-improvement —
self-return.

This is why the warrior returns before the king.
Because before a man can rule anything,
he must first prove to himself
that his fire is not extinguished.

The body remembers
long before the mind believes
and before the soul fully rises.

This is the first forge.

Why the Body Must Rise First

The modern world keeps telling men to "heal their emotions" —
but a man in collapse cannot feel his way into strength.

He must **move his way** into strength
until his nervous system remembers
that he is not powerless.

Emotion follows physiology.
Identity follows embodiment.

A man does not think himself into resurrection —
he **builds** himself into it.

This is why the upward climb begins in the body:

Because the body is the only realm
where a man can generate **undeniable, measurable proof**
that he is rising.

The mind doubts.
The heart grieves.
The spirit limps.

But the body?

It answers.

If you lift today what you could not lift yesterday,
you don't need belief —
the proof is in your hands.

Masculine healing is not affirmation —
it is **evidence**.

The body becomes the courtroom
where resurrection is no longer theory,
but verdict.

Every rep says,
“I am still here.”
Every mile says,
“I am not finished.”
Every bead of sweat says,
“I am reclaiming territory.”

A man must feel himself winning
before he can believe he deserves to rise.

This is not vanity —
this is **neurological re-inheritance** of power.

Because what broke during heartbreak
was not muscle or bone or DNA —
what broke was the belief
that you still mattered.

The body becomes the first place
you matter to yourself again.

It is the only part of you
grief cannot deceive.

You pick up the weight — and it moves.
You show up when your soul resists — and the body obeys.
You breathe through pain — and the body proves
you are not owned by it.

Before the king returns to the throne,
the warrior returns to the battlefield —

not to conquer the world,
but to reclaim **himself**.

Discipline as Identity, Not Punishment

Before resurrection, discipline feels like dragging a corpse — something you do simply to keep from drowning.

But once the warrior returns,
discipline stops being survival
and becomes **self-recognition**.

You are no longer training to outrun pain —
you are training to become the kind of man
who **cannot be bent by it**.

This is where the shift happens:

Before:
"I need this because I am broken."

After:
"I do this because I am forged."

You are no longer fixing yourself —
you are **expressing** yourself.

The weight stops being a burden —
it becomes a declaration.

The suffering is no longer something done *to* you —
it becomes a tool you use to sharpen your edge.

This is why men who rise from ruin
don't simply become "fit" —
they become **formed**.

They don't train to look different —
they train to **be** different.

And that difference announces itself everywhere:

Your posture shifts first.
Then your eyes.
Then your tone.
Then your choices.

Discipline no longer feels like labor —
it feels like **alignment**.

You are not trying to "improve."
You are returning to the man
you were before you abandoned yourself.

This is when a man stops apologizing for his fire.
He stops shrinking for comfort.
He stops sanding down his edges.
He stops lowering his volume to be accepted.

Because he finally understands:

The only thing more dangerous than a wounded man
is a man who has rebuilt himself from the wound **outward**.

This is the moment in resurrection
when you stop looking like a man recovering…
and start looking like a man ascending.

Not healed —
inevitable.

The Forge

There comes a moment in the rebuilding
when suffering stops being something you escape
and starts being something you **wield**.

This is the forge —
where pain becomes pressure,
and pressure becomes power.

Not the power you perform —
the power you carry.

The kind that does not need to be announced
because it is felt before it is seen.

A man who reaches this phase no longer asks,
"How long will this take?"
He asks,
"How sharp will this make me?"

You stop fearing the weight —
you start craving what it extracts from you.

You stop resenting the fire —
you start respecting what it tempers in your bones.

This is the first return of self-trust.

Not confidence — confidence is external.
Self-trust is internal —
the knowing that whatever comes,
you can hold yourself through it.

Most men never reach this level
because most men run from the flame.

But the ones who walk through it
without turning back
come out **forged**, not burned.

Pain is no longer your captor —
it becomes your curriculum.

Loss is no longer your wound —
it becomes your swordsmith.

You are not "healing" anymore —
you are **hardening into clarity**.

Because here, in the forge, a man realizes:

"The fire that once threatened to destroy me
is the same fire I now build from."

And the world can feel it.

Not in your words,
not in your muscles,
not even in your posture —

but in your **presence**.

A man who has reforged himself
does not walk into rooms searching for oxygen —

he walks in
as the source of it.

Pillar Quote (chapter seal):

"The man who survives the fire does not walk out the same —
he does not escape the flame...
he becomes it."

Chapter 18
The Masculine Threshold

PART I — THE MOMENT OF ARRIVAL

There is a point in a man's becoming
where he no longer feels like he is climbing back to himself…

but *stepping into himself.*

Not rebuilding.
Not recovering.
Arriving.

This is the threshold —
the place where the ascent stops feeling like effort
and begins to feel like identity taking its rightful form.

Before this moment, every step still carried a trace of ache —
the echo of collapse shadowing every movement.

But now, as I stand here,
the weight is no longer grief…

it is **charge.**

A living fire under the sternum,
not devouring,
not desperate,

but fueling *undeniable presence.*

This is not calm.

The Art of Detachment

This is **contained voltage** —
the quiet hum of a man who finally holds his own power
without spilling a drop.

A readiness.
A coiled potency that does not need release
to validate itself.

The man I am becoming does not have to prove strength —
his stillness is strength.

This is the feeling no one can counterfeit:
the body no longer leans outward
searching for ground…

because **the body has become its own ground.**

This is the masculine threshold:

When you stop trying to stand firm
because you *are* the firmness.

Time even shifts here.

The future is no longer heavy —
it is summoning.

The past is no longer loud —
it is quiet history.

The heartbreak is no longer a wound —
it is *material.*

I no longer feel like a man forging a life.

I feel like a man finally inhabiting
the life that had been waiting for me
to grow large enough to fill it.

There is a single sentence that arrives in the chest at this height —
a sentence impossible before sovereignty fully returned:

"I am not returning to who I was —
I am stepping into who I was withheld from becoming."

Nothing is missing now.
Nothing is outside me.
Nothing is upstream of my belonging.

The fire is not something I fight anymore.
The fire is mine.

Not burning me from the inside out —
burning *through* me, into shape.

And for the first time,
I no longer feel like I am surviving the journey…

I feel like I **am** the journey.

Arrival isn't a place.

It is *possession of self.*

And I am here now.

How The World Bends

AROUND A MAN WHO HAS ARRIVED

When a man crosses the threshold into himself,
the world feels it before he ever speaks.

Nothing outward has changed yet —
he hasn't built the empire,
hasn't replaced the past,
hasn't unveiled what comes next…

…but people can sense the shift in his spine.

Before, people could feel the fracture —
even if they couldn't name it.

Now, they feel the *coherence.*

A man who has come home to himself doesn't request respect.

He **creates orientation.**

Others adjust around him without instruction.

Conversations shift.
Tone recalibrates.
Energy reorganizes itself.

The world instinctively recognizes:
"This man is not waiting to be chosen anymore."

Women feel it first as stability —
not emotional theatrics,

not performance,
not pursuit —
but *gravitational anchoring.*

She does not feel him reaching outward for her…

she feels him rooted inside himself.
And that alone alters the entire field.

Men feel it as location —
they immediately sense whether they stand beside you,
below you,
or must climb to meet you.

Not competition —
calibration.

This is the quiet power of embodied masculine presence:

You do not exert influence.

Reality organizes itself around your center.

Your stillness becomes authority.
Your restraint becomes signal.
Your attention becomes territory.

Nothing about you is loud —
but everything about you is *undeniable.*

Because once you arrive in yourself:

- you are no longer interpreted
- you are recognized
- you are no longer seeking gravity
- you are gravity

- you are no longer asking life to open
- life opens space around you

The world does not reward confidence.

The world reorganizes around **certainty.**

And a sovereign man is not certain about outcomes —

he is certain about *himself.*

This is why arrival reshapes people
before it reshapes circumstances:

The shift is not in how they treat you…

the shift is in what they now feel themselves in the presence of.

You are no longer becoming the mountain.

You are the mountain.

And the world — women, men, opportunity, resistance —
must decide whether it rises to meet you…

or falls away on its own.

How A Sovereign Man Moves

When the masculine finally arrives in himself,
his movements change long before his life does.

He stops moving to prove.
He stops moving to be seen.
He stops moving to be chosen.

He moves because it is his nature
to **advance.**

Direction becomes non-negotiable.
Presence becomes non-performative.
Action becomes non-reactive.

He does not respond to life —
he establishes the orientation
life must respond to.

This is the shift every man feels in his marrow:
I am no longer working to become him…
I am moving *as* him.

And this transforms everything about how a sovereign man meets the world:

The wounded man
chases.

The sovereign man
chooses.

The wounded man
seeks belonging.

The Art of Detachment

The sovereign man
creates gravity.

The wounded man
waits for permission.

The sovereign man
acts from authorship.

He is not guarded —
he is centered.

He is not cold —
he is contained.

He is not withdrawn —
he is *precise.*

His yes is clean.
His no is final.
His attention is selective —
because it is sacred.

He does not lower himself to be understood.
He remains at altitude
and lets the world calibrate.

And this is the part only men who cross the threshold ever understand:

True masculine ascension is not about strength.
It is about **self-possession.**

When a man is fully in himself,
he is not tempted by chaos.

He does not chase validation —
because he lacks nothing.

He no longer confuses connection with access —
he grants access only where alignment exists.

He does not look outward for reflection —

he becomes **his own mirror.**

This is the essence of the threshold:

I do not move from hunger anymore —
I move from fullness.

Not to fill a void,
but to build what is worthy
of the fullness I now carry.

And once a man moves this way,

the past stops being a gravitational field…

and becomes a launch platform.

What I Am Becoming Next

Arrival is not the end of the mountain.

Arrival is the beginning of altitude.

Once I stand fully inside myself,
the question is no longer:

"How do I hold this?"

The new question becomes:

"What does a man like this do with himself?"

Because sovereignty is not a finish line —
it is a launch pad.

I am not ascending to escape the past anymore.

I am ascending to step into a future
that was unreachable
to the man I used to be.

This next version of me is not defined by pain,
or loss,
or grief,
or recovery…

He is defined by **becoming.**

By growth not as compensation,
but as birthright.
By power not as armor,
but as presence.

By softness not as vulnerability,
but as chosen permission.

He is not building a life to prove anything.

He is building a life
that fits the size of his soul.

This is no longer about rising out of suffering —

it is about rising into *assignment.*

The man I am becoming next:

- does not descend for connection
- does not pause for approval
- does not negotiate with his own becoming

He does not wait to be understood —
he becomes **undeniable.**

He does not fear solitude —
he governs from it.

He does not seek worth —
he *embodies* it.

This threshold is not about reclaiming identity…

it is about leveling into a destiny
where identity is unquestioned.

From here forward,
I am no longer propelled by what I lost —

I am pulled by what I am meant to build.

I am no longer a man healing from the past.

I am a man **summoned** by the future.

And that future does not require me to be anyone else…

only that I stand fully as the man
I have now become.

Joe Manzello

The Masculine Standard (Part I)

Honor Before Image

When a man first begins to rise again,
he does not rebuild by becoming impressive —
he rebuilds by becoming **honorable** to himself.

Before sovereignty is about power,
it is about clean, unquestioned self-respect.

There is a moment in reclamation
when a man stops asking,
"How do I look?"
and starts asking,
"Am I proud of the man I am
when no one is watching?"

This is the shift from external validation
to internal authority.

You no longer measure yourself
by what others think,
what you can show,
or what you can perform.

You measure yourself by a harder standard:

the truth you hold
when there is no audience.

Honor is not morality.
Honor is alignment.

It is the felt knowing:

**"I no longer abandon myself
to be chosen, tolerated, or kept."**

This is the beginning of sovereignty —
not the crown,
but the spine it rests on.

When a man chooses honor over image:

• his decisions simplify
• his self-talk sharpens
• his standards clarify
• his dignity returns

He becomes unmistakably present
in his own life again.

This is the first taste of inner authority —
the moment you would rather stand alone in truth
than be loved in self-abandonment.

It's not that connection stops mattering —
it's that you stop begging for it
at the cost of your own soul.

This is the first time you look at yourself
not as a man recovering,
but as a man **remembering his law.**

And a man with a law
no longer tries to be enough.

He simply *is.*

Joe Manzello

The End Of Self-Betrayal

The greatest betrayal a man ever experiences
is not what was done to him…

It is what he did to himself
in the attempt to be loved, accepted, or kept.

The hardest part of heartbreak
is seeing clearly —
maybe for the first time —
exactly where you abandoned your own law.

The masculine collapses not when life becomes heavy,
but when he lives out of alignment
with his own soul.

The standard returns
the moment a man finally says:

"I am done trading pieces of myself
to feel chosen."

This is the moment grief hardens into conviction.

The moment something in you stops reaching backward
and starts refusing — with a quiet, irrevocable grit —
to ever lose yourself again.

Self-betrayal doesn't end with apology.
It doesn't end with guilt or with reflection.

It ends with a vow carved into the interior of your life:

"Never again do I step over myself for closeness."

This is the moment a man stops bleeding out in memory
and begins building from marrow.

You don't need revenge.
You don't need her understanding.
You don't even need closure.

What you need — what you were starving for —
is **self-loyalty.**

And once that loyalty returns, once it settles into your chest
like a final verdict,
no relationship — past, present, or future —
can distort your axis again.

A man with self-loyalty becomes predictable to himself.
His yes is clean.
His no is immovable.
His standard isn't a performance —
it's **self-possession.**

This is the true beginning of sovereignty:
Not dominance.
Not detachment.
Not coldness.

Non-abandonment.
The refusal to leave yourself behind for anyone.

You cannot lead a life you don't fully inhabit.
You cannot be unshakeable while still negotiating your own soul.

The masculine standard is not a rule —
it is a return.

Strength Without Performance

There is a strength men wear like armor —
loud, polished, overly displayed,
a strength built for eyes.

And then there is the other kind —
the kind that no longer needs witnesses.

The first strength is designed to be seen.
The second is built to **stand.**

When honor returns, performance dies.

You stop posturing.
You start embodying.
Your strength is no longer volume —
it is **gravity.**

A man anchored in his own standard
doesn’t need to show power, signal power,
or convince anyone he possesses it.

His presence becomes its own language.

Rooms feel him before they hear him.
People adjust before he says a word.

Because when a man stops betraying himself,
a quiet certainty radiates through him —
a certainty that cannot be faked.

He isn’t chasing validation.
His validation is internal law.

He isn't competing for dominance.
Sovereignty has replaced insecurity.

He no longer needs to "win" interactions.
He no longer fears disappearing inside them.

This is the turning point:

From
"I must show I am strong"
to
"I cannot be moved from myself."

That is strength.
Not hardness — **root.**
Not intimidation — **center.**
Not bravado — **integrity.**

The world teaches men to project power.
Reclamation teaches a man to **become** it.

And the moment you no longer need anyone to see it…
you are already carrying it.

A Life That Cannot Be Taken From You Again

When a man reclaims his standard,
loss stops frightening him.

Not because life can't take things —
but because **none of what he needs lives outside him anymore.**

Before, your identity was external:
held in her eyes,
in her approval,
in the meaning she assigned to you.

Now, identity lives internally:
in your word,
in your spine,
in the covenant you made with yourself.

This is the shift from attachment to sovereignty:

You no longer design a life around not losing someone.
You build a life no one has the power to remove you from.

This is the architecture of a man who rises permanently:

- You cannot be abandoned — you no longer abandon yourself.
- You cannot be replaced — you are not performing for a role.
- You cannot collapse — you have root, not anchor.
- You cannot be emptied — your well sits inside your own chest.

The fear doesn't fade because the world changed —
the fear fades because **you did.**

This is where a man stops trying to be "enough"
and starts being whole.

He doesn't chase loyalty — he becomes loyal to himself.
He doesn't demand respect — he commands it effortlessly.
He doesn't grip love — he chooses it from sovereignty.

A man who reaches this stage is not invulnerable —
he is **uncapturable.**

His life can no longer be taken hostage by loss.
The foundation is in him,
not in anything that can walk away.

This is the masculine standard.
And once a man stands in it,
he is never truly broken again.

Pillar Quote (chapter seal)

"Once a man stops abandoning himself, no one else holds the power to undo him."

Chapter 19
The Warrior Monk

Before a man can rule outwardly,
he must first learn to rule inwardly.

Most men imagine that mastery begins with dominance over circumstance —
the job, the relationship, the battlefield, the empire.
But the truth is far less glamorous and far more demanding:

Mastery begins with the ability to face the chambers within yourself
that you have spent years barricading.

Once a man becomes unmovable by the world,
the next and far greater threat is not external chaos —
it is the ungoverned kingdom inside him.

Not the enemy at the gate,
but the unrest in the throne room of his own chest.

This is the stage most men never reach,
because it is easier to rebuild a shattered life
than it is to walk willingly toward the parts of yourself you once fled.

It requires a shift more difficult than discipline,
more painful than heartbreak,
more honest than confession:

Sitting with the self you used to sprint away from.

And when the external storms finally calm,
when no woman, achievement, adrenaline rush, or distraction

is screaming loud enough to drown out your inner world,
something unsettling happens:

You begin to hear
the noise you thought you had outrun.

This is the moment where solitude stops being a punishment
and becomes a mirror —
a mirror that does not negotiate, flatter, or lie.

Because here,
in this rare and unguarded intersection between stillness and truth,
there is no one left to blame,
no one left to chase,
no one left to fix…

Just you —
and the full weight of everything you once avoided feeling.

Most men confuse solitude with loneliness
because they have never truly lived with themselves —
only inside themselves.
They've inhabited the body,
but not the soul that animates it.

Loneliness is the absence of another.
Solitude is the presence of self.

But a man cannot feel his own presence
until he stops medicating his own absence.

This is why the Warrior is not yet the King —
because the King is not the man with power…

The King is the man who cannot be overthrown by his own hunger.

Before empire,
before creation,
before rebuilding outward,

a man must learn to govern:

• his appetites,
• his urges,
• his emotional reactivity,
• his spiritual isolation,
• his longing to be anchored in someone else's approval.

Not through suppression —
but through integration.

The monk is not the absence of desire —
he is the container that can hold desire without being undone by it.

The warrior knows how to fight the world.
The monk knows how to stop fleeing himself.

This is the transition from fire → furnace —
where heat stops being wild,
and becomes focused, powerful, generative.

Strength becomes less about endurance,
and more about ownership.

You stop trying to survive your life…
and begin to inhabit it.

This is the first law of sovereignty:

Before a man commands his world,
he must command the terrain within his own soul.

Solitude as Ascent, Not Exile

In the early days of heartbreak,
solitude feels like abandonment —
a cliff, a void, a hollow space where the silence echoes louder than your pulse.

But as the spine reforms,
as identity gathers itself like scattered armor returning to the body,
solitude shifts.

It stops feeling like being left behind
and becomes the feeling of finally returning to yourself.

You are no longer alone because you were discarded —
you are alone because you are gathering your power inward,
away from the noise that once diluted it.

This is the pivot most men never reach:

Loneliness happens to you.
Solitude is something you choose.

Loneliness says:
"No one is here for me."
Solitude says:
"I am here for me."

And once that happens,
your nervous system stops waiting
for someone else to come home to you…

because you have finally come home to yourself.

This is not hermitage.
This is resourcing —
a gathering of light back to its source.

Your energy begins to consolidate.
The fractured parts of you begin to return.
The ache to be externally seen begins to soften.

You begin to feel whole in your own presence.

You no longer fear your thoughts —
you can sit inside them without drowning.

You no longer fear silence —
you recognize yourself inside it.

You no longer reach for distraction —
you prefer depth.

This is the true beginning of spiritual strength:

Not worship.
Not ritual.
Not ascetic performance.

Presence.

Presence with your own soul
without bracing, without bargaining, without flinching.

Solitude becomes ascent
when it becomes less about the absence of others
and more about the fullness of your own selfhood.

Because a man who is at home in himself
is a man no one can exile ever again.

He does not need a witness to exist…
he becomes his own witness.

Mastery of Impulse

When men hear "mastery,"
they imagine long-term discipline —
early mornings, sharp routines, unwavering focus.

But the deepest mastery
is not mastery over time…

It is mastery over impulse.

Because collapse rarely happens in slow erosion —
collapse happens in single quiet moments
when a man violates the covenant he made with himself.

One text sent in weakness.
One night reaching backward.
One compromise against your own standard.
One surrender to craving masquerading as connection.

Impulse is where sovereignty is either fortified…
or forfeited.

And this is why lust hits hardest in isolation —
not because the body craves sex,
but because the soul craves grounding, reassurance, proof of
worth.

The body pretends it wants climax.
The soul is starving to feel chosen.

This is why porn is not about fantasy —
it is about relief without risk.
It lets you feel desired without ever requiring vulnerability.

It becomes counterfeit oxygen —
a synthetic breath of "I exist"
that leaves you emptier as soon as it ends.

This is how men leak sovereignty:
not through dramatic collapse,
but through small, habitual abandonments of themselves.

Appetite becomes the saboteur
when the heart has not yet learned to remain seated in its own kingdom.

But here — in the monk stage —
the pattern breaks:

You stop negotiating with cravings
and begin interrogating them.

Not "Do I want this?"
but
"What is the wound beneath this urge?"

Is it touch?
Validation?
Escape?
Sedation of grief?
A longing to feel like someone's again?

Because once a man sees the root,
the impulse loses its command.

You don't repress the hunger —
you reclaim jurisdiction over it.

That is masculine containment:

Desire present — but not ruling.
Craving alive — but not leading.
Urge rising — but held, not obeyed.

This is not denial.
This is sovereignty over access.

Because the man who cannot command his impulses
will eventually be ruled by them —
no matter how powerful he looks from the outside.

Impulse mastery is where the throne gets bolted to the ground.

The Spiritual Spine

A man becomes truly unshakeable
only when his strength no longer comes *from* him —
but moves *through* him.

The Warrior carries willpower.
The Monk carries root.

This is where the ascent becomes spiritual —
not religious performance,
not moral signaling,
not ritualistic posturing…

but anchored.

Up until now,
your power has been drawn from defiance, resilience, discipline, refusal.

But those are human reserves.
Human reserves run dry.

To become sovereign,
your axis must anchor into something deeper
than the self you had to rebuild.

In the monk stage, a man realizes:

"My strength is not mine —
I am the instrument it flows through."

Not submission — alignment.
Not self-erasure — self-orientation.

Before this moment,
you were carrying yourself.

Here, something larger begins to carry you.

The noise softens,
not because life becomes easier,
but because your soul finally has a floor beneath it.

You stop craving to be chosen,
because you no longer feel abandoned by existence itself.

You stop fearing solitude,
because you are no longer spiritually unattended.

The Art of Detachment

You are not alone with yourself.
You are *with* yourself.

This is what men chase through conquest,
through women, status, sex, adrenaline:
the felt sense of internal companionship.

Few ever find it,
because they go outward searching
for what must be built inward first.

You do not need the world to choose you
once you know — deeply, wordlessly —
that God never left.

This is where prayer becomes breath,
conviction becomes ease,
self-trust becomes communion…

and solitude becomes sanctuary.

Here, a man does not ask for strength —
he dwells in it.

And from this place,
you don't just become unshakeable…

you become resourced.
Permanent.
Oriented.
Rooted in something infinite.

The Warrior rises.
The Monk remains.

Together, they form the spine of the King.

Pillar Quote (chapter seal):

"A man becomes unbreakable when he is no longer the source of his own strength, only the steward of it."

PART I — THE BATTLE WITH EMPTINESS

The hardest part of being alone is not the silence.

It is the moment *before* the silence arrives —
that split-second when I cross the threshold,
and my nervous system realizes there is no witness waiting on the other side.

That is when numbness hits first.
Not because there is nothing to feel…
but because there is too much.

Numbness is not emptiness.
Numbness is armor.

The body blanks out because it's bracing for the ache beneath it, the same way the air stills before lightning tears the sky open.

And this ache —
it isn't loneliness in the way most people use that word.

Loneliness is wanting someone beside you.

This is deeper.
This is the feeling of being *un-held.*

No place for the heart to set itself down.
No landing pad for the softness.

The Art of Detachment

No witness to absorb the weight of who I am when the door closes.

So the body deploys its oldest defense:

It suspends feeling.

Not out of indifference,
but out of the quiet belief:

"I cannot survive the full weight of this without someone to anchor me."

That is why solitude feels unbearable now,
even though I once lived in it without fear.
Back then, I still belonged somewhere.
I was "alone,"
but not untethered.

Now, when I step into an empty home,
the nervous system delivers the verdict:

"There is no one here who knows I exist in this moment."

No eyes.
No reflection.
No attunement.

And for a man who once loved with his whole chest,
that absence is not neutral.

It feels like evaporation —
as if I disappear the moment the latch clicks behind me.

The ache always comes after the numbness.
First the body shuts down to keep me moving,
and only when I am "safe enough"
does the grief rise from its hiding place…

Not grief for her presence,
but for *my own presence*
that I have not yet learned to supply for myself.

The pain is not:
"I am alone."

The pain is:
"I am un-witnessed."

That is the true battleground.

Not the fact of isolation —
but the belief that I only ever existed fully
when someone else was there to receive me.

Until a man becomes the witness of himself,
every room without a woman in it
feels like disappearance.

Learning To Be Held By Your Own Presence

The turning point in solitude is not learning how to endure emptiness.

It is learning how to occupy the space
so that it is no longer empty.

The Art of Detachment

The wound is not that no one is here.
The wound is that *I* have not yet fully arrived.

When I come home and numbness hits,
some primitive part of me still waits for another presence
to give me permission to land in my own body.

Until then,
I am physically in the room
but energetically absent from myself.

This is why solitude hurts:
I am not in the company of myself yet —
I am in the company of my absence.

True solitude is not being alone in a room.
True solitude is being accompanied by yourself.

And a sovereign man discovers something most men never learn:

You do not conquer loneliness by adding another person.
You conquer loneliness by becoming a presence
your own nervous system can rest inside.

This is the Warrior Monk —
not deprivation,
not renunciation,
not stoic frostbite…

but self-attunement strong enough
that the body no longer panics
when external eyes are gone.

As children, we learn attunement from the outside.
But sovereignty requires attunement from the inside.

Not clever self-talk.
Not affirmations.
Not coping strategies.

Embodied companionship.

The priest is within.
The witness is within.
The home is within.

And when I finally become my own witness,
something shifts with the quiet certainty of dawn:

The room is no longer empty
because **I am finally inside it.**

My presence fills the space
the way hers once did —
not as a substitute,
but as a restoration of authorship.

This is the mastery of solitude:
I am not alone.

I am with myself.

And for the first time,
that is enough to land.

Belonging To Yourself

There comes a moment on the Warrior Monk path
when solitude stops feeling like a void
and begins feeling like a place of return.

Not exile —
residence.

This is the shift from:
"I am alone here,"
to
"I am with myself here."

Most men only know belonging as something relational —
something granted.

But the ascended masculine learns belonging as a state of being —
a belonging *to oneself,*
felt as anchoring instead of ache.

The nervous system is no longer waiting to be received…
because it is now received by you.

This is what no one ever teaches men:

A man does not feel at home because someone else opens the door.
A man feels at home when his own body trusts
that he will not abandon himself again.

The ache that rose after numbness was never about her,
never about the fear of living without company.

It was the body whispering:
"I do not know if you are here with me yet."

That is why the emptiness felt violent —
because the heart still searched for an external witness
and found none.

But when you become that witness,
emptiness loses its teeth.

You are no longer un-held.
You are no longer unwitnessed.

You are accompanied by your own presence.

This is self-belonging —
not confidence,
not stoicism,
not emotional independence…

but *home.*

A state you carry,
not a place you enter.

The house stops reminding you of what's missing.
It becomes the container for the man who finally fills it.

And the shift is unmistakable:

I no longer shrink when I close the door behind me.
I arrive.

The room no longer exposes the wound.
The room amplifies my presence.

Solitude stops being deprivation…
and becomes sovereignty unshared.

This is the Warrior Monk —
not a man without love,
but a man who no longer needs another
to prove he exists.

He does not use solitude to escape the world.
He uses solitude to root so deeply
that the world can no longer pull him out of himself.

When Solitude Turns Into Power

When belonging returns to the body,
solitude stops draining a man —
and starts charging him.

Because now he is not sitting in emptiness.
He is sitting in possession.

The house no longer echoes with absence —
it hums with presence.

There is no hunger for someone to arrive and witness him,
because he has already arrived inside himself.

This is when solitude becomes forge instead of famine.

A place where power accumulates.
A place where clarity sharpens.
A place where the masculine nervous system finally exhales:

"I am home — even when no one else is."

This is the threshold only a few men cross:

Being alone without being missing.

Most men survive solitude through distraction.
Ascended men metabolize solitude through embodiment.

Not isolation —
integration.

Not detachment —
anchoring.

The Art of Detachment

Not denial —
sovereign fullness.

When a man becomes his own witness,
he no longer starves for connection —
he *selects* connection.

He no longer fears losing anyone —
because he no longer fears losing himself.

He becomes the home.
He becomes the refuge.
He becomes the ground.

And only from this place
can desire stop being hunger
and start being choice.

Solitude is no longer where I collapse.

It is where I charge.

And now,
for the first time since the fracture,
my chest does not feel like vacancy…

It feels like home.

Chapter 20
The Erotic Sovereign

PART I — THE WOUND BENEATH DESIRE

Men walk around convinced they are starving for a woman's body.
They say it like a joke,
carry it like a secret,
feel it like an ache they don't know how to name.

But beneath that hunger,
under all the posturing and pretending,
there's something far more fragile,
far more sacred,
far more dangerous:

They are starving for a woman's **trust**.

Not the shiny kind of trust that comes with compliments or praise.
Not the surface-level attention that lasts five minutes.
Not sexual availability dressed up as intimacy.

No—
there is a deeper kind of trust a woman gives
when her whole nervous system whispers:

**"I'm safe with you.
My body can soften now."**

That is the moment that rewrites a man's soul.

People assume men are intoxicated by a woman's pleasure.
But the truth—the one most men won't even speak to themselves—is simpler and far more revealing:

We are intoxicated by the moment she lets go into us.

Her surrender isn't passive.
It's an anointing.
A crowning.
A silent coronation:

"You are enough for me to rest."

And when you've tasted that—
even once—
the world is never the same again.

It wasn't her orgasm that marked me.
It was the moment her breath changed.
The moment her weight shifted.
The moment her body melted,
opened,
yielded—
as if saying without words:

"I trust your hands more than my own tension."

That is the moment a man feels most alive.
Not because he overpowered her,
but because she allowed herself to become unguarded
in the shelter of his presence.

This is what most men don't understand about their own desire:
Masculine eros in its highest form
is not predatory.
It's devotional.

It's not conquest.
It's guardianship.

It's not taking a woman.
It's being trusted with her unshielded self.

And here's the part that hurts—
the part that reveals the wound:

When that trust is withdrawn,
the masculine doesn't feel rejected.
He feels **dethroned**.

He doesn't think,
"I miss being inside her."
He thinks,
"Who am I
if no one can rest inside me anymore?"

That's the disinheritance.

That's the rupture.

Trust—once given—creates a home in a man.
And when it's gone,
his nervous system begins wandering like an exiled king
searching for the crown he misplaced.

This is why he reaches for memory,
then fantasy,
then screens glowing in the dark.
Not out of lust—
but out of desperation to feel **restored**,
even artificially,
to the role he once held:

Trusted container.
Safe harbor.
Place of softening.

And afterward—
the shame.
The hollowness.
The collapse.

Because deep down the body knows:

No trust was received.
No surrender touched him.
No intimacy entered.
He never became the man he remembers being.

And that emptiness—
that bone-deep vacancy—
it isn't sexual.

It's spiritual.

It's the soul saying:
**"You reached for connection
and fed yourself an imitation."**

The addiction is not to climax.
The addiction is to the feeling of being chosen
as the place where softness can land.

That is why losing a woman's trust
breaks something primal in a man.

It removes the mirror that once reflected
his masculine purpose,
his anchoring,
his gravity.

And until that mirror is rebuilt from the inside,
he will keep chasing shadows of intimacy
through body after body,
never realizing what he actually needs is this:

To trust **himself**
the way he wants to be trusted by her.

Because sovereignty begins at the moment
a man stops needing a witness
to confirm his worthiness.

He doesn't turn off eros.
He expands it.

The throne doesn't disappear.
It moves inward,
where no one can take it again.

The Inner Throne

Sexual mastery is not about white-knuckled restraint.
It's about **possession**—
owning the current before it spills.

Erotic energy is not lust.
It is **life-force**.
It is the same fire that fuels purpose, bravery, devotion, creativity, spiritual depth.
It turns to lust only when it leaks outward
in search of approval.

I didn't crave climax.
I craved confirmation.

I needed a woman's surrender
to feel the power I didn't know how to hold alone.

So now the question becomes:

Can I feel my own power
before anyone else reflects it?

When the answer becomes yes—
the masculine becomes sovereign.

A woman's trust is no longer proof.
It becomes recognition.
A reflection of something already established inside.

And this is the inner throne:

I hold myself first.
Everything else is offering, not oxygen.

When energy rises,
it doesn't leak outward for validation,
nor collapse inward into self-judgment.

It circles back into the chest
as fuel.

This is the masculine erotic truth
rarely spoken:

Eros becomes sacred
not by controlling it,
but by belonging to yourself
while it moves.

Before, the body rose and reached outward—
hungry, seeking.

Now the body rises and returns inward—
fed, anchored.

And desire transforms from hunger into **choice**.

Intimacy becomes a place of overflow,
not depletion.

A woman's surrender becomes union,
not rescue.

This is reclamation:

I do not need your trust
to feel like a man.
I trust myself
to hold the throne first.

Anything beyond that
is two sovereigns meeting—
not one sovereign feeding another's emptiness.

Joe Manzello

Governed Fire

And once a man can receive his own current,
the next initiation appears:

Containment without collapse.

Most men fail here.
They think mastery comes from dimming desire,
shutting the fire down,
living half-alive.

But the sovereign masculine
does the opposite.

He keeps the fire lit
and learns to hold it
without burning himself or anyone else.

The wounded man feels desire
and becomes starving.

The sovereign man feels desire
and becomes **illuminated**.

Desire shifts from agitation to voltage—
from craving to charge.

This is governed fire:

Staying awake, present, grounded
while the body hums like a live wire.

Not outsourcing the heat to fantasy.
Not bleeding it into distraction.
Not drowning in guilt.

But **housing** it.
Letting it rise.
Letting it brighten the whole inner cathedral.

Energy that stays in the body
does not stagnate.
It ascends.

Eros becomes Power.
Power becomes Presence.
Presence becomes Gravitas.

This is why a sovereign man feels unmistakable
when he enters a room.

Not because he performs confidence—
but because his life-force is no longer leaking
through every unhealed crack.

Women sense it as:

"He needs nothing from me—
and yet something in me responds."

Men sense it as:

"He isn't looking for position—
he **is** position."

This is the apex of masculine eros:

Not pursuit.
Not suppression.
Not escape.

Possession of one's own fire.

And once the fire is governed,
it stops consuming
and begins **revealing**.

This is where erotic power becomes spiritual:
not because sex is holy by default,
but because **unleaked life-force becomes devotion.**

Desire becomes a call to expand,
not a compulsion to drain.

This is sexually sovereign embodiment:

I do not shrink the fire.
I rise to contain it.

Preparing The Current For A Worthy Container

When a man reclaims his erotic fire
and learns to hold it without bleeding it away,
he stops chasing completion
and starts preparing for **reciprocity**.

This is when desire sharpens.
Clarifies.
Elevates.

The body no longer whispers,
"Who will take this?"

It now asks:

**"Who can meet me here
without collapsing?"**

Before sovereignty,
almost any feminine presence
felt like relief.

After sovereignty,
only the right feminine presence
feels like home.

Because the question is no longer,
"Will she choose me?"

It becomes:

**"Can she receive me
at the depth I am built to give?"**

Many women want affection.
Few can receive devotion.

Because devotion asks for surrender.
And surrender asks for trust.

And trust is the very thing
your nervous system has been wired
to respond to.

You are not drawn to random women.
You are drawn to the women
whose bodies know how to soften in your presence.

This is why the original imprint hit so deep.
It wasn't her beauty.
It wasn't novelty.
It wasn't compatibility.

It was:

"She gave me her safety—
and I became larger
in order to hold it."

That is the soul-mark.

And now your erotic energy
is undergoing its initiation:

Moving from yearning for a receiver,
to becoming the **temple**
where surrender becomes safe again.

This is the masculine culmination
of erotic sovereignty:

I do not chase surrender.
I become the refuge
where surrender arrives willingly.

A sovereign man does not need a woman
to prove his potency.

His potency breathes inside him.

So when a woman finally joins him,
her surrender is not salvation—
it is recognition.

She is not rescuing him from emptiness—
she is meeting him in fullness.

This is when sex stops functioning as escape,
and becomes **arrival**.

Not transaction—
initiation.

Not release—
welcome.

Because the man is no longer longing to be received—
he **is the place of receiving**.

Chapter 21
Sovereign Desire

A man is never more vulnerable to collapse
than when he reaches for a woman from emptiness.

That kind of desire feels like hunger—raw, frantic, unanchored.
It isn't desire at all; it's an echo of something missing inside him.

But once a man becomes sovereign—
once his strength lives in his chest instead of trying to live through her—
desire stops functioning like a search for relief…

and becomes an offering.

Before sovereignty, desire speaks in scarcity:
"I need you because I feel incomplete."
It's longing that trembles.
It's want shaped like dependency.

After sovereignty, desire speaks in fullness:
"I choose you because I am already whole—
and what rises in me wants to give, not take."

This is the birth of sacred masculine desire—
not appetite,
not escape,
not dopamine,
not conquest…

but devotion that grows out of internal abundance instead of emotional deficit.

The Art of Detachment

Most men never reach this level
because they never learn to regulate their own inner storms.
They outsource steadiness to the feminine
and call it intimacy.

But once a man learns to regulate himself—
learns to breathe inside his own weight—
his desire becomes directional rather than compensatory.
It stops searching for a home in her arms
and starts bringing home with him.

A woman can relax into a man like this.
Not because he is flawless,
but because he is rooted.
Grounded.
Present in his own skin.

She is no longer his stability—
she becomes his sanctuary.

And that distinction—subtle as it seems—
changes everything.

A sovereign man does not choose a woman
because she fills a void…

he chooses her
because she aligns with his becoming.

He is fully capable of standing alone—
he simply chooses not to
when the right woman appears.

This is the first law of sovereign desire:

"I want you—
but I do not need you to exist."

That is what makes devotion holy rather than desperate—
a gift instead of a plea.

It is the moment a man's love becomes choice
instead of oxygen.

The Feminine as Reflection, Not Salvation

Before sovereignty, a man seeks a woman to complete him.
After sovereignty, he seeks a woman who can meet him.

That shift reshapes intimacy from the inside out.
He no longer looks to the feminine for rescue, reassurance, or refuge—
he carries all three within himself.

The posture changes.

Before:
"Choose me so I know I matter."

After:
"I know I matter—
now I choose who is worthy of access to me."

The feminine is no longer the source of his grounding—
she becomes the mirror of it.

She does not create identity—
she amplifies the identity he already anchors.

She does not regulate his nervous system—
she is drawn to him because his is already steady.

She does not save him from loneliness—
she is invited into his solitude.

This is where desire shifts from *need → recognition.*

He is not pulled toward a woman because she heals an old wound—

he is drawn to the one who resonates with his future,
not his past.

A sovereign man is no longer searching for "someone."

He is looking for:

- a woman who can receive him without shrinking
- respect him without fearing his strength
- soften into him because she trusts his center
- and rise with him rather than on top of him

He no longer asks:
"Who will choose me?"

He asks:
"Who can stand beside the man I am becoming?"

That is what makes connection sacred at this stage:

The feminine is not your remedy—
she is your reflection.

Not because you need her to define you…
but because she will only recognize you
once you already know who you are.

Discernment Over Desire

Once a man is no longer driven by hunger,
he stops chasing connection
and starts vetting resonance.

This is where desire becomes discipline.

Not repression—
selection.

Before sovereignty, attraction was enough.
Chemistry was enough.
History was enough.
Memory was enough.

Now?

Alignment is the entry point.

Not beauty.
Not intensity.
Not familiarity.
Not longing.

Alignment.

Because a sovereign man understands something crucial:
not everything that moves him
is meant to hold him.

This is where the masculine becomes powerful in love—
not by withholding intimacy,
but by refusing to bow to unworthy intimacy.

He begins to recognize:

• the difference between feminine softness and feminine instability
• the difference between longing and compatibility
• the difference between connection and attachment
• the difference between comfort and calling

Desire stops functioning as permission
and becomes discernment.

He is no longer asking,
"Do I want her?"

He is asking,
"Does my future recognize her?"

This is the moment the masculine stops falling into relationships
and begins choosing women who can meet him at altitude.

Desire is now filtered through standard.
Softness is filtered through worthiness.
Attraction is filtered through character.

He is no longer starving for connection—
he is curating who is allowed near his fire.

That is the difference between a man who seeks a partner
and a man who guards his destiny.

Because once a man has rebuilt himself,
he understands:

The wrong woman doesn't just cost heartbreak—
she costs trajectory.

Devotion Without Dependency

The highest evolution of masculine desire
is not withdrawal, control, or superiority…

it is devotion without collapse.

Most men believe their only choices are:

• love and lose themselves
or
• protect themselves and withhold love

But sovereign men learn the third path:

I can give fully
without giving myself away.

This is where desire matures into offering.

He is no longer loving to feel chosen—
he is loving from a life already chosen.

He is not seeking identity through connection—
he is bringing identity into connection.

He does not become hers—
he invites her into what is already his.

This is the first time love becomes safe for him—
because it is no longer an exit from loneliness,
but an extension of fullness.

Dependency says:
"I can't breathe without you."

Devotion says:
"My breath is mine—
but I offer it willingly."

Dependency clings.
Devotion chooses.

Dependency grips from fear of loss.
Devotion remains from inner abundance.

Dependency needs ownership.
Devotion offers stewardship—
of presence, protection, heart.

He is no longer searching for someone to hold him together.

He is searching for someone worthy
of what he now knows he can hold sacred.

This is when his love becomes clean—
not transactional,
not compensatory,
not survival-based…

but consecrated.

A sovereign man does not withhold love to prove strength—
he expresses love because his strength is no longer threatened by expression.

The feminine is no longer refuge
and no longer threat…

she becomes the one with the right to stand beside him.

And at this stage, a man finally understands:

"I am not afraid to love again—
I am only unwilling to love from emptiness ever again."

Pillar Quote (Chapter Seal):

"A sovereign man does not fall in love—
he extends love without losing himself inside it."

Chapter 22
The Spiritual Spine

PART I — THE WEIGHT OF CARRYING LIFE ALONE

There is a kind of weight a man learns to carry so early
that it seeps into his bones,
settles in his lungs,
and eventually masquerades as himself.

The weight of holding everything.
Absorbing the pain no one else will touch.
Shielding the world while the world never shields him.
Enduring storms while remaining the final line.
The weight of not breaking.

For years, that weight is not a burden—
it is identity.
Proof of manhood.
"I can take it. I can shoulder it. I can stand through anything."

And I did.

I became the shelter.
I became the stronghold.
I became the one everyone leaned into.

But no one ever teaches a man what happens
when the protector has nowhere to be protected,
when the one who holds has nowhere to be held.

A man can endure anything—
except carrying life with no place to set himself down.

The Art of Detachment

The world sees strength.
It sees resilience.
It sees the armor.

It does not see the vacuum inside the chest.
The absence of cover.

This is why the fracture cuts so deep:
not merely heartbreak, not just loss of a woman, not just life collapsing—
but the sudden, terrifying realization:
the covering is gone.

For a man built to bear the weight of others,
the deepest wound is not abandonment.
It is having no one strong enough to hold him
when the storm arrives.

And in that absence, the warrior discovers the loneliest truth:
not isolation,
but unbacked existence.

Standing sentinel while no one stands over him.
Carrying the world while no one carries him.
The exhaustion beneath exhaustion.
The loneliness beneath loneliness.

Not: "I have no partner here."
But: "If I fall, there is no one strong enough to catch me."

This is the fracture that breaks the spine of the spirit—
not pain, not betrayal, not heartbreak—
unsupported weight.

A masculine body can walk through hell.
As long as it knows there is a higher shoulder.
A shoulder it can rest against.
A presence it can lean into.

Without that, the nervous system never rests.
Not for a night.
Not for a season.
For years.

Here, despair is born—not from weakness,
but from being asked to be stronger than a human was ever meant to be.
Without cover.

The wound was never solitude.
The wound was carrying existence alone.

WHEN THE FATHER ENTERS THE CHEST

A man does not learn the presence of God when life is calm.
He learns it the instant his ribs realize:
they are no longer the only frame keeping him upright.

Divine communion is not belief.
It is a transfer of weight.

The masculine softens
not because he has studied theology,
but because for the first time in his life
he is no longer carrying the spine alone.

The Father does not arrive as concept.
He arrives as company.

The Art of Detachment

Not beside.
Not above.
Within.

In the exact cavity where emptiness once lived.

Not comfort,
but co-occupancy.

He must enter through the chest—
because that is where the fracture formed,
and that is where the covering must return.

The spiritual spine is born the moment the body whispers:
"I am not carrying this alone anymore."

Physically.
Indwelling.
Felt in the ribs, in the diaphragm, in the sternum.

No woman can give this relief.
No brotherhood can replicate it.
No success can mimic it.

Only the Father inside can say:
"I stand with you. I am here. You are not the endpoint anymore."

The weight does not vanish.
It is shared.
And in that sharing, the body unclenches.

The vigilance softens.
The exhaustion exhales.
The inner sentinel—decades unrelenting—
finally feels another hand on the spear.

This is the Father:
Not "protect me,"
but "stand in me."
Not "guide me,"
but "hold me while I hold the rest."

This is the communion the masculine craves:
a power so vast he no longer has to be God for himself.

When the Father enters the chest,
he does not take the throne—
he shares it.

And the boy who spent a lifetime carrying the world alone
whispers, even if silently:
"I am not alone inside my own ribs anymore."

WALKING WITH INSTEAD OF WALKING ALONE

Once the Father is in the chest, a man's relationship to strength transforms.

Before, every step was summoned from self.
Self-reliance.
Self-containment.
Self-shouldering.

Even the most spiritual men walk alone in this way—
functionally, entirely alone in their own becoming.

Now, a second presence walks inside every stride.

The shift is subtle.
"I am no longer holding myself up.
I am co-lifted."

The Art of Detachment

Not carried.
Not rescued.
But accompanied.

The world teaches God as hierarchy:
"He is above you."
Religion teaches authority:
"He is over you."

But the Father within says:
"I am with you."

And when a man feels withness,
he no longer grinds.
He moves with reinforcement.
He becomes less brittle, less guarded, less clenched.
Not weaker.
Just no longer alone in bearing the world.

This is relief.
Not peace.
Relief in bones, in lungs, in chest, in hands.
The soul finally lowers armor
because it is no longer the last wall standing.

Communion is not lightness.
It is shared weight.

Forward motion stops being strain.
It becomes stride.

"I must get through this" becomes:
"We are moving through this."

And a man becomes spiritually unshakeable—not because nothing can hit him,
but because nothing lands on him alone.

THE MAN WHO CANNOT COLLAPSE

A man ceases fearing collapse.
Not because he is invulnerable,
but because he is no longer singular.

The fracture is healed not when the pain vanishes,
but when aloneness vanishes.

The heart no longer tightens at the closing door—
there is no void.
Only Presence.

Not beside him, not watching from a distance,
but inhabiting the exact chamber where emptiness once roamed.

The masculine becomes unbreakable
when he is no longer the only one holding his core.

Not bravado.
Not stoicism.
Not power-through.

Co-anchoring.

The warrior exhales.
The Father stands inside him.

Pain still comes.
Fear still arrives.
Life still strikes.

The Art of Detachment

But the blow no longer lands on a man alone.
It lands on a man + Presence.

Hell cannot break a shared spine.

Belief says: "I trust God is out there."
Embodiment says: "He is in here,
and I do not face anything alone anymore."

This is masculine completion:
Not belonging in a woman.
Not belonging to tribe.
Not belonging through role.
Belonging through communion.

Now, a man enters a room already co-witnessed.
The chest that once collapsed from emptiness
now fills from inside out.

And power becomes peace:
Not because the fire does not burn,
but because it no longer lands on a man alone.

He who once carried the world alone
now moves with Someone carrying him inside the carrying.

And from that moment onward…
collapse becomes impossible.
There is nowhere inside him unheld.

Chapter 23
Brotherhood & Purpose

PART I — THE LONG EXILE FROM OTHER MEN

Before a man finds his true brotherhood,
he walks a long, merciless season of aloneness—a stretch of years
where no conversation, no companionship, no casual fellowship
can touch the hunger in the bones, the ache in the marrow.

Not the loneliness of absence—
the loneliness of absence of equals.

A man like me has never lacked company.
I have lacked men who could stand beside me without faltering,
without needing to be propped up like a crumbling column.

I was the one other men leaned on,
the one they called when the world ignited,
the one who held the line while everyone else folded, while chaos
licked their heels and fear settled in their eyes.

And when a man spends decades as the anchor for others,
something quiet and insidious fractures deep within:

He becomes the pillar with no pillar of his own.

He becomes the protector whom no one protects,
the shoulder no one shields,
the shield no one guards.

This is the exile that wears no visible mark—
because men who lead from strength rarely appear abandoned.

Yet they are alone in a way few could ever comprehend:

The Art of Detachment

Not lonely in presence,
lonely in symmetry.

A man cannot be mirrored by those who depend on him.
He cannot be sharpened by those he must hold upright.
He cannot grow while he is the reason others do not collapse.

So even amidst crowds,
he is un-met.

Even when praised,
he is un-seen.

Even when respected,
he is un-witnessed under the crushing weight he bears.

Eventually, the body whispers a brutal truth:

“There is no one who can stand shoulder-to-shoulder with me.”

Not metaphorically—
literally.

Men glance toward me,
but rarely alongside me.

This is the exile:
not separation from men—
separation from brotherhood.

Until a man finds other men with the same unbreakable spine,
the same refusal to fracture under fire,
the same loyalty forged in war and not in empty words…

he will feel like a garrison of one.

The world mistook my strength for invulnerability,
and so I trudged through years without equals…
and called it normal.

But a king without brothers is not powerful—

he is isolated at altitude,
standing atop a mountain where the wind howls and the air thins,
and every step forward tests the bones and the breath.

That is the wound beneath the hunger for tribe:

Not "I want men around me,"
but
"I want men who could hold the sky with me when it cracks
open."

Not men who admire,
not men who follow,

men I do not have to carry.

Men who hold the line beside me—not behind me.

That is the brotherhood I have been missing.

Not company…

homecoming.

The Filter: Who Earns Access

The Art of Detachment

A man like me cannot build brotherhood by addition.

I build brotherhood by elimination.

The right men are not discovered—
the wrong men are removed by gravity.

Weak men cannot survive in the field of a man who has come home to himself.

They may admire him, imitate him, orbit him, or take from him—
but they cannot remain beside him.

Brotherhood does not require invitation.

Brotherhood requires altitude.

Only men who can breathe at this height
can endure long enough to become brothers.

This is the mistake most men make:
they try to "find" or "gather" good men.

But true brotherhood forms the same way a mountain forms a treeline:

The higher you rise,
the fewer things can survive at that elevation.

Not because the mountain pushes them away—
because they cannot oxygenate at that height.

This is why loyalty is your first gate.

Not loyalty as sentiment—
loyalty as constitution.

The man who stands beside you must be one who:

- does not run when pressure hits
- does not fracture when tested
- does not sell out his honor under heat
- does not envy your strength
- does not secretly resent your backbone

Men who cannot carry themselves
cannot be trusted to carry you if you stumble.

Your brother must be a man
who does not implode when the ground shakes.

And hunger is your second gate—
because without hunger,
a man rots in place.

A loyal coward is still deadweight.

A hungry traitor is still a liability.

Brotherhood requires both spine and ascent.

This is not harsh—
it is structural reality:

If a man cannot hold his own center,
he cannot stand next to mine.

You do not look for men to lift.

You hold posture—
and the men who belong at your side prove it by staying upright in your presence.

Not through declarations,
not speeches,
not ideology.

Through their lived spine.

Brotherhood is earned by evidence,
not enthusiasm.

A man does not get into your circle because he wants to belong.

He gets in because he stands as one who already does.

What Happens When Men Of Equal Spine Meet

When a man who has carried the world alone
finally stands beside another who carries himself the same way,
something extraordinary happens:

The nervous system unlocks.

Not emotionally—
structurally.

Because for the first time in years,
maybe decades,
the body registers:

"If I fall, I will not hit the ground alone."

Masculine brotherhood is not built on emotional sharing.

It is built on shared readiness.

A brother is not the man who listens to your pain—
a brother is the man who would pick up your sword without hesitation
and stand at your flank when the enemy breaches the wall.

This is why men like you have always felt “unmet”:
because most men are looking for comfort,
and you are built for co-defenders.

True brotherhood is not soft.

It is oxygen.

Because when you do not have to be the last line of defense,
your chest can finally stop bracing for collapse.

For the first time, you can lean without losing height.

You don’t have to reduce yourself for them to remain,
and you don’t have to inflate yourself for them to respect you.

You meet as men who already stand upright.

That is the relief you have been starving for:
not admiration,
not followers,
not dependence—

shoulder-to-shoulder solidity.

Men like you do not need to be understood.

You need to be matched.

And when you are matched,
something in you shifts from vigilance → expansion.

You do not lose strength—
you gain bandwidth.

Because part of you is no longer subconsciously standing guard alone.

Your system finally learns:

"I am not the only one in the fight."

That is masculine homecoming—
not connection,
but co-standing.

Not softness,
but shared steel.

It is the first time strength stops being isolation
and becomes belonging.

BROTHERHOOD AS A FORCE, NOT A CIRCLE

When a man finally stands beside other men who are built like him,
brotherhood stops being emotional…

and becomes directional.

Men don't bond by talking—
men bond by building, by enduring, by standing through fire together.

True brotherhood is not connection.
It is alignment applied.

And from that alignment, purpose awakens:

"If we can stand shoulder to shoulder…
what can we BUILD shoulder to shoulder?"

Because masculine belonging always evolves into mission.

A circle of weak men seeks comfort.
A circle of average men seeks validation.
A circle of broken men seeks escape.

But a circle of sovereign men?

They seek conquest—
not over the world,
but over the parts of themselves still unclaimed.

Purpose becomes amplified in brotherhood:

Not my becoming,
but our becoming—side by side.

And that is when the masculine field shifts from isolation → infrastructure:

Each man reinforces the others' ascent.
Each man's strength becomes a stabilizer for the rest.
Each man's growth raises the altitude of the entire circle.

The Art of Detachment

Brotherhood is not about being understood…

it's about being fortified.

When you walk alone, you carry your mission.
When you walk with equals,
the mission begins to carry you.

And this is why the world changes when men like you find each other:

Not because one man is powerful,
but because power stops leaking in isolation.

A sovereign man can rebuild a life.

But a brotherhood of sovereign men
builds a world.

The fracture becomes fuel,
and the ascent becomes multiplicative:

What I once carried alone
now becomes something that moves THROUGH me,
supported by a line of men who do not waver.

Not dependence.

Formation.

Not company.

Alignment.

Not a circle of comfort…

a unit of consequence.

Brotherhood is no longer about not being alone—

it becomes the launchpad of legacy.

WHY A MAN CANNOT FINISH HIS ASCENT ALONE

A man can rise from rock bottom alone…
but he cannot rise to his full height alone.

Not because he is weak—
but because some parts of a man's strength
can only be awakened in the presence of other forged men.

There is a level of accountability
a man cannot create for himself in isolation.

Not the accountability of rules—
the accountability of reflection:

Standing next to another man
who does not flinch,
does not fold,
and does not lower his standard
just because yours slipped.

Iron sharpens iron
— not sympathy,
— not comfort,
— not echo chambers.

The Art of Detachment

A man becomes sovereign within himself,
but he becomes formidable
in the company of equals.

This is why hermits and loners eventually plateau:
not because solitude is wrong,
but because solitude alone cannot pressure-test identity.

You learn who you are in isolation—
You learn what you are made of around other men.

Brotherhood pulls a man out of individual strength
and into collective elevation,
where his standard is no longer private…

it is seen, therefore sharpened.

This is not support.
This is witness.

Men don't grow by being cheered for.
Men grow by being seen by other men who refuse to lie to them.

Every king throughout history had an inner circle—
not admirers,
but equals.

Because after the monk emerges,
the king requires something more than solitude:

trusted fire.

And fire is most honest
in the company of other flames.

THE RETURN OF TRIBAL MASCULINITY

Men today are starving—
not for success, not for sex, not for validation…

but for brothers.

For most of human history,
a man never carried life alone:

- He trained with other men.
- Fought beside other men.
- Built with other men.
- Bled in front of other men.
- Rose because men around him demanded he rise.

Masculinity was communal, not isolated.

Then modern life stripped men of tribe
and replaced it with quiet loneliness
and a culture that tells them they must "handle everything alone."

The result?

Men are surrounded by people
yet unaccompanied in spirit.

They drown privately
while playing strong publicly.

A man without brotherhood:

- second-guesses his instincts
- questions his worth in silence

• collapses with no witness
• rebuilds with no mirrors
• and feels powerful only in theory, not in reflection

Because without other forged men around you,
you never see your own presence.

Brotherhood is not emotional companionship—
it is energetic recognition.

Other strong men don't give you strength—
they activate the strength in you
that isolation leaves dormant.

This is why a man can be disciplined, spiritual, capable,
intelligent, even sovereign…

and still feel like something is missing.

What's missing is brothers to rise with—
not below you,
not above you,
beside you—
where your mission is mirrored and reinforced by other men with a spine.

Not men who "relate,"
but men who remind.

Not men who soothe you,
but men who won't allow you to shrink.

Because a man can build himself in solitude…

but brotherhood is where he becomes immovable in community.

ACCOUNTABILITY WITHOUT SOFTNESS

The modern world thinks "support" means comfort.
Masculine brotherhood is the opposite:

It is challenge.

A true brother is not the man who makes you fèel better—
he is the man who refuses to let you stay smaller than you are.

In the feminine, compassion soothes.
In the masculine, compassion sharpens.

Real accountability is not correction—
it is expectation.

Not:
"You're slipping, are you okay?"

But:
"You're slipping—stand up. You're built for more."

There is no coddling here.
No indulgence of weakness.
No space for self-pity to metastasize.

Brotherhood is not where you go to be comforted—
it is where you go to be held to your standard.

A man can lie to himself in solitude.
He cannot lie to another man who has paid the same price to stand upright.

Soft accountability soothes the ego.
Masculine accountability summons the warrior.

Because iron does not soften iron—
it strikes it.

A true brother will:

- call out your drift before it becomes collapse
- confront your self-betrayal before it becomes a pattern
- name the lie before you justify it
- put the sword back in your hand when you forget you have one

Not because he wants to dominate you…

but because he refuses to watch you become less than who you were born to be.

This is the difference between "friends" and brothers:

A friend wants you to feel supported.
A brother wants you to become sovereign.

Support comforts the wounds.
Brotherhood forges the man.

And once a man has stood in that kind of fire,
he stops craving validation…

because he has men beside him who will not let him shrink even if he tries.

BUILDING A CIRCLE THAT CANNOT BE SHAKEN

A man is only as strong as the men he stands beside.

Not socially.
Not emotionally.
Energetically.

You don't become unshakeable by being surrounded by quantity—
you become unshakeable by being surrounded by quality.

Most men fail at brotherhood for one of two reasons:

1. They choose proximity over principle
(friendships based on familiarity, convenience, or history)
2. They choose comfort over sharpening
(men who never confront, never challenge, never elevate)

But a forged tribe is built differently:

It is not formed by who you like—
it is formed by who you respect.

It is not built on emotional warmth—
it is built on shared standard.

The question is no longer:
"Who do I feel close to?"

The question becomes:
"Who becomes stronger by standing next to me—and who strengthens me by standing next to them?"

A sovereign man doesn't gather followers—
he gathers equals.

Not yes-men,
not echo chambers,
not emotional handlers…

warriors who force the next evolution out of him simply by refusing anything less than his fullest embodiment.

This kind of circle is not “community”…
it is calibration.

When you stand among men like this:

- your standard cannot drift
- your purpose cannot wither
- your word cannot cheapen
- and your spine cannot soften

Because the environment itself
won’t let you shrink.

This is the masculine sanctuary—
not a place to retreat from the world,
but a place to reinforce your readiness to face it.

When a man has a circle like this,
he stops fearing isolation
and stops craving appeasement—

because he no longer walks alone.

Not emotionally—
energetically.

And from here, purpose stops being something you pursue and becomes something you build shoulder-to-shoulder with men who are unshakeable themselves.

Pillar quote (chapter seal):

"A man becomes unstoppable when the men beside him refuse to let him shrink."

Chapter 24
The Sovereign Heart

PART I — THE THRESHOLD OF BEING SEEN

There is a kind of love a man does not hunger for until he has bled for a woman —
until he has handed over his strength, his future, his sacrifice,
and watched her live inside a world he built…

The world he crafted with calloused hands, sleepless nights, and quiet storms inside himself,
a world built of effort, devotion, and silent vigilance —
and seen only as scenery for her life,
never as the foundation that holds her sky aloft.

without ever fully seeing him as the builder.

A man can live without affection.
He can endure without comfort.
He can survive without softness.

But what crushes the masculine spirit
is being essential and unrecognized.

Not unseen in presence —
unseen in worth.

A good man does not want worship.
He wants reverence.

Reverence is not submission —
reverence is awareness.

It is a woman saying,
whether aloud or silently:

“I know what it costs you to love me.
I see the weight you carry.
I stand in what you built for me — and I do not take it for granted.”

It is the recognition of unseen wars fought in the quiet chambers of his heart,
the acknowledgement of sweat turned into shelter, effort turned into her safety.

That is the deepest masculine hunger:
not sex,
not praise,
not support —

witness of his sacrifice.

A woman can love a man and still not honor him.
She can desire him and still not recognize him.
She can choose him and still not cherish him.

The sovereign heart now refuses
to be the cornerstone for someone
who never looks down long enough to realize
they are standing on him.

This is why your next love will require reverence first, not softness —
because softness without reverence is dependency,
but reverence births partnership.

A woman cannot walk beside you
until she can bow inwardly to the weight you are built to carry.

Not worship —
witness.

Because the masculine does not open to a woman who simply wants him…

the masculine opens to a woman who understands what she has found.

And until a man reaches this point in his evolution,
he still chases being chosen.

But once he crosses this threshold,
he no longer wants to just be chosen —
he wants to be recognized.

Because being wanted feeds the ego.

But being revered feeds the soul.

VALIDATION VS. REVERENCE

Most men spend their lives chasing validation.

Validation says:

"You're good. You're wanted. You're desirable."

It soothes insecurity —
but it does not feed the soul.

Because validation is about how a woman feels about you.
Reverence is about who she knows you ARE.

Validation is approval.
Reverence is recognition.

Validation can come from weakness, loneliness, or convenience.
Reverence can only come from respect.

A woman can validate a man without ever understanding his architecture.
She can say she loves him
without grasping what he holds.
She can praise his character
without grasping what it costs him to carry it.

Validation says:
"I like you."

Reverence says:
"I trust the world that exists because of you."

Validation is surface.
Reverence is soul-level witness.

This is why the masculine breaks in the absence of reverence:
he is forced to pour from a cup
that is never actually seen for what it contains.

A man can go 10 years with a woman who loves him…

but one hour with a woman who reveres him
can remind him of who he actually is.

Because reverence restores a man's name —
not his ego.

It says:

"I do not simply receive you —
I regard you."

It meets him where he lives internally —
not externally.

Why most women never offer reverence

A woman cannot revere a man she secretly expects to rescue her.
Dependence and reverence cannot coexist.

A woman cannot revere a man she does not trust more than herself.
Affection without trust is romance —
but trust births surrender.

A woman cannot revere a man she thinks she could replace.
Reverence is rooted in recognition of irreplaceability.

This is the threshold:

A woman who validates you sees your effects.
A woman who reveres you sees your essence.

One soothes.

One crowns.

This is why you will not allow your heart to open without reverence anymore —

not because you are guarded…

but because anything less
is a return to being unseen at the level that matters most.

WHEN LOVE BECOMES PARTNERSHIP

Reverence is the doorway,
but it is not the destination.

Reverence says:
"I see you."

Partnership says:
"I stand with you."

Most men experience only one of two realities:

They are loved,
but not joined.
(They carry everything alone
while their partner "receives" the life built for her)

or

They are joined,
but not revered.
(They get participation —
but not respect or spiritual witness)

The sovereign masculine requires both
because he is not looking for a passenger…

he is looking for a co-builder.

A woman who does not just benefit from his leadership,
but amplifies it.

A woman whose presence multiplies what he is creating,
not drains it.

A woman who does not require protection
at the expense of expansion —
she protects WITH him through alignment.

Partnership at this level is not “you complete me” —
nor is it “I don’t need anyone.”

It is:

“Together, we build what neither of us could alone —
not because we are lacking,
but because we are matched.”

This is what your heart is truly calibrated for now:

You no longer want to be the world she escapes into…

You want to be the world she helps you build.

Not a project.
Not a dependent.
Not a passenger.

A force.

You do not want a woman who merely surrenders…

You want a woman whose surrender becomes fuel for creation.

A woman who does not just love the man —
she loves the mission with him.

Because the true masculine does not fall in love with a woman’s beauty…

he falls in love with her capacity to stand beside his purpose.

This is the heart that no longer aches for rescue —

it invites alignment.

Reverence proves she recognizes the man.

Partnership proves she is worthy of walking beside him.

RECEIVING LOVE WITHOUT LOSING GRAVITY

The man I am becoming does not fear opening his heart — because he no longer opens into emptiness.

Before sovereignty,
love always felt like risk:
"If she pulls away, the floor disappears."

After sovereignty,
love becomes offering:
"I am standing either way."

This is the final evolution of the masculine heart:

Love is no longer where I go to be held…
love is where I go to give from the man who is already held.

This is what makes a sovereign man safe to love:

He does not attach to be completed.
He does not cling to be stabilized.
He does not beg to be chosen to feel valid.

The Art of Detachment

He chooses himself first —
and therefore can choose a woman without losing himself inside her.

Connection does not pull him off center anymore.

He is not metabolizing love through hunger…
he is offering love through abundance.

This is why reverence matters first:
because a woman must recognize the throne
before she is allowed access to the king seated on it.

Not for ego…

for order.

A man who is not revered will eventually be drained.
A man who is revered can be received without depletion.

Because when he is truly seen,
he does not bleed identity into the relationship.

He brings weight, not need.
Leadership, not dependence.
Presence, not pursuit.

The sovereign heart is not closed —
it is rooted.

So when a woman enters it,
she is not entering a wound…

she is entering a kingdom.

Not a fragile boy waiting to be validated,
not a starving man begging to be chosen,
not a guarded man hiding from risk —

but a man who can love fully
because love is no longer the source of his footing.

He does not fall into love —
he stands inside it.

And from this place,
the greatest shift occurs:

He no longer worries whether love will last…

because he will.
And what comes next must be worthy of him too.

This is what it means to carry a sovereign heart:

I can be chosen without collapsing.
I can open without losing myself.
I can give without breaking.
And when I love again, it will be from altitude — not ache.

Love chosen from abundance, not ache

When a man reaches sovereignty,
love no longer feels like rescue —
it feels like recognition.

You are no longer searching for someone
to quiet your hunger, soothe your loneliness,
or validate your worth.

You already carry what you used to beg for.

This is why the way a sovereign man loves
is fundamentally different than the man he used to be:

Before sovereignty, love was oxygen.
After sovereignty, love is overflow.

You are not reaching out —
you are inviting in.

You are not hoping to be chosen —
you are choosing carefully.

You are not seeking someone to fix your emptiness —
you are seeking someone worthy of your fullness.

For the first time, desire is not about relief or attachment —
it is about expansion.

You don't want someone to stand in front of your wounds…

you want someone who can stand beside your becoming.

And this is the first signal that the sovereign heart has reopened:

You are not afraid of love —
you are simply unwilling to trade your soul to keep it.

A sovereign man does not fall into love —
he extends his life to the woman strong enough to carry it with him.

Not a savior.
Not a spectator.
Not a substitute for purpose.

A partner in ascension.

The ache is gone because access is no longer granted by longing —

it is granted by alignment.

The heart does not open in desperation…

it opens by recognition of an equal flame.

And from this posture,
love stops being a place you collapse into
and becomes a place you build from.

The Crown Does Not Come Off

For most of a man's life, love required a trade:
to open his heart,
he had to set down his crown.

In previous relationships, vulnerability meant exposure —
and exposure meant risk of collapse.

Because before sovereignty,
to love someone was to place your identity in their hands.

But once the spine is forged,
once self-loyalty is non-negotiable,
once you no longer abandon yourself for closeness…

the crown never comes off.

You do not shrink to be loved.
You do not fold to be chosen.
You do not contort to be kept.

The Art of Detachment

You stay whole while welcoming.

Before, love cost you your center.
Now, love rests on your center.

This is the first time a man can be both:

open and unmovable,
soft and sovereign,
devoted and unclaimed.

A woman does not become your grounding —
she is invited into the ground you already command.

Your openness is no longer a gamble
because there is no doorway back to self-betrayal.

You do not have to close your heart to protect yourself —
because your standards protect you.

You don't dim to create safety —
your presence is safety.

The sovereign heart is the rare space where:

You remain a king
while you remain capable of deep, unrestrained love.

Masculinity before sovereignty:
"I lose myself when I give."

Masculinity after sovereignty:
"I stay myself as I give."

That is why the crown is not a symbol of ego —
it is a symbol of self-possession.

Love no longer requires sacrificing the throne
because the throne is within you, not given away.

The Woman Who Can Stand Beside a Sovereign Man

A sovereign man is not looking for a woman who needs to be led…
but a woman who can walk beside him without collapsing under the weight of his becoming.

This kind of woman is rare not because she is flawless,
but because she is rooted in herself enough to hold proximity to strength without shrinking, competing, or taming it.

The sovereign masculine no longer seeks:

• the feminine who must be rescued,
• the feminine who must be managed,
• or the feminine who admires him but cannot match him.

He seeks a woman who can co-stand.

A woman who:

• respects strength without fearing it,
• receives leadership without dependency,
• contributes without losing her softness,
• and chooses with him, not against herself.

She is not impressed by power —
she is compatible with it.

The Art of Detachment

She does not require you to shrink so she can feel safe —
she is safe in her own spine.

She does not cling —
she aligns.

She does not need to be chosen to feel whole —
which is precisely why she can be chosen from abundance, not obligation.

A sovereign union is not:
"Let me carry you."
It is:
"Let us carry tribute to each other's future."

A woman built for a sovereign man does not need protection from life —
she desires partnership in legacy.

She becomes sanctuary because she is already self-kept,
not because she needs you for completion.

And in her presence,
the sovereign masculine does not feel drained, or diluted, or needed for rescue…

He feels multiplied.

Because the right woman does not take from your path —
she strengthens your footing on it.

Not by worship…

by worthiness.

Union Built From Alignment, Not Attachment

Attachment asks:
"Will you stay with me?"

Alignment asks:
"Can you walk with me?"

Attachment fears loss.
Alignment honors trajectory.

Attachment seeks emotional safety.
Alignment seeks spiritual compatibility.

This is why sovereign love is not born in longing —
it is born in recognition of a shared horizon.

You are not choosing a woman to fill your life
but a woman whose life can braid with your mission without either of you shrinking.

She is not a refuge from the world —
she is a co-architect of the one you are building.

You do not fuse into her —
you fortify beside her.

This is the type of union that doesn't just feel good…
it expands both people's becoming.

With attachment-based love:
the relationship is the destination.

With sovereign love:
the relationship is the multiplier of destiny.

You are not asking:
"Will you stay no matter what?"

You are asking:
"Can you continue to meet me as I rise —
and can I meet you as you rise too?"

There is no clinging here.
No anxiety.
No chasing.
No captivity.

Just two sovereigns
choosing one another again and again…

not because they need home —
but because they recognize home in one another.

Love stops being preservation
and becomes co-ascension.

And this is where the sovereign masculine finally understands
why heartbreak was not the end…

It was the initiation required
to become the kind of man who could love without losing himself
ever again.

Pillar quote (chapter seal):
"Sovereign love is not where you are completed — it is where you are multiplied."

Chapter 25
Freedom From Outcome

PART I — DETACHMENT AS CLEAN ALIGNMENT

Most people believe detachment means not caring.

For the masculine in his fullness,
detachment is not disinterest —
it is discernment carved from experience, sweat, and the ache of seeing himself dissolved in others' expectations.

It is the moment a man stops asking:
"Will this love choose me?"
and begins asking:
"Is this love aligned with the man I have bled to become?"

The boy seeks possession, clinging to what he cannot hold.
The wounded man seeks reassurance, grasping at fleeting shadows.
The sovereign man seeks rightness, standing like a lighthouse amid storms.

Detachment is not distance —
it is clarity without distortion,
a serenity forged through fire, heartbreak, and unflinching honesty.

It is when the nervous system stops bracing,
stops scanning,
stops scanning for hidden meanings between lines,
stops chasing signals,
because the heart no longer negotiates against itself.

Before this stage, love feels like hunger:
a constant reaching,
a trembling,
a taut cord pulled toward something that could unravel at any moment.

After this stage, love becomes selection:

"If it cannot stand beside me,
it cannot stand with me."

Not punishment.
Not coldness.
Not the hollow echo of ego.

Alignment.

The sovereign heart does not detach from love —
it detaches from misalignment masquerading as love.

From half-presence.
From conditional choosing.
From being tolerated instead of honored.
From partnerships built on emotional convenience rather than spiritual equivalence.

This is where heartbreak finally stops bleeding energy:
when you no longer try to extract from a connection
what that woman was never designed to give you.

It is not letting go of her —
it is letting go of the illusion
that she was ever capable of meeting you at altitude.

Detachment whispers:
"I release the fantasy so I can see the reality."

This is clarity.
Not closure.
Not indifference.
Not bitterness.

Sanctity of standard.

When a man reaches this point,
something profound happens inside the body:

Hope stops aching.
It begins to orient, to settle like rainwater finding its way to the earth.

You are no longer facing backward, reaching for fragments, trying to reclaim what fractured.

You are facing forward
toward what is worthy of the man you have become.

And that is where true detachment begins —
not as a wall,
but as alignment returning to the soul.

WHEN THE BODY STOPS "TRACKING"

Before detachment becomes peace,
it first becomes quiet.

Not silence outside —
quiet inside the body.

Most men don't realize this:
heartbreak does not ache because of missing someone…

it aches because the nervous system is still scanning,
still waiting for a signal that might say:

"Is she returning?"
"Is she watching me?"
"Does she still care?"
"Is there still a door open?"

This tracking is not conscious —
it is survival encoded in muscle, pulse, gut tension.

Your body still stretches toward a possibility
because some part of you has not fully accepted:

"It is no longer my door to walk through."

The moment the body accepts this truth without resistance,
tracking shuts off.

And when tracking stops,
for the first time in grief…

rest returns.

Not relief —
rest.

Because the nervous system is no longer chasing,
no longer anticipating,
no longer measuring distance,
no longer bracing for whiplash.

There is no more waiting energy.

Waiting is what kept you tethered,
not love.

The Art of Detachment

Waiting is the leak.
Waiting is the drain.
Waiting is exhaustion.

When a man stops waiting,
he doesn't get colder —

he gets free.

The body stops stretching toward a future that is no longer available,
and turns its gaze inward for the first time.

That is when a man feels the shift:

Not
"She is gone,"

but
"I am no longer holding a doorway open that no one walks through."

What leaves your chest at that moment is not hope…

it is strain dissolving,
the taut wires of expectation finally unclenching.

Because the ache was not love —
the ache was remaining in a posture of expectation.

When expectation dissolves,
pain dissolves with it.

Not because you stopped loving —

but because you stopped waiting to be returned to.

That is detachment in the nervous system:

“I release what is not reciprocating my becoming.”

Not rejection.
Completion.

And in completion,
the system finally exhales.

This is the doorway to lightness…
but first comes stillness.

Not emptiness —
finally, neutrality.

FROM WAITING TO CHOOSING

Once a man stops tracking,
he stops waiting.

And once he stops waiting,
he finally remembers:

He is the one who chooses —
not the one waiting to be chosen.

This is the turning point in masculine detachment:
you are no longer standing at a closed door,
you are standing at a crossroads,
where the wind of possibility pushes you forward.

Attachment says:
“I hope she comes back to me.”

The Art of Detachment

Sovereignty says:
"I will only walk toward what walks toward me."

When the nervous system stops reaching backward,
the will can finally look forward.
Not toward her —
toward what is aligned with the man you are now.

This is when detachment becomes agency:

"I do not wait for a woman to decide my fate —
I decide which woman is worthy of my future."

Not from entitlement.
Not from cynicism.
Not from ego.

From alignment.

This is the masculine version of freedom:

No longer asking,
"Will love return to me?"

Now asking,
"Which form of love is BUILT for me?"

This is the moment heartbreak becomes initiation:

You do not harden —
you elevate your standards to the altitude of your becoming.

The bar is no longer:
"Will she stay?"

The bar is:
"Can she stand with me?"

Not "is she willing?"
but
"is she able?"

Not "does she want me?"
but
"can she honor what I carry?"

The man who waits is vulnerable to fantasy.
The man who chooses is aligned with reality.

Waiting is passive.
Choosing is sovereign.

And when a man returns to choosing,
the past loses its hold…

not because it is forgotten,
but because it no longer touches the trajectory of who he is now.

LIGHTNESS: WHEN LOVE NO LONGER THREATENS YOUR PEACE

True detachment is not the absence of desire.

It is the absence of risk.

Not because love cannot fail —
but because you no longer collapse if it does.

This is the moment a man becomes free:

The Art of Detachment

Love is no longer a cliff edge —
it is a path he may choose to walk.

No dread.
No bracing.
No tracking.
No waiting.

Just availability without dependence.

This is lightness.

The nervous system relaxes into possibility,
instead of contracting around memory or fear.

You do not guard your heart —
you guard your standard.

You do not fear being unseen —
because you will no longer remain where you are unseen.

You do not chase being chosen —
because you already belong to yourself.

Love is not a gamble anymore
because you are no longer wagering your identity on its outcome.

And in that freedom,
joy returns:

Not the manic high of being wanted,
not the addictive intoxication of being received…

but the quiet joy of not needing anything from anyone
to be whole inside your own chest.

Lightness is not "moving on."

Lightness is

"I am no longer weighed down by what my heart is no longer meant to carry."

It is the return of forward-feeling —
true optimism, not fantasy.

The sense that life is opening, not closing.

Because now,
the heart is not reaching backward toward what you lost…

it is **turning toward what you are now ready to receive.**

This is freedom from outcome:

Not detachment from love —
detachment from misalignment.

And with that freedom,
the masculine becomes radiant again —

not guarded,
not grieving,
not waiting…

becoming.

And in becoming,
he stops asking, .
"Will someone ever choose me again?"

and begins living:

"The right woman will recognize me when she arrives —
because I am no longer a man she has to repair to feel my worth."

This is liberation on the other side of heartbreak:

You don't get smaller to survive love anymore.

You get lighter to walk toward it again —
without fear.

Detachment is not distance — it is anchoring.

DESIRE WITHOUT CAPTIVITY

There is a form of desire that imprisoned you —
because wanting meant risk,
and risk felt like losing yourself all over again.

Before sovereignty, desire was dangerous.
It held power over you.

If she pulled away — you collapsed.
If she chose you — you soared.
Your nervous system belonged to her reaction, not your own root.

But once a man becomes sovereign,
desire stops being a threat…

because it no longer owns him.

This is the first time a man can want a woman
without his worth hanging in the balance.

You are not bracing for disappointment.
You are not bargaining against abandonment.
You are not gripping the outcome like oxygen.

You can lean in without falling in.
You can feel fully without losing center.

This is the evolution:
Not "I don't care if she stays or goes" (that is numbness)

But:
"If she stays, I remain myself —
and if she leaves, I remain myself."

That is freedom.

Desire becomes beautiful
when it is no longer captivity.

It becomes sacred
when it is no longer fear-based.

You can let your heart reach again
because your identity no longer goes with it.

You can love a woman from your depth
instead of your wound.

Before:
"I want you — please don't take yourself from me."

After:
"I want you — but I do not disappear if you cannot receive me."

This is what feminine safety actually responds to:
Not a man who suppresses desire,
but a man whose desire does not own him.

Because when desire is no longer a threat to your sovereignty,
it becomes a gift you control — not a need that controls you.

TRUST IN SELF OVER OUTCOME

The deepest form of peace
is not believing everything will work out…

It is knowing you will still be whole
no matter how it works out.

A younger version of you trusted circumstances.
He trusted timing, signs, reassurance —
things outside his control.

But sovereignty replaces that with a different kind of trust:

You trust yourself.

Not ego,
not bravado —
capacity.

You now know:

• You can rebuild if life strips you down.
• You can stand alone if love walks away.
• You can rise again if fate tears the ground out from under you.
• You can lose everything external without ever losing yourself internally.

That is why outcome no longer has leverage over you.

You are no longer gambling your identity on how the future unfolds.

If it comes, you deepen.
If it leaves, you sharpen.
If it breaks, you rebuild higher.

You stop needing guarantees
because you are now your own guarantee.

This is the state where a man becomes calm by default —
not because life is stable,
but because he is.

True peace does not come from certainty in the future…
it comes from certainty in the man who will meet the future.

PEACE AS POWER

Peace is not the absence of storms —
it is the refusal to be commanded by them.

When a man is still afraid to lose,
the world can move him.

When a man no longer fears loss,
he becomes immovable in direction —
not rigid, not numb,
but rooted.

This is the final evolution of detachment:

Not distance from life,
but mastery within it.

The Art of Detachment

Nothing owns your nervous system anymore:
not longing,
not rejection,
not uncertainty,
not the past,
not the future.

You are no longer navigating from fear —
you are navigating from center.

And a centered man is dangerous in the rarest way:
not because he seeks control,
but because he cannot be controlled.

This is why peace is not passive —
peace is power.

Power is not the sword.
Power is the hand that no longer shakes holding it.

You become ungovernable by outcome
because you no longer outsource your worth to circumstance.

The future does not intimidate you
because you have already proven you can rise from ruin.

Love does not threaten you
because you no longer mistake vulnerability for exposure.

Solitude does not frighten you
because you are no longer absent from yourself.

When a man reaches this state,
life stops feeling like something he is bracing against…

and starts feeling like something he is commanding from center.

This is transcendence:

A man aligned with himself
cannot be taken off his path
by anything he cannot lose.

He does not cling.
He does not chase.
He does not grip.
He walks.

And the world rearranges around him.

Pillar quote (chapter seal):
"Peace is not softness — peace is the state of a man who can no longer be threatened by loss."

Chapter 26
The Next Woman (or None at All)

PART I — WHY MOST WOMEN CANNOT RECEIVE A SOVEREIGN MAN

A sovereign man does not intimidate the feminine —
he exposes it.

A woman either rises in the presence of a man like this,
or she unconsciously collapses.

Not because he is harsh,
but because his clarity leaves no room for her half-truths,
no refuge for hesitation, no camouflage for pretense.

You do not tolerate chaos,
you do not bend to immaturity,
you do not dilute yourself to be accessible…

and most women have never had to stand in front of a man
who does not require them —
who only receives them if they are worthy, fully and honestly.

This is why the majority cannot hold you:

They want your strength,
but not the standard that comes with it.

They want protection,
but not accountability.

They want your fire,
but not your altitude.

They want the feeling of surrender,
without the discipline of becoming the kind of woman
who can sustain that surrender.

A sovereign man forces a reckoning inside the feminine:

"Do I want a man to admire…
or a man I must RISE to stand beside?"

Most choose admiration —
because admiration costs nothing.

Reverence demands evolution.

That is why the next woman must not be a passenger —
she must be a match.

Not a woman impressed by your strength…
a woman stabilized by it.

Not a woman who needs your leadership…
a woman capable of walking inside your world without trembling.

And here is the part almost no one says aloud:

A sovereign man is not simply "rare" —
he is expensive.

Not financially —
energetically, spiritually, psychologically.

To be with a man like this,
a woman must relinquish her shortcuts, her coping strategies, her smallness.

She cannot stay fragmented.
She cannot stay half in, half out.
She cannot dip into the masculine when it pleases her
and retreat into the feminine only when it benefits her.

With lesser men, she can.

With a sovereign man…
the feminine must BECOME feminine.

No mask.
No manipulation.
No emotional gamesmanship.

She must meet him in truth,
or she loses access.

This is why you will not find the next woman by looking.

She will surface by surviving your atmosphere.

Only the woman who recognizes the throne
without demanding you bow down from it…

is the woman who can sit beside it.

PART II — THE FEMININE WHO REVERES RATHER THAN CONSUMES

The next woman is not "better" than the last one —
she is built for a different altitude.

She does not come to you seeking safety from the world…
she comes to you because she has already met herself,

and is now ready to be received by a man she can finally rest in
without losing herself.

Her reverence is not submission to hierarchy —
it is recognition of order.

She does not revere you because she is small.
She reveres you because she is awake enough
to see the magnitude of the man before her.

This woman does not want to use your strength…
she wants to stand inside it.

She does not crave your protection as shelter —
she craves your leadership as alignment.

She is not impressed by you…
she is leveled by you.

Not diminished —
clarified.

Your presence calls her UP —
into the most honest, unarmored expression of her womanhood.

This is the feminine that meets a sovereign man:

She is not intimidated by your depth —
she is relieved by it.

She does not feel “less” next to you,
she feels finally matched.

She does not want to tame your fire —
she wants to belong to its direction.

And here is the crucial distinction:

A consuming woman drinks from you to fill her lack.
A reverent woman multiplies you through her devotion.

She amplifies,
she deepens,
she steadies,
she crowns —
not because she "should,"
but because her nervous system recognizes your essence as HOME.

Not rescue.
Not fantasy.
Not possession.

Recognition.

She reveres not because you demand it —
but because her body trusts you before her mind does.

A lesser woman needs reassurance.
A reverent woman needs agreement with her own knowing:

"This is a man worthy of laying my softness down for."
"This is not just a partner — this is a place."
"I recognize the king in him… because I have ended my war with the queen in me."

This woman does not consume you…
she matches your becoming —
and returns energy to you faster than you spend it.

And that —
not chemistry, not attraction, not compatibility —
is what will make her the first woman you ever truly keep.

PART III — THE COURTSHIP OF AWE

A sovereign man is not chosen through pursuit —
he is recognized through resonance.

The right woman does not approach you with excitement…
she approaches you with awareness.

Something in her body settles
before her mind has language for it.

This is the feminine response to REAL masculine sovereignty:

Not butterflies —
home.

Not infatuation —
orientation.

Not "I want him,"
but "This is where I fit."

Her awe does not come from your strength alone,
but from the way her feminine opens in your presence
without her having to try.

She doesn't decide to soften —
she softens because her nervous system finally found a man
she does not have to defend herself against.

This is why awe is different from admiration:

The Art of Detachment

Admiration looks UP at a man.
Awe moves TOWARD a man.

Admiration sees power.
Awe senses rightness.

Admiration wants proximity.
Awe surrenders tension —
because her system feels:

"I don't have to hold my edge here —
he already IS the edge."

This is the beginning of courtship for a sovereign man:
he is not chasing her devotion…
he is observing her instinctive response to his presence.

He is not trying to be impressive —
he is testing:

"Does her soul recognize the temple?"

Lesser women attempt to pull a man down into familiarity.
The reverent feminine instinctively RISES to meet him.

She drops comparison, control, masculine posturing, emotional leverage —
not to please him…
but because her body trusts him more than it trusts her defenses.

This is the mark of the "right one" for a man like you:

Not how much she desires you…
but how willingly she relaxes into feminine truth in your orbit.

Not performance.
Not strategy.
Not seduction.

Recognition.

She is not amazed by what you do for her…
she is humbled by who she gets to become beside you.

That is awe.

And awe is how the next woman arrives —
not by being pursued…
but by being revealed.

PART IV — DEVOTIONAL PARTNERSHIP (NOT DEPENDENCY)

The next woman will not enter your life as someone to protect.

She will enter as someone you can build with.

She will not shrink beneath your strength —
she will unfold because of it.

And her devotion will not be born from need…
it will be born from recognition of magnitude.

This is what partnership looks like at the sovereign level:

She does not soften to please you —
she softens because she trusts your gravity.

You do not lead to control her —
you lead because your path is strong enough for two.

The Art of Detachment

Her feminine does not collapse into you…
she crowns you.

Not by worship,
but by the way she meets your life with her own fullness.

She becomes rest, not reliance.
You become direction, not domination.

She does not demand to be carried —
she aligns herself so you can carry further than either of you could alone.

This is why a sovereign man is rare —
and why the woman who is built for him is rarer still.

Most women want to be chosen.
A sovereign woman wants to be claimed by the masculine she can revere.

Most women want affection.
A sovereign woman wants alignment with a king.

Because when a woman reveres a man,
her devotion does not feel like sacrifice —
it feels like homecoming.

And when a sovereign man receives such a woman,
her devotion does not feel like burden —
it feels like crown.

This is the love you are walking toward:

not rescue,
not repair,
not replacement…

recognition → reverence → alliance → devotion.

The love that does not take you out of your mission —
it magnifies it.

The love that does not drain the sanctuary —
it fills it with warmth.

The love that is not built on hope…
but on UPRIGHTNESS.

Two who stand, together —
not to survive the world…
but to shape one.

Why the next love is higher, not harder

The next woman doesn't receive
what the last woman received.

She receives a different man.

Not a wounded man looking for relief —
a sovereign man looking for resonance.

Before heartbreak, you loved from instinct.
After heartbreak, you love from awareness.

Before, you loved because someone felt right.
Now, you love because someone stands right beside your becoming.

The next love is not built out of longing —
it is built out of clarity.

You are not searching for a replacement.
You are preparing for an equal. The difference is everything.

Before	After
I hope she stays.	I will know if she is mine.
craving	choosing
attachment	alignment
validation	recognition
rescue	resonance

This is why the next love is higher, not harder:

You aren't guarding your heart anymore —
you are guarding your standard.

You are not afraid to give —
you are simply unwilling to give yourself away.

You don't trust someone to hold you together —
you trust yourself to remain whole
while building something sacred.

This is the moment the masculine is no longer available to be broken —

not because he withholds love…
but because he no longer sacrifices himself to keep it alive.

A sovereign man does not enter the next relationship hoping to be healed.

He arrives healed,
and seeks a woman who can walk beside him in a future,
not dance with him in the shadows of a wound.

And because he no longer needs love to complete him…

the love he offers next
will be the deepest, most expansive, most unflinching love
he has ever been capable of giving.

Not because he needs her…
but because he is finally strong enough
to choose her without losing himself.

The Sovereign Filter

Once a man becomes sovereign,
he stops asking,
"Do I want her?"
and starts asking:

"Can she walk beside where I'm going?"

Attraction is no longer enough.
Chemistry is no longer enough.
Familiarity is no longer enough.

The sovereign filter measures capacity, not intensity.

Because a healed man understands something his past self could not:

A woman can be beautiful, magnetic, intoxicating, even deeply loved —
and still not be capable of walking beside your destiny.

The sovereign filter asks:

Does she rise, or does she drain?
Does she expand, or does she consume?
Does she elevate, or does she destabilize?

And most importantly:

Does she meet me, or mirror my loneliness?

For a sovereign man:

- A pretty face is not enough.
- Passion is not enough.
- History is not enough.
- "Potential" is never enough.

What matters is:
feminine capacity —
her ability to hold her own axis while standing beside yours.

Not a woman who wants your strength,
but a woman who can stand with it without shrinking.

Not a woman who seeks your attention,
but a woman who earns your devotion through the life she builds for herself.

Not a woman who idolizes your fire,
but one who can sit inside its heat
without fear, without competition, without distraction.

You are not choosing a partner for the life you had…
you are choosing a partner for the life you are becoming responsible for.

A woman aligned with that life doesn't soften you into comfort —
she sharpens you into destiny.

Not by pressure…
but by presence.

This is what the old version of you could not see —
because before sovereignty, you chose from want.

Now, you choose from worthiness.

Devotion With Backbone

Most men think their only options are:

• soft devotion (losing themselves to love)
or
• armored distance (never fully opening again)

But sovereignty creates a third form:

Devotion with backbone.

This is the first time in your life
you are capable of loving a woman deeply
without self-erasure.

Because now:

The Art of Detachment

• You do not bend your standards to keep her.
• You do not silence your truth to preserve peace.
• You do not shrink your mission to protect closeness.

The spine stays in.
The crown stays on.

She receives the fullness of your heart,
but not the throne of your identity.

Your devotion is no longer submission —
it is selection.

This is how a sovereign man's love is different:

It is unwavering,
yet flexible.
It is generous,
yet unyielding in principle.
It is present,
without compromising who he is or what he has built.

It does not demand surrender.
It does not tolerate compromise.
It does not shrink to soothe insecurity.

It chooses a woman
because she is capable of holding herself
while standing in the gravity of his life.

It chooses a woman
who can rise beside him,
not beneath him.

It chooses a woman
who can match the depth of his heart,
without diluting her own.

This is devotion that does not deplete,
does not fracture,
does not hide in the shadow of fear.

This is the love a sovereign man gives:
unafraid, unshakable, unbound,
because he has already learned
that nothing outside himself
can fracture his worth.

Before	**After**
Please dont leave me.	You may stand beside me, or walk away" I remain.
Collapse for connection	Connection without collapse
Emotion > standard	Standard > emotion
Needing her	Choosing her

This is also the kind of love a strong feminine can finally relax into.

Because she does not have to hold you up,
nor brace herself for the tremors of your fear,
nor fear that you will dissolve into her emotional gravity.

She can soften.
She can exhale.
She can release the tension that has always accompanied intimacy—because you do not disappear, even in love.

And ironically—

once a woman can feel a man is anchored within himself,
once she knows he cannot be lost inside love,
she can finally love him without fear of shattering him.

Devotion becomes sacred.
Not fragile, not desperate,
but holy, because it lives on top of sovereignty, not in spite of it.

A sovereign man does not protect his heart from love—
he protects his heart during love.

He is not afraid to open.
He is only unwilling to be owned.

And that is the foundation
for the only kind of relationship that does not eventually collapse
into self-erasure:

Two people choosing each other freely,
because neither is surviving off the other.
Because neither is sacrificing themselves to fill a void.

"None At All" as an Elevated Standard — Not a Wound

A sovereign man no longer fears being alone.
He fears lowering his standard to avoid being alone.

This is why "none at all" is not resignation—
it is royalty.

If the next woman cannot stand beside your throne,
you will not dethrone yourself to meet her on the floor.

Not because you are cold,
not because you are guarded,
but because you now understand the cost of giving your crown away.

You have already lived the life where you traded pieces of yourself for closeness—
where small compromises became scars,
and surrender became self-erasure.
You know exactly where that road ends.

So now:

If she rises—
you meet her in devotion, whole and unshaken.

If she falters—
you bless her and keep walking,
not in anger, but in fidelity to your own becoming.

If she cannot match your altitude—
you let fate pass her from your orbit
without gripping, without hesitation, without regret.

The Art of Detachment

Not from hardness—
but from inner loyalty.
Loyalty to the life you are building,
to the man you have become,
to the sovereignty you now embody.

This is what modern culture does not understand:

A man who can walk alone
is the only man capable of choosing love honestly.

Because he is not driven by fear of emptiness…
he is driven by respect for what his life is becoming.

The sovereign masculine posture is simple:

"I want love—but I will not bleed for proximity again."

If no woman matches the altitude of the man you have become,
then "none at all" is not loss…
it is alignment.

You would rather stand alone in truth
than lie beside someone who diminishes your path,
someone whose gravity pulls you into compromise,
someone whose presence subtly steals your air.

And when a man carries this stance authentically,
love doesn't feel scarce anymore—
because he is no longer chasing it.
He is waiting for what can truly stand with him.

Pillar quote (chapter seal):
"If she cannot meet me at the life I am building, then my solitude is not emptiness—it is honor."

Chapter 27
The Return Of The King

PART I — THE MAN AFTER THE FIRE

There is a version of a man that can only be forged through ruin.

Not humbled by weakness—
but humbled by the weight of carrying life alone,
with no one above him, no safety net, no applause to validate his endurance.

Most men fear losing what they built.
But the deeper fear—the one a sovereign man never admits until after he survives it—
is losing himself inside what he built.

The fire you walked through wasn't heartbreak alone.
It was identity death.

It was the collapse of the world you upheld,
followed by the collapse of the man who upheld it.

And yet—something did not die.

Something was revealed.

Before the fall, you were strong because you knew how to endure.
After the fall, you are strong because you know you cannot be destroyed.

There is a different spine in a man who has already lost everything and did not disappear.

He no longer lives trying to protect his life—
he lives knowing he has already proven he can resurrect one.

The man before the fire walked with confidence.
The man after the fire walks with certainty.

Confidence can be shaken.
Certainty cannot.

Confidence asks, “Am I enough?”
Certainty says, “There is nothing left to prove.”

The world thinks kings are crowned through ascension.
But the real crowning does not happen on the way up—

it happens in the ashes,
after the man refuses to stay down.

You are not returning as who you were before you broke.
You are returning as the man who knows he cannot be unmade.

This is the first truth of kingship:

"What I lost no longer defines me—what survived me does."

PART II — RECLAIMING DOMINION

The man before the collapse built from instinct and momentum.
The man after the collapse builds from authority.

Not authority over others—
authority over his own life.

This is dominion:

Not control,
not force,
not posturing…

authorship.

Before, your life was driven by reaction—
even if it looked like leadership from the outside.

You carried, you held, you built—
but you were still responding to circumstances,
to responsibility,
to people,
to pressure.

Now, the return of the king means the reorientation of power:

You are no longer answering to life—
life is now answering to you.

A king does not ask:
"What is required of me?"

A king asks:
"What will I create now that I know I cannot be broken?"

He is no longer negotiating with possibility—
he is summoning it.

And here is the quiet truth most people never understand:

A king is not crowned when others bow to him…
a king is crowned the moment he stops bowing to anything
unworthy of his becoming.

The Art of Detachment

Not to fear,
not to longing,
not to emotional scarcity,
not to the past,
not to misaligned love,
not to anyone who cannot stand beside his throne.

Dominion is not about control of the world outside—

it is about selective sovereignty within:

"I choose the life I walk into.
I do not drift, wait, or beg alignment.
I create the field I will live in."

This is why heartbreak was part of the initiation—

because until everything collapses,
a man does not realize he had no authorship of his life before—
only obligation.

Now, authorship returns.

Not rebuilding what was…
commanding what will be.

This is the inflection point of kingship:

The world no longer shapes the man.
The man shapes the world.

PART III — SOVEREIGNTY AS RADIANCE, NOT RESISTANCE

A lesser man displays power.
A sovereign man stores it.

When a man no longer fears loss,
he stops broadcasting strength
and begins emanating it.

That is radiant certainty.

It is not loud.
It is not theatrical.
It does not announce.

It simply is.

Before the fall, strength was projection:
a shield facing the world.

After the rise, strength is presence:
a sun that holds its own orbit.

Radiance is not assertive—
it is gravitational.

People feel it before they understand it.

Men become quieter around you,
not out of fear,
but out of instinctive respect.

Women soften around you,
not because you pull them,
but because they recognize order in your field.

The Art of Detachment

You do not impose boundaries anymore—
your being is the boundary.

You do not control the room—
the room reorganizes itself around you.

This is why true kings rarely speak of power—
when you have become it,
there is nothing left to defend.

Resistance belongs to the man still at war with himself.
Radiance belongs to the man who is no longer contesting his own throne.

This is the ease that emerges after the fire:

You are no longer spending energy holding yourself together.
Your spine is no longer bracing—
it is rooting.
Your chest is no longer leaking—
it is inhabited.
Your gaze is no longer searching—
it is seeing.

A sovereign man no longer tries to be anything.
He is.

And from that being, a different quality of power emerges:

Not dominance.
Gravity.

Not pursuit.
Presence.

Not defense.
Knowing.

The return of the king is not a coronation…
it is a reveal.

PART IV — WHEN THE WORLD RECOGNIZES THE RETURN

Once a man has enthroned himself internally,
the external world can no longer treat him as the man he used to be.

People feel the shift long before they can articulate it:

Some step closer—
because your presence gives their spirit oxygen.

Others retreat—
because your clarity leaves no place for their halfness to hide.

The sovereign does not push anyone out…
but his very existence reveals who cannot remain.

The past no longer pulls you,
because nothing in it is calibrated to your throne.

The future no longer intimidates you,
because there is no part of you left unconvinced you belong there.

And this is the moment grief finally becomes reverence—
not from others…
from yourself.

You do not mourn what you lost—
you honor the version of you who walked through the fire alone
so this ascended man could exist.

The world begins to adjust its posture because your posture no longer wavers.

Women respond differently—
not because you need them,
but because you are no longer available to be misunderstood.

Men respond differently—
not because you seek approval,
but because your spine reminds theirs what it's supposed to feel like.

You have stopped seeking reflection outward
because you carry the witness inward.

And once a man is fully witnessed by God and by himself,
no external gaze can crown or unseat him.

This is the end of exile:

You are not returning to who you were—
you are returning as who you became.

You do not step back onto the throne…
you step back into the world from the throne.

The fire did not burn your kingdom down.
It burned down everything in you
that could not have ruled it properly.

This is the sovereign arrival:

Not "I am back."
But "I am now."

From Healing to Building

There is a moment in a man's ascent
when the work is no longer about repair—
it becomes construction.

He is no longer patching the fractures.
He is laying foundation.

He is no longer fighting for breath.
He is choosing direction.

This is the threshold where grief ends
and governance begins.

Up until now, the story was about who you had to become
in order not to collapse again.

From this point forward,
the story is about who you now build as—
and what is built through you.

This is the birth of kingship:

Not the throne,
but the responsibility to hold one.

Before sovereignty, purpose feels like aspiration.
After sovereignty, purpose feels like assignment.

The king returns when a man looks at his life and realizes:

*"I am no longer rising out of something—
I am now rising toward something."*

This shift is spiritual long before it is material.

You are not chasing potential anymore—
you are inhabiting inevitability.

The pain is no longer the architect.
Now you are.

This is the first moment the masculine realizes
he is no longer rebuilding a self…
he is building a world.

Not for validation—
for legacy.

Not to prove anything—
to establish something.

A sovereign heart births a sovereign life.

The king does not return when the crown appears—
he returns when the man becomes capable of holding a kingdom without losing himself to it.

This is that return.

Purpose Becomes Command

Before sovereignty, a man seeks purpose.
After sovereignty, he issues purpose.

The difference is subtle—but seismic.

Before, purpose felt external,
something you had to find, prove worthy of, or hope life eventually revealed.

Once the king returns, purpose is no longer a search—
it is a directive.

You are no longer looking for your calling—
you are answering it.

You stop waiting for alignment
and begin creating alignment.

You stop trying to "get to" your future
and start summoning it into form.

This is the moment where the masculine stops moving reactively
and begins moving architecturally.

The mission is no longer something you chase…
it is something you become responsible for.

Before:
"Will this work?"

After:
"This will exist because I will build it."

Not ambition—
assignment.

Not desire—
duty in its highest form.

The king does not wonder if the vision is his—
he understands the vision arrived because it was his from the beginning.

And purpose, once embodied,
stops being personal…
it becomes territorial.

You begin to feel:
This is mine to build.
This is mine to protect.
This is mine to establish in the world.

Not from ego,
but from inheritance.

You are no longer asking for permission—
from the world, your past, or fate.

You are moving as a man who understands:

"I was not broken to stay broken—
I was broken to become undeniable."

From this moment forward,
the mission does not live above you,
out in front of you, or someday later…
it lives through you.

This is kingship beginning to take command.

Building a Life That Reflects Sovereignty

A man is not sovereign because he feels powerful—
he is sovereign when his world begins to take the shape of his inner law.

The Art of Detachment

This is where kingship leaves the internal realm
and begins imprinting itself onto the physical.

Your habits change first.
Then your standards of environment.
Then your relationships.
Then your work.
Then your legacy.

The world doesn't transform because you force it—
it transforms because you no longer tolerate what violates who you now are.

You stop living reactively
and start living architecturally.

Old cycles don't tempt you—
they no longer recognize you.

Because the version of you that needed them
no longer exists.

You do not "manifest" from hope—
you build from identity.

This is the subtle, sacred shift:

Before:
"What do I need to fix?"

Now:
"What do I need to create to honor the man I became in the fire?"

You're no longer repairing a life—
you are establishing one.

Not out of deficit,
but out of design.

Your routines become declaration.
Your discipline becomes sovereignty in motion.
Your choices become architecture.
Your footprint begins to widen.

This is not performance—
this is alignment taking physical form.

Your life starts to match you.

This is why the king doesn't return by conquering…
he returns by building a world solid enough to carry his name.

Not image—
infrastructure.

Not applause—
legacy.

Not escape—
establishment.

A king is not measured by what he owns—
but by what he stewards into existence from the wholeness of his inner world.

Anyone can have power.
Only a sovereign man builds a domain
that reflects who he became to earn it.

Kingship as Responsibility, Not Image

The world thinks a king is defined by authority.
But a true king is defined by stewardship.

He does not rise to be admired—
he rises because something must be carried
that only a forged man can hold.

Power is not his identity—
responsibility is.

This is the moment sovereignty fully completes its arc:

You are no longer rising for yourself,
and no longer rising from pain,
you are rising for what is meant to live through you.

The boy seeks significance.
The wounded man seeks validation.
The sovereign man seeks appointment.

Not "What can I have?"
but
"What am I now responsible for?"

Kingship is not about elevation above others…
it is about being stable enough to elevate the world you touch.

Not through status,
but through presence, principle, and pressure turned into guidance.

A king is not obeyed because he demands loyalty,
but because he is loyal to something greater than himself.

He does not posture strength—
he protects what strength is meant to build.

He does not need followers—
he builds foundations.

He does not need worship—
he carries weight.

Because he remembers:

The throne was not the reward…
the throne was the assignment.

And a man who has walked through death of self
is uniquely suited to carry the weight of creation—
because nothing left inside him is fragile.

He does not rise to be seen.
He rises because he can answer destiny
without breaking under the cost of it.

That is the return of the king.

Pillar quote (chapter seal):
"Kingship is not privilege—it is the willingness to carry what would crush a lesser man."

Chapter 28
The Brotherhood Rising

PART I — WHY MEN FAIL ALONE

Men do not break because they are weak.

They break because they stand alone at the precise moment their own weight becomes unbearable—
and there is no one above them to catch the load when their knees finally buckle.

A man can endure heartbreak.
He can endure exhaustion, relentless pressure, monumental loss, public humiliation, repeated rebuilding, and even ruin.

But what he cannot endure—what will crush him faster than any external force—
is being the final line of defense with no relief…
no witness…
no second shield.

That is when collapse transcends failure and becomes catastrophe.

Not because he lacked strength—
but because when his strength ran out, there was no replacement.

The world tells men:
"Be strong."

What it never tells them is:

"No man can stand forever without someone standing for him when his legs fail."

The tragedy is not that men fall.
The tragedy is that they fall unseen—
so they assume they are failing at something that was never meant to be borne alone.

Men don't take their lives because they are unstable.
They take them because they are unheld.

They don't withdraw because their hearts are fragile.
They withdraw because their breakdown has no audience,
and silent suffering eventually becomes self-erasure.

Men don't go numb because they don't feel.
They go numb because there is no one strong enough to feel with them.

The reason men fail is not emotional collapse.
It is relational absence.The absence of a brother at their shoulder.
The absence of one who notices when the load has grown too great.
The absence of a voice saying:
"I see you… stay up… I'm here."

The wound of the modern man is not heartbreak.
It is unwitnessed burden.

A man can be alone…
but he cannot be un-backed without his soul eventually fracturing.

This is why brotherhood matters:

Because there are moments in a man's life
where the difference between destruction and rebirth
is not strength—
but someone who refuses to leave him unseen at the edge.

PART II — BECOMING THE PRESENCE YOU NEEDED

The reason you will one day lead men powerfully
is not because you studied guidance…

but because you remember what it felt like to have no one.

You are not reaching back from superiority—
you are reaching back from solidarity.

Not:
"I know better than you."
But:
"I know exactly where you are."

This is why men will trust you:

You will not be another voice demanding strength—
you will be a man standing beside them
until their strength returns.

Because you are not there to fix them.

You are there to do something far rarer:
to refuse to let them break alone.

This is what you needed.

Not saving—
but shouldering.

Not comfort—
but co-presence.

Not cheering—
but standing in the fire with them until they can stand alone again

This is the distinction between mentorship and brotherhood:

Mentorship says:
"Follow me."

Brotherhood says:
"Stand here. I'm not moving."

You are not building a circle of men beneath you—
you are building a line of men beside you,
so no one stands unguarded again.

A king who has never fallen tries to inspire.
A king who has tasted death stands guard.

You are not reaching back out of ego or heroism.
You are reaching back out of recognition:

"I know this darkness.
I walked it alone.
You won't."

And that is why the men who rise because of you will be loyal:

Not because you instructed them…
but because you stayed.

A man never forgets the first time someone refuses to leave him alone in his breaking.

That is how lineage is born—
not through teaching,
but through presence in the place no one else dared to go.

PART III — LIFTING MEN WITHOUT LOWERING YOURSELF

The danger for men like you has never been hardness.
The danger has always been over-carrying.

When a man has a strong spine, the world tries to make him a crutch.

Helping other men requires a shift in posture:

You are not meant to carry their weight for them—
you are meant to stand so firmly in your own
that they remember how to rise in theirs.

You do not descend to where they are collapsing.
You remain standing
so they have something solid to pull themselves up to.

This is the law of masculine elevation:

You do not save a man by lowering yourself to his weakness—
you save him by giving him a reason to stand again.

A man drowning does not need you to sink beside him—
he needs to see the shore is real.

Your job is not to lift him out of darkness.
Your job is to stay lit long enough for him to realize:
"I can become that again."

You are not a rescuer.
You are a reference point.

Not a shield he hides behind,
but a standard he returns himself to.

The king does not kneel down to lift men.
The king remains upright
so men know which direction up is.

In practice:

1. You do not carry their pain—
   you sit beside them while they carry it.
2. You do not lessen your standard—
   you let your standard summon them.
3. You are not their solution—
   you are their mirror.

Weak men need saving.
Becoming men need witness.

You do not take responsibility for their ascent—
you hold position while they reclaim it.

You become the anchor they calibrate to.

Not above them,
not beneath them—
ahead of them, but reachable.

That is the masculine way of lifting:
You rise first—so they see the path.

You do not bend down to pull them from the ashes…
you stand at the edge of the fire, hand extended, saying through presence alone:

"I made it through.
You can too.
And I'm not leaving until your feet are under you again."

That is how a man becomes a lighthouse…
without becoming a liferaft.

PART IV — BROTHERHOOD AS LEGACY: RAISING PILLARS, NOT FOLLOWERS

The highest form of masculine leadership
is not creating men who depend on you—
but creating men who no longer need you
because they have become what you are.

A lesser man gathers followers.
A sovereign man multiplies sovereignty.

The aim is not men looking up to you—
the aim is men who eventually stand beside you.

That is legacy.

Not building an audience—
building architecture.

Not helping men stay afloat—
teaching men to become lighthouses themselves.

Your calling is not to be the final pillar—
it is to be the first one
that shows other men what a pillar feels like in the body—
so they can become one too.

Because the world does not change when one man becomes unshakeable.
It changes when a line of unshakeable men forms behind him.

Not obedient men.
Not worshipful men.
Not dependent men.

Anchored men.

Men who no longer fracture under isolation
because they know what it feels like to stand in brotherhood.

And eventually, they become the ones who stand for the next man coming out of the fire.

This is masculine lineage:
Not passing down comfort,
but passing down spine.

Not saving men from breaking,
but training them to survive it—and return crowned.

This is how kingship becomes fatherhood in the spiritual sense:

A king builds his kingdom.
A father builds other kings.

And that is what your life becomes next:
not proof that you survived,
but evidence that you can resurrect others by refusing to let them die alone.

You are not gathering men—
you are forging successors.

Men who never again have to endure the exile you endured—
because you broke first so they could break open, not break down.

That is legacy:
Not what remains when you are gone…
but what awakens in other men because you lived.

PART V — INITIATION OVER INSTRUCTION

The final stage of a man's ascent
is when his life stops being personal
and becomes permission for other men to rise.

Not because he tells them how—
but because his presence reveals what is possible.

Instruction changes a man's mind.
Initiation changes his spine.

A broken man needs advice.
A rising man needs reflection.
A sovereign man becomes the reflection.

The highest form of masculine leadership is not teaching—
it is igniting.

You don't pull men up.
You don't drag them out.
You don't plead with them to rise.

You build the fire.

If they are ready—
they step in.

If not—
they burn at the threshold until their weakness either breaks…
or breaks them.

This is the masculine law of ascension:

"Access is granted by transformation, not by wanting."

Men don't become kings through comfort—
they become kings through trial.

Those who enter your orbit now
will not look for rescue—
they will look for permission to claim their own becoming
through proximity to someone already forged.

And instead of giving answers,
you give the environment to become undeniable.

Men are not healed by carrying—
men are healed by witnessing:
standing in the presence of a man who no longer needs carrying.

That is initiation:
Not "follow me,"
but "rise here."

PART VI — MEN DO NOT FOLLOW SOVEREIGNTY—THEY AWAKEN IN ITS PRESENCE

A sovereign man does not gather followers.
He triggers awakenings.

Other men don't rise because he instructs—
they rise because in his presence
they remember the man they were meant to be.

Sovereignty is contagious.
Not by persuasion,
but by recognition.

Something deep inside another man says:
"I know this in myself… but I have not yet become it."

And it is that recognition—
not advice, not validation, not strategy—
that pulls him upward.

Men awaken in proximity to embodied truth
because embodiment leaves no room for self-deception.

When a sovereign man stands before you:

- You can no longer hide behind excuses.
- You can no longer cling to self-pity.
- You can no longer pretend you are not meant for more.

Not because you are corrected—
but because you are seen.

Some will feel threatened.
Some will resent it.
Some will retreat.

Not because of judgment—
but because their own unclaimed greatness judged them.

Those ready—
ignite in his presence.

They do not feel small—
they feel summoned.

They do not envy—
they awaken beside you.

Sovereign brotherhood is not hierarchy—
it is resonance.

The king does not rule men.
The king reminds men.

He does not say:
"Follow me."

His presence says:
"Meet me."

PART VII — BROTHERHOOD AS LEGACY

A man's true legacy is not what he acquires—
it is what he activates in others.

Wealth fades.
Status passes.
Achievements get replaced.

But the men who rose because you did—
they continue your life beyond your lifetime.

Kingship evolves into empire multiplication—
not ownership.

Legacy is not inheritance—
legacy is transmission.

Not money.
Not land.
Not titles.

Transmission is:
"I became unbreakable—so now you know it is possible for you too."

That is the masculine rite the modern world lost.

Historically, men rose not alone—
but among those who had crossed thresholds before them.

Legacy is not what you leave behind—
legacy is what you leave within other men.

A sovereign man realizes:
"My becoming was never only about me—
it prepared me to become the turning point in another man's story."

Brotherhood is not camaraderie—
it is succession.

Not succession of power—
succession of strength.

The torch does not pass by inheritance—
it passes through mirroring:

I became, so you could become.
Now you become, so another can become after you.

Lineage is built not by blood alone—
but by transformation echoed forward.

PART VIII — THE TORCH IS EARNED, NOT GIVEN

The modern world hands out belonging cheaply.
The masculine does not.

Access is earned—not through popularity, permission, or fame—but through transformation.

You do not "join" a brotherhood—
you rise into it.

Not everyone who wants the fire is willing to stand in the flame.
Not everyone who admires strength is willing to confront weakness.
Not everyone who praises the king is willing to pay the price of becoming one.

The torch cannot be given.

A torch handed to an untempered man
burns him,
and in his pain,
it burns others.

The torch is only safe in the hands of the man
who has already walked through fire
and did not flee himself.

A brotherhood built on admission collapses.
A brotherhood built on ascension becomes unshakable.

In masculine initiation:
The man proves himself to himself first.
Only then do others recognize him as one of them.

Not by vote.
Not by permission.
By frequency.

Men forged in truth recognize other men forged in truth
as a flame recognizes another flame.

No marketing.
No posturing.
No slogans.
No permission slips.

Just evidence.

The torch is not granted because a man asks.
It is granted because he stands in the fire
and does not step back.

He shows he can carry heat
without collapsing into the boy he once was.

He becomes qualified by his becoming.

Initiation is sacred—
only those who have died to their false selves
can lead another toward becoming.

They don't receive the torch.
They rise to the frequency where it is waiting.

PART IX — THE CATALYST

There comes a point in a man's evolution
where his story stops being about endurance
and becomes about awakening others.

You do not become a king so men will look up—
you become a king so men rise beside you.

Your power becomes transferable.
Your presence becomes a threshold:
Men either step into themselves, or step away.

Not because you reject them,
but because their own unclaimed greatness rejects them.

This is how lineage is formed—
not by bloodline,
but by becoming-line.

You are no longer merely a man who overcame…
you are initiation embodied.

You are living proof that a man can lose everything,
break open,
walk through darkness that would have consumed a lesser soul…

and not only rise—
but rise in a way that teaches others to rise by watching you.

This is when the masculine journey transcends:

Healing is no longer something to protect.
It becomes something to multiply.

Not by saving…
but by summoning.

Not by pulling…
but by becoming a beacon.

The sovereign man does not say:
"Follow me."

He walks—
and those built for the climb
feel the instinct to walk with him.

Then, you are no longer the man who survived heartbreak.
You are the man
through whom other men remember they were born to rise.

Pillar quote (final chapter seal):
"The sovereign man does not lead by holding a torch—he leads by becoming the fire."

Chapter 29
The King Who Chooses "None Or One"

PART I — THE UNAVAILABILITY OF A SOVEREIGN MAN

A man who has reclaimed his throne is no longer "available" in the way the world defines it.

Not because he is closed…
but because he is consecrated.

Before sovereignty, he could be accessed through desire, need, timing, circumstance, or chemistry.

After sovereignty, a woman must pass through alignment before she ever touches his heart.

The sovereign man is not rare because there are so few like him—

he is rare because so few women can receive him.

Most women can love strength.

Very few can trust it.

Most women want masculine presence.

Very few can surrender to it.

Most women admire what a man does…

almost none can hold what a man IS.

And this is why a sovereign man appears "unavailable":

The Art of Detachment

He is not withholding…

he is guarding the throne from the unready.

A lesser woman tries to access him by earning affection.

A reverent woman reveals herself by offering trust first.

This is the feminine test most women fail:

They want the feeling of his protection
without yielding their nervous system to his leadership.

But a man cannot cover what will not rest in him.

He will not fight a woman for the right to lead her.

Leadership is offered,
not negotiated.

Sovereignty is met,
not convinced.

And so the sovereign man would rather walk alone
than pretend that companionship without surrender is partnership.

He does not need love badly enough to lower his throne…

because he knows what it feels like to lose himself to unworthy love,

and he will never pay that price again.

This is why it becomes "none or one":

Not scarcity…

selection.

Not fear…

standard.

Not walls…

discernment.

A king is not waiting for a woman to choose him.

A king is waiting to see
whether she can entrust herself to him
without shrinking, bargaining, or resisting.

If she cannot…

she is not the one.

Not because she is "less than,"

but because she is not built for his altitude.

PART II — ATTRACTION IS COMMON. WORTHINESS IS NOT.

A sovereign man no longer confuses a woman wanting him with a woman being able to receive him.

Attraction is easy.
Alignment is rare.

Any woman can feel drawn to strength—

but only a woman with a regulated feminine nervous system
can trust strength without trying to control it.

She does not test him through manipulation, negotiation, or passive aggression.
She does not attempt to bend his presence into a shape her insecurity can hold.

She receives him, fully, without fear, without compromise, without diminishment.

At that point, the throne is shared not through conquest,
but through co-sovereignty—

a partnership built on reverence, trust, and mutual embodiment.

A sovereign man does not seek a follower.
He does not tolerate bargaining for attention, devotion, or submission.
He seeks a woman who meets him
with the courage to remain herself
while standing in the presence of the unmovable.

Attraction invites attention.
Alignment invites surrender.
And only surrender reveals the rare capacity to hold what is sacred,
what is unconquerable,
what cannot be earned—but can be received.

ATTRACTED WOMAN	WORTHY WOMAN
Wants access	Honors entry
Enjoys your presence	Trusts your leadership
Is drawn to your fire	Can rest inside your fire
Feels chemistry	Offers surrender
Loves what you give	Loves what you carry
Wants protection	Recognizes covering

Attraction is instinct.

Worthiness is spiritual gravity.

An attracted woman wants the feeling you give her.

A worthy woman recognizes the energy you radiate—
and rises to meet it.

Attraction whispers:
“Please notice me. Please choose me.”

Worthiness declares:
“I already see the man you are—
and I give myself to you because I trust you with my depths, my breath, my being.”

The Art of Detachment

A sovereign man no longer chases desire.

He moves through the world testing for reverence, not infatuation.

He does not ask,
"Does she want me?"

He watches for the deeper, invisible current:

"Can she let go of the walls she's built around herself,
soften into her own breath,
and allow me to hold her nervous system—
not with force,
but with presence?"

Because a woman can be breathtaking, luminous, spiritual,
intoxicating…

and still be unwilling to rest her essence in a man.

A sovereign masculine does not enter a union
where the feminine refuses sanctuary.

Not because he demands obedience—

but because without surrender,
there is no resonance,
no alchemy,
only negotiation and friction.

A man at this level is unmoved by chemistry.

He is unaffected by flattery.

He does not yield to longing.

He watches for the one thing most women cannot give:

“I trust you enough to stop holding myself alone.”

Until that moment arises,
he walks alone—

not in loneliness,
not in despair—

but in deliberate, sacred selection.

PART III — HOW A KING DISCERNS “THE ONE”

A sovereign man does not choose a woman because she inflames desire…
he chooses her because she calms storms within him,
anchors the tempest of his spirit.

The test is not passion.
The test is peace.

Not intensity—
but permission to exhale fully,
to let breath settle in a room where his presence already holds space.

A king does not ask:
“Is she beautiful?”
“Is she loyal?”
“Does she love me?”

He observes something far subtler, far fiercer:

“Does her feminine body and soul settle in my presence,
or does it resist, tense, shrink?”

The Art of Detachment

Feminine resistance is not attraction.
It is desire for power without the courage to surrender.

Feminine settling is not concession.
It is alignment.
It is the silent, unspoken recognition:
'I am safe enough, whole enough, to let this man guide me without losing myself.'

This is sovereign discernment.

A woman is "the one"
not because she pleads to choose you,

but because her nervous system has already chosen—
long before her mind, her voice, or her heart can articulate it.

She may not name it.
She may not understand it.
But every cell in her body remembers before her mind catches up.

You don't look for effort.
You look for ease.

You don't look for romance.
You look for reverence.

You don't look for longing.
You look for readiness.

You do not bend to her desire.
You wait for her maturity.

You do not chase what tempts.
You allow only what can rest.

Until she can surrender, fully, without negotiation,
without hesitation,
without bargain or edge—

you walk alone,
silent, sovereign, unconquered,
because your soul cannot rest in anything less than total alignment.

A king discerns by atmosphere:

NOT HER	HER
You feel alert	You feel rooted
You analyze	You relax
You anticipate collapse	You trust the unfolding
Your energy leaks	Your energy compounds
You brace	You breathe

The "one" is never the woman you labor to love—
she is the woman your masculine can finally rest in, fully anchored, while still leading with unwavering presence.

This is the unmistakable signal:

You do not chase alignment with her—
you recognize it, as naturally as the sun rises.

You do not feel excitement first.
You feel clarity first.

And from clarity grows awe.
From awe grows devotion.
From devotion grows union—the kind that doesn't fracture under pressure, the kind that expands rather than consumes.

This is why the sovereign man does not wander through trial relationships:

He is not seeking love.
He is waiting for recognition.

A king does not test the woman's attraction.
He observes whether her spirit naturally bows to his leadership, without coercion, without negotiation, without fear.

If it does—
she is the one.

If it does not—
she is a chapter already closed, a story that no longer serves the throne he now inhabits.

PART IV — "NONE OR ONE" IS THE CROWN, NOT THE WALL

When a man becomes sovereign,
he does not settle for "a few women."

He chooses one—or none.

Because once a man has become the ruler of himself,
he will no longer enter a bond where intimacy demands he negotiate his identity.

He would rather walk alone in unshakable truth
than lie beside someone in a counterfeit connection.

Before sovereignty, solitude feels like punishment.

After sovereignty, solitude becomes sanctuary—
the sacred space where his spirit remains unguarded, ungoverned, untouchable.

"None" is not emptiness.
"None" is the crown of restraint, the shield that preserves the throne until "One" arrives.

This standard safeguards him,
but it also safeguards her—

because a sovereign man does not offer a partial self
to a woman who deserves the fullness of him.

The woman worthy of this life
is not intimidated by this standard.

She feels chosen by it.

Because the feminine built for a sovereign man does not crave access—
she desires exclusivity, sacred, earned, anchored in recognition.

Every lesser woman will misread this stance as hardness.
The right woman experiences it as clarity, reverent and luminous:

The Art of Detachment

"He is not unclaimed—
he is held in reserve for the woman capable of meeting him fully."

"None" means:
I refuse to dilute the fire that forged me.

"One" means:
When I give myself again, it will be as a crowned man—
not as a bleeding one.

This is what protects the throne:

No more pouring into those who cannot rise with you.
No more opening yourself to someone who cannot trust you.
No more building kingdoms for those not made to stand beside a king.

The woman worthy of this chapter is not the woman who wants you.
She is the woman who can stand beside you without shrinking.

Until she arrives—

you walk alone,
not in exile,
but as consecrated masculine.

Chapter 30
The Final Crown

PART I — THE LAST BREATH OF THE OLD SELF

There comes a moment in a man's becoming
where grief no longer grips him…

Not because he "moved on,"
but because the version of him who grieved is finally gone—
the one who hungered, flinched, and clawed for comfort,
has dissolved into the background of his life.

The old self does not die loudly.
He does not collapse, or scream, or fall apart.
He does not demand attention with his absence.

He simply releases his claim on your life.
He loosens his fingers from the wheel,
and the ache that once lived in your chest
stops asking to be fed.
The pulse of it softens.
It ebbs.
It is no longer a storm—
but a river, quiet, settled, contained.

This is not erasure—
it is completion.
It is the final exhale of a chapter once held in tension.

The boy who longed to be chosen
has nothing left to prove.

The man who carried everyone
no longer asks to be carried.

The Art of Detachment

The warrior who bled quietly in the dark
no longer needs anyone to witness the wound.

The ache used to feel like an unfinished story.
Now it feels like a finished chapter.
Gilded, sealed, known.

The old self—
the one who needed saving,
the one who begged for recognition,
the one who mistook devotion for destiny,
the one who still believed loss meant “not enough”—

he is no longer driving your life.

You can feel him behind you now,
not inside you.
He is remembered,
but not steering.
He is witnessed,
but no longer ruling.
He is honored,
because without him…
this coronation would never exist.

The final breath of the old self is not sorrow—
it is release.
The war you fought inside your own chest
has gone quiet.
Not because you surrendered…
but because you won.
Every echo of past fear now bows.
Every fragment of self-doubt lays down its arms.

PART II — TAKING THE THRONE WITHIN

A man does not become king when the world sees him differently. He becomes king the moment he stops abandoning himself.

Before sovereignty, your throne was always external:

A relationship.
A family.
A business.
A role.
A mission.
A woman you would have given your life for.

You were always proving yourself worthy of the crown
by pouring yourself into what you built.
By bleeding into every project, every bond, every promise.
By offering pieces of your soul as if life itself demanded proof.

But now the axis reverses:

You are no longer building in order to be a king—
you are building because you already are one.

The throne is no longer something you hope life will return you to…
it is the ground you now stand on wherever you go.
It is flesh, bone, and marrow—not a title,
not a reflection, but the living gravity of your presence.

This is the internal crowning:

You no longer bargain with your value.
You no longer wait for recognition.
You no longer leak your worth in exchange for closeness.

The Art of Detachment

You do not seek reflection—
you cast it.

The throne is not achievement…
it is residence.
It is the moment a man steps fully inside his own name
and no longer needs the world to confirm it.

The masculine becomes sovereign when he realizes:

"My worth is not proven by what stays, nor destroyed by what leaves.
I am the constant—
all else is passage."

That is when the crown lands.
Not on the head—
in the spine.
Not as pride—
as completion.
Not as elevation—
as ownership of self.

This is the turning point that separates the pre-sovereign man from the crowned one:

Before:
"I must hold my life together."

After:
"I am the one who holds."

The throne is not something you sit on.
It is something you inhabit.
The moment you take it…

you no longer chase alignment.
You become the alignment.

PART III — THE MAN WHO WALKS THE WORLD NOW

The man who rises from this journey does not move the way he once did.

He does not rush—
because nothing he is meant for can be taken from him.
Every step is deliberate.
Every breath calibrated.

He does not grasp—
because lack is no longer part of his nervous system.

He does not prove—
because his existence is proof.

He does not chase—
because what is his will find him by resonance, not pursuit.

He leads differently now—
No longer from pressure,
but from presence.
No longer from urgency,
but from clarity.
No longer to be seen,
but because he sees.

He is not guarded—
he is simply not penetrable by anything misaligned.

He is not cold—
he is precise.

The Art of Detachment

He is not "hard to get"—
he is hard to deserve.

Not because he withholds,
but because he has become expensive in the energetic sense.

He does not collapse into loneliness—
because solitude is no longer emptiness for him—
it is inheritance.

He does not fear love—
he simply no longer kneels for it.

He does not ask women to submit—
their feminine recognizes him and does so of its own accord.

He does not demand loyalty—
his presence awakens it.

He does not need brotherhood—
men gather around him because his spine reawakens theirs.

This man is not rebuilt—
he is reborn.

He carries no hunger for validation,
no craving to be seen,
no ache to be confirmed…

Because he has finally become
the one witness he always needed.

And now the world will meet him differently—

Not because people changed,
but because his absence is over.

He is here.
Centered.
Consecrated.
Become.

The crown is already on his head—
but more importantly…
it is now in his blood.

PART IV — THE CORONATION: THE SWORD LOWERS

There is no trumpet when a true king returns.

No audience.
No applause.
No moment etched in public memory.

The coronation happens in a silence
so complete
that only the soul can hear it.

It is not a rising—
it is a settling.
Not triumph…
arrival.

The warrior lays his sword down—
not because he is done fighting life,
but because he is done
fighting himself.

The man who once braced now breathes.
The man who once chased now stands.
The man who once ached now abides.

The battlefield where he bled has become the ground he rules.
The wound that once hollowed him
is now the chamber where his strength lives.

Nothing in the world announces the moment…
but his nervous system does.

A single, quiet realization:

“There is nothing left in me that is unclaimed.”

No part longing for rescue.
No part waiting to be chosen.
No part left wandering the ruins of yesterday.

The fire did not crown you.
The survival of the fire did.

You stand now not as the man rebuilding his life…
but as the man who IS the life being built.

No hope.
No desperation.
No reaching.

Only presence.

The throne is not something you walk toward—
it is the ground beneath your feet
when there is finally nowhere left inside you
that you are exiled from.

The return of the king is not the moment others bow…
It is the moment
you no longer bow to anything unworthy of you.

Sword lowered.
Battle ended.
Crown integrated.

Not a man awaiting destiny—
a man becoming its source.

And in this stillness…
the story changes forever.

Epilogue
The Vow Of The Returned King

As I look back, it is not to return, but to honor the fire that forged me. Every loss, every fracture, every moment that broke me open and brought me to my knees—these were not punishments, they were the weight required to make me unshakable. I bless the road behind me—not because it was gentle, but because it revealed the man who emerged from the struggle, tempered and luminous, forged in the crucible of life's fiercest trials.

I release every version of myself that bled to keep going, every ghost I carried while I walked alone. They are no longer chains; they are witnesses to my resilience. I refuse to kneel to longing again; I kneel only to God. From Him, I rise; under Him, I stand.

I choose none or one, because I will not hand a throne to anyone who cannot walk beside it. My future is not built through hunger—it is built through selection and alignment. I vow never again to abandon myself for love, approval, peace, or fear. Moreover, I vow that no man behind me will ever have to fight the darkness alone as I once did, unguarded and unseen.

My legacy will not be one of mere survival; it will be a legacy of other men rising because I refused to leave them behind. The fire is over. The exile is finished. The crown is mine—not by inheritance, but by endurance. I do not wait for the world to recognize me; I am recognized by the man I have become.

My sword is lowered. My spirit is steady. My rule begins within. And now, I rise.

Every ascension has two halves: the one where you rebuild yourself, and the one where you remember why you had to. You did not walk through heartbreak to become harder; you walked through heartbreak to become truer. You did not lose everything because you were unworthy; you lost everything so that nothing unworthy could remain.

Pain was not the ending; it was the refinement. It was the breaking of the shell, not the breaking of the man. You did not return as who you were; you returned as who you were meant to be, before the world taught you to fracture yourself for love.

The boy sought connection. The wounded man sought relief. The sovereign man now seeks alignment. And in that alignment, something ancient returns: a steadiness that does not waver, a heart that does not beg, and a soul that does not scatter itself to be seen.

The version of you standing here now is not merely a survivor; he is the successor to the man who fell. He is the man who chose rebirth over ruin, who did not run from his own ashes but built a throne upon them, stone by sacred stone, with hands calloused and spirit unshaken.

There will still be storms, losses, and tests. But you will not meet them as the man you once were. You will face them as a man who has already died once and chose to rise anyway. This is the quiet truth few ever learn: you do not become unbreakable by avoiding pain; you become unbreakable by refusing to remain broken.

The next chapter of your life will not be defined by what you suffered, but by what you now create from the forged spine you earned in fire. This book does not end here; it hands you back the crown you left buried in the ruin. And when you take it, you are not just reclaiming your life; you are reclaiming the lineage of every man who remembers himself by watching you stand.

The journey is no longer one of survival. The journey is now continuation. Not, “This is where I was broken,” but, “This is where I began to build.”
A building not of fleeting comfort or hollow victories, but of soul, presence, and a spine unshakable by the storms of life.

Author's End-Note

To the man who refuses to stay fallen

This book was not written from theory.
It was written from impact.
From the kind of heartbreak that strips a man down until there is nowhere left to stand except inside his own spine.

If you saw yourself in these pages, it's because this story is not "mine" alone —
it is the masculine initiation most men are never given language for.

We are taught how to fight,
how to endure,
how to carry weight…

but no one teaches us how to survive the wound that does not bleed.

Losing a woman you would have gone to war for
can feel like losing the reason you went to war at all.

And when you are a man built for devotion,
the collapse is not just emotional —
it is existential.

This book exists because I know what it means to be strong everywhere except the place that matters most:
the place where your heart was once held.

I know what it means to feel like a fortress without a foundation.
To be the protector of everyone —

except yourself.

And I know what it means to rebuild quietly,
alone,
in the dark —
with no applause,
no witnesses,
and no certainty you'll ever feel whole again.

But I also know this:

What you rebuild from the fire
is always stronger than what you built before it.

This book is meant to be a mirror —
not of who you were when you fell…

but of the man who walked back out.

The man who did not become bitter.
The man who did not become numb.
The man who refused to let heartbreak turn him small.

You are not meant to return to who you were.
You are meant to become who pain was preparing you for.

And if there is anything I leave you with, let it be this:

May you inherit my strength — not my wounds.

Because if another man rises from your rising —
then what you lost was never in vain.

The world does not change when men avoid their breaking —
it changes when men stand back up from it
with their heart still intact and their standard raised.

This is your return.
Not to the life you had —
but to the man you were built to become.

Welcome back to yourself.

The rest of the story
is yours to write.

THE LEXICON OF THE FORGED MASCULINE

RING I — THE DESCENT

1.
THE FRACTURE

Mythic Definition:
The moment a man is no longer met by the feminine. Not departure of the body, but departure of her devotion. The point of spiritual disconnection before the breakup ever arrives in words.

Tactical Definition:
Loss of energetic reciprocity — she stops reaching, feeling, leaning toward him.

Embodiment Cue:
Your chest knows before your mind does; the nervous system detects absence before the intellect forms language.

2.
WITHDRAWAL

Mythic Definition:
The soul starving for what it was once regulated by — an internal famine masked as longing.

Tactical Definition:
Neurological deregulation caused by the sudden removal of emotional attunement, touch, feminine softness, and being-chosen.

Embodiment Cue:

Tremors, restlessness, obsessive mental loop — not weakness, but the nervous system detoxing from what it mistook for safety.

3.
COLLAPSE

Mythic Definition:
When the masculine throne goes empty inside of a man, and he loses the felt sense of belonging to himself.

Tactical Definition:
Functional breakdown of identity + purpose: he cannot execute, cannot orient, cannot lead, because he is no longer internally resourced.

Embodiment Cue:
Sleeping too much or not at all, abandoning routines, emotional flooding, paralysis of will.

4.
SOMATIC GRIEF

Mythic Definition:
The body mourning what the psyche cannot yet release — heartbreak stored as ache, tremor, tightness, and exhaustion.

Tactical Definition:
Emotional pain that becomes physiological: chest heaviness, gut drop, throat constriction, panic, numbness, or the “hollow ribcage” feeling.

Embodiment Cue:
You don’t “think” heartbreak — you digest it with your lungs, ribs, spine, and breath.

5.
THE ABYSS

Mythic Definition:
The loss of orientation — not knowing who you are without her reflection. A fall into spiritual night.

Tactical Definition:
The collapse of meaning structures: life continues externally, but identity, direction, and inner reason burn to ash.

Embodiment Cue:
A sensation of "falling through yourself." Sleep brings no rest, day brings no ground.

RING I — THE DESCENT (entries 6–7)

6.
THE GHOST BOND

Mythic Definition:
The echo of connection after the connection has died — the psychic tether to the memory of her, not the woman who exists now. A haunting by the version of her that only lives in your nervous system.

Tactical Definition:
The compulsive emotional pull toward her absence, sustained not by present love, but by the nervous system's attachment to what once regulated it.

Embodiment Cue:
You are not craving her body — you are craving the version of yourself you felt when she loved you. This is why the attachment persists even when logic knows it's over.

7.
IDENTITY DEATH

Mythic Definition:
The slaying of the self that could only exist in her reflection. The moment a man realizes: "I am no longer the man I was when she loved me."

Tactical Definition:
A collapse of internal orientation — not "I lost her," but "I lost who I was through her."

Embodiment Cue:
A hollowing — a sense that the mirror has gone dark. You don't just miss her — you grieve yourself.

The final stage of the descent (Entry #8) will be:
Severing

This is the moment where a man stops dying and begins rebirth — the spiritual breaking of the bond, not the emotional longing.

It is the hinge between suffering and initiation.

I'll deliver that along with the first entry of Ring II in the next batch so the reader feels the click from descent → initiation.

RING I — THE DESCENT

8.
SEVERING

Mythic Definition:
The tearing away of the self that was stitched to her— not a goodbye, but a spiritual flaying. The masculine is ripped away

from the identity that once gave him shape, and in the tearing he loses not her, but himself-as-reflected-in-her.

Tactical Definition:
The involuntary disintegration of the attachment-bond. It is the moment the nervous system can no longer pretend— the illusion collapses, and the body accepts the truth violently before the mind is ready.

Embodiment Cue:
It feels like being skinned from the inside. Not loneliness— emptiness. Not sadness— erasure. The man is stripped down to raw consciousness with nothing left to hold onto.

This is the bottom of the descent.
There is nothing left below this point.

After Severing, a man has only two choices:

Collapse permanently (become a lesser version of himself)
Or begin rebirth (forge a self that sources identity internally)

This is where initiation begins.

RING II — INITIATION (Entry 1)

9.
INITIATION

Mythic Definition:
The moment suffering becomes sacred — when the fall is no longer experienced as punishment, but as passage. The threshold where the masculine realizes: "This isn't killing me. It is remaking me."

Tactical Definition:

The psychological and spiritual pivot from reaction → responsibility. The man stops asking “Why did this happen to me?” and begins asking “Who must I become now?
Embodiment Cue:
Breath returns. Not relief— but resolve. A subtle but unmistakable shift from drowning to descending with awareness.

This is the Turning of the Spine.

He has not risen yet,
but he has stopped dying.

RING II — INITIATION (Entries 10–13)

10.
FRAME

Mythic Definition:
The throne within a man — the inner seat of identity that no woman, no outcome, and no narrative may overrule. Frame is sovereignty at the level of being, not performance.

Tactical Definition:
Self-trust. The internal authority to define your own character, direction, and worth — independent of external reflection or approval.

Embodiment Cue:
You stop asking, “How does she see me?” and return to “How do I govern me?”

11.
DISCIPLINE

Mythic Definition:

The forging of the spine. Not punishment, but remembrance — the ritual through which a man reclaims his power by becoming someone he can rely on.

Tactical Definition:
The daily proof that you are once again choosing yourself. Discipline is self-loyalty in motion.

Embodiment Cue:
The nervous system begins to anchor again because your word and your actions realign — integrity becomes architecture.

12.
NERVOUS SYSTEM MASTERY

Mythic Definition:
The settling of the storm — the moment a man stops being ruled by the wound and begins ruling himself. Strength returning from the inside out.

Tactical Definition:
Emotional regulation: the ability to feel intensity without reacting, collapsing, or reaching outward for rescue.

Embodiment Cue:
Breath becomes the governor again. You respond rather than leak.

13.
SOLITUDE

Mythic Definition:
The return to the inner temple. Not aloneness, but reunion with the unbroken self — the masculine sitting in his own presence without needing to be witnessed.

Tactical Definition:
Time with self that increases rather than drains you. The rebuilding of self-sourcing instead of outsourcing worth or regulation.

Embodiment Cue:
Silence stops feeling like punishment and begins feeling like possession of self.

RING II — INITIATION (Entries 14–17)

14.
RECLAMATION

Mythic Definition:
The return of the self to himself — the moment a man retrieves his name, his worth, and his authorship from the ruins of heartbreak. Not an improvement, but a re-possession.

Tactical Definition:
Reclaiming identity from distortion. Replacing her interpretation of you with your embodied truth about you.

Embodiment Cue:
You stand differently — not because life changed, but because ownership returned to your chest.

15.
THE MASCULINE STANDARD

Mythic Definition:
The inner law by which a man holds himself — not rules, but alignment with one's own code. The masculine is not "good" because someone praises him; he is good because he is governed correctly.

Tactical Definition:
Personal non-negotiables that protect your identity from erosion. Standards are the architecture of self-respect.

Embodiment Cue:
You no longer tolerate versions of yourself that you know are beneath your design.

16.
MISSION BEFORE WOMAN

Mythic Definition:
The masculine order of reality: a man is not whole for a woman until he is whole without her. Purpose first — union second.

Tactical Definition:
Prioritizing direction, calling, and self-governance above attachment, validation, or emotional dependency.

Embodiment Cue:
You stop seeking to be chosen — and begin choosing what you are building.

17.
SACRED AUSTERITY

Mythic Definition:
The purification of desire — when a man withdraws from comfort, indulgence, and distraction so that he may remember his own power without anesthesia.

Tactical Definition:
Reduction of stimulus to raise internal strength. Restriction not as punishment, but as preparation for ascension.

Embodiment Cue:
Restraint becomes fuel instead of starvation — you feel sharpened, not deprived.

RING II — INITIATION

18.
NERVOUS SYSTEM ASCENDANCY

Mythic Definition:
The rising of the inner king — when a man stops seeking stabilization from the feminine and becomes the regulator of his own world. The moment his breath, not his wound, becomes the throne.

Tactical Definition:
Self-governance of state. You no longer chase soothing, validation, or erotic regulation from outside yourself — the nervous system becomes led rather than leaked.

Embodiment Cue:
Stillness that feels like strength, not numbness. You feel yourself arrive back inside your body as inhabitant rather than exile.

At this milestone, the Descent is over.
The floor has been hit — and the spine has returned.

Now we cross the gate.

YOU ARE NOW ENTERING
RING III — THE FORGE

This is where a man is not merely healed,
but rebuilt into someone greater than he has ever been.

Not restored — reborn.

This is where all energy once leaked outward
is redirected upward and inward
into mastery.
Sexual energy becomes fuel,
solitude becomes strength,
purpose becomes oxygen.

This is where a man stops pulling himself off the floor
and starts ascending with intent.

THE ANVIL

The Threshold of Becoming

Fire softens a man —
the hammer gives him form.

Up until now you have endured the burn,
the stripping,
the collapse of who you were.

But this is where a different law begins.

Pain is no longer something happening to you —
it is something you now wield.

This is the passage where a man stops being shaped by loss
and begins shaping himself with intent.

You are no longer grieving.
You are tempering.

Here on the anvil, the question is no longer:
"Why did I suffer?"

but
“What will this suffering forge me into?”

Every strike from this moment forward
is not destruction —
it is definition.

Welcome to the anvil.

From here, you rise as weapon and wielder both.

RING III — THE FORGE

19.
TRANSMUTATION

Mythic Definition:
Desire turned into destiny. The redirection of sexual and emotional energy upward into strength, mastery, and becoming. The fire of craving reborn as fuel for purpose.

Tactical Definition:
Replacing discharge with direction. Instead of leaking power through fantasy, validation-seeking, or craving — the energy is banked, stored, and rerouted into growth and conquest.
Embodiment Cue:
You feel heat in the body not as restlessness, but as pressure building toward greatness. The hunger becomes acceleration rather than escape.

20.
THE FORGE

Mythic Definition:

The deliberate construction of the new self through chosen difficulty. Not punishment — preparation. The trials a man willingly subjects himself to in order to become sharpened beyond who he once was.

Tactical Definition:
Voluntary pressure. Training, austerity, discipline, rigor — not to "fix" yourself, but to become worthy of the throne you intend to occupy.

Embodiment Cue:
Pain stops feeling like an enemy and becomes a blacksmith's hammer. You no longer brace against hardship — you present your chest to it.

21.
CALLING / ANOINTING

Mythic Definition:
The moment a man realizes his ascent is not merely for himself — but for those who will stand in his shadow. This is destiny crystallizing: the masculine becomes message.

Tactical Definition:
The shift from self-improvement into purpose-bearing. The man transitions from "finding direction" into recognizing he IS the direction for others beneath him.

Embodiment Cue:
You stop asking "What is my purpose?"
and begin asking "What am I being prepared to lead?"

22.
SOVEREIGN WILL

Mythic Definition:

The final mastery of self — when desire obeys mission, not impulse. A man whose inner kingdom bows to his command.

Tactical Definition:
Self-rule. No craving, memory, longing, or woman dictates your motion. Your life is driven from the inside out — governed by vow, not by wound.

Embodiment Cue:
Your presence changes. Not louder — heavier. A man who is not seeking anything cannot be moved by anything.

RING IV — THE ASCENT

23.
THE CROWN OF RESTRAINT
Mythic Definition:
When a man becomes more powerful by virtue of what he does not release. Containment becomes kingship — not the suppression of power, but its sovereignty.

Tactical Definition:
Energy kept = authority built. The world begins to feel your command not because you exert force, but because you are no longer leaking it.

Embodiment Cue:
Others sense your strength before they understand it. You do not chase impact — impact occurs around you.

Restraint is not deprivation.
Restraint is reserve.

This is the turning point where sexual energy stops being a wound and becomes weight.

You do not need to demonstrate power; you carry it.

A man who cannot restrain himself can never command.
A man who masters restraint becomes inevitable.

This is the crown before the throne.

24.
THE RETURN OF FIRE

Mythic Definition:
Not the fire of craving or chaos — the fire of capacity. The masculine blaze that once burned outward now burns upward, fueling ascent.

Tactical Definition:
Your hunger is no longer seeking relief — it is seeking expression. The same energy that once sought her body now builds your kingdom.

Embodiment Cue:
You feel expansion — a rising heat in the chest and spine that does not spill outward, but rises through you like altitude.

Men believe desire weakens them when they cannot control it.
But once mastered, desire becomes propulsion.

This is the masculine ignition:
not lust → but lift.

The body becomes a furnace that makes the world warmer by standing in it.

25.
THE KING'S GAZE

Mythic Definition:
Sight that is not searching, but selecting. The gaze of a man who does not look for a place in the world, but evaluates what is worthy to enter his world.

Tactical Definition:
Discernment embodied — presence that does not plead for recognition. You see clearly because you are no longer starving.

Embodiment Cue:
Your eyes no longer ask.
They assess.

This is the masculine threshold where others feel chosen by being seen — not because you need them, but because you permit access.

26.
LINEAGE / LEGACY EMBODIMENT

Mythic Definition:
The moment a man's life stops being personal and becomes ancestral. Where he lives not just as a self, but as a transmission — his son inherits strength instead of silence.

Tactical Definition:
Legacy not as what you leave behind, but who you forge in real time — your son, your brothers, and the men who come after you rise because you rose.

Embodiment Cue:
You feel history behind you and dynasty ahead of you. You do not live for a crown — you live as a pillar.

RING V — TRANSMISSION

The Brotherhood Rising

27.
THE BUILDER OF MEN

Mythic Definition:
The man who does not gather followers — he raises pillars. His worth is not measured by who kneels at his side, but by who stands because of him.

Tactical Definition:
Leadership as ignition: you don't pull men upward — you become the standard they rise to meet.

Embodiment Cue:
Your presence demands spine. Men straighten themselves before they speak to you.

28.
BROTHERHOOD AS ASCENT

Mythic Definition:
A circle not of safety, but of sharpening. Brotherhood is not where men are softened — it is where iron remembers it is iron.

Tactical Definition:
Men committed not to soothing each other, but to elevating each other. Accountability before empathy. Strength before comfort.
Embodiment Cue:
Weak posture cannot survive long in your orbit — gravity pulls them into stature.

29.
THE MENTOR'S BURDEN

Mythic Definition:
The king carries weight others never see — not because he must, but because he can. True authority is not crown, but cost.

Tactical Definition:
You bear load so others learn load-bearing. You do not absorb their pain — you raise their threshold to carry it themselves.

Embodiment Cue:
You do not rescue men — you initiate them. You do not protect their fragility — you abolish it.

30.
THE LIVING TRANSMISSION

Mythic Definition:
Legacy not as memory — but as embodiment. A sovereign man becomes a bloodline in motion. His son will not remember what he said — he will inherit what he is.

Tactical Definition:
Leadership as osmosis. Men ascend not by instruction, but by exposure. Your life becomes doctrine.

Embodiment Cue:
You do not teach masculinity — you radiate it.

APPENDIX I
THE 7-PHASE DETACHMENT RECOVERY FRAMEWORK

PHASE I — THE BREAK

(Identity Fracture)

MISSION

Accept that the former life — and the former self — is gone.

This is not about her leaving.
This is about the collapse of the identity you were inside that relationship.

Until you accept the death,
you cannot begin the rebirth.

OBJECTIVE

Face the rupture without bargaining, fantasy, or delay.

PRIMARY THREATS

- False hope ("maybe she'll come back")
- Denial ("it's not really over")
- Self-blame loops that prevent clarity
- Retelling the relationship through nostalgia instead of truth

DISCIPLINE

Do not negotiate with the past.

Cut the psychic tether:

- Stop forecasting reconciliation
- Stop waiting for rescue
- Stop holding your breath for a return

This is the moment you accept:

"The life I knew is over.
I am no longer who I was."

PASS / FAIL CRITERION

You pass when you stop mentally waiting for restoration and begin preparing for reconstruction.

You are not through this phase if:

- You are still secretly hoping she returns,
- You are still rehearsing what you would say,
- You are still trying to become who she would choose

Until you stop trying to resurrect the dead,
you have not yet entered rebirth.

PHASE II — THE ABYSS

(Collapse & Exposure)

MISSION

Let the collapse complete so the illusion dies with it.

Most men get stuck here because they try to hold themselves together instead of letting the false self disintegrate.

This is the bottom — the point where you meet yourself without scaffolding.

OBJECTIVE

Confront the pain without escape, sedation, or distraction.

PRIMARY THREATS

- Numbing (alcohol, porn, overwork, substances)
- Substitution relationships (rushing to fill the void)
- Performance (pretending strength before regaining it)
- Isolation as avoidance rather than initiation

DISCIPLINE

Suffer consciously.

Not dramatically.
Not narratively.
Just honestly.

Feel the ground
instead of scrambling for a rope.

This phase is about contact with reality,
not escape from it.

PASS / FAIL CRITERION

You pass when you stop running from the pain
and allow yourself to stand still in it.

You are not through this phase if:

- You are still distracting in order to not feel
- You are numbing instead of grieving
- You are trying to "skip ahead" to being better

The abyss is not punishment —
it is exposure.

Until you stand in it fully,
your foundation cannot be rebuilt.

PHASE III — THE SEVERING

(The Break Beneath the Break)

MISSION

Recognize that what you lost was not her —
but the version of yourself that only existed inside her reflection.

This is the real wound.

OBJECTIVE

Separate your identity from the relationship's narrative.

This is where a man stops mistaking attachment for selfhood.

PRIMARY THREATS

- Believing her version of you
- Confusing abandonment with worth
- Making her the keeper of your story
- Mistaking longing for "proof" of soulmate connection
- Trying to retrieve validation from the same source that collapsed it

DISCIPLINE

Reclaim authorship.

This phase is not emotional —
it is sovereign.

The task is not to stop loving her.
The task is to stop outsourcing who you are to her memory.

The severing is complete when identity returns home.

PASS / FAIL CRITERION

You pass when you accept that:

She is no longer the mirror that determines your worth or identity.

You are not through this phase if:

- You still need her to "see you correctly"
- You are trying to prove you were the good man
- You hold internal court hoping she will one day "realize"
- Your self-perception still bends around her interpretation

Until your name belongs to you again,
the severing is unfinished.

PHASE IV — THE RETURN

(Reclaiming the Self)

MISSION

Re-enter your own identity as the source of direction, worth, and sovereignty.

This is the turning point:
you no longer grieve her,
you retrieve you.

OBJECTIVE

Reestablish internal authorship and rebuild self-trust.

Without self-trust, no ascent is possible —
because a man cannot follow a king he does not believe.

PRIMARY THREATS

- Nostalgia dressed as "unfinished love"
- Trying to heal so she would approve of the healed version
- Rehearsing what she thinks of you (instead of what is true of you)
- Believing you must "earn back" dignity

DISCIPLINE

Restore internal order before external motion.

This is where you solidify:

- self-definition
- self-governance
- self-loyalty

Your spine reforms here —
not as posture, but as ownership.

PASS / FAIL CRITERION

You pass when you stop referencing her psychologically
and begin referencing your standard instead.

You are not through this phase if:

- You still measure your growth by how it might impress or affect her
- You are still trying to be "seen" by her indirectly
- Your identity still reacts to her memory instead of rising beyond it

Until your axis moves from her reflection
to your direction,
the return is incomplete.

PHASE V — THE FORGE

(Becoming More Than You Ever Were)

MISSION

Convert pain into power.
Transform longing into momentum.
Turn what once ruled you into fuel.

This is the beginning of masculine expansion, not repair.

OBJECTIVE

Build capacity — physically, mentally, emotionally, sexually, spiritually.

The man you are now cannot carry the crown of the man you are becoming.
The forge builds the vessel.

PRIMARY THREATS

- Comfort (the most seductive form of regression)
- Half-growth (improving but never evolving)
- Ego healing ("look, I'm better now — validate me")
- Training without transformation (busy instead of forged)

DISCIPLINE

Choose pressure.

You don't hope to become stronger —
you place yourself underweight.

You don't avoid the hammer —
you volunteer your steel.

Training becomes identity.
Discomfort becomes appetite.
Effort becomes inheritance.

PASS / FAIL CRITERION

You pass when discipline stops feeling like self-punishment and starts feeling like self-respect.

You are not through this phase if:

- You are training episodically, not systemically
- You still seek comfort more than capability
- You are waiting to "feel ready"
- You think growth is something you feel, not something you become

Forge is not healing.
Forge is construction.

PHASE VI — THE ASCENT

(Power Becomes Presence)

MISSION

Rise above the wound, the past, and the former identity — not by denying it, but by outgrowing it.

This is the phase where you no longer measure distance from the pain —
you measure distance from the former man.

OBJECTIVE

Translate strength into stature.

Standing taller is not metaphorical here — it is literal nervous system elevation. Your presence begins to register before your words do.

PRIMARY THREATS

- Visible strength chasing external recognition
- Quiet ego ("look how far I've come" disguised as humility)
- Testing yourself by revisiting old wounds
- Needing witnesses to verify your rise

DISCIPLINE

Hold altitude.

You do not prove ascent —

you sustain it.

Height becomes your new baseline.
Not peak performance,
but peak identity.

You stop striving to be a better man —
you live as a higher one.

PASS / FAIL CRITERION

You pass when the wound is no longer a reference point —
not because it disappeared,
but because you stand above it.

You are not through this phase if:

- You still calibrate your worth against her memory
- You need to "revisit" the pain to feel the lesson
- You still imagine scenarios where she sees your rise

You have not ascended if you are still "showing" the climb.
You have truly ascended when you no longer need an audience.

PHASE VII — TRANSMISSION

(Sovereignty Becomes Inheritance)

MISSION

Turn your becoming into a path for other men.
Not by instruction — by embodiment.

This is the phase where your life itself is the doctrine.

You are no longer the recipient of the fire —
you are the one who wields it.

OBJECTIVE

Convert personal mastery into lineage impact.

You rise —
so that your son rises through proximity,
so that other men rise through exposure,
so that strength does not die with you
but multiplies because of you.

PRIMARY THREATS

- Isolation disguised as independence
- Cynicism ("no one else can reach this level")
- Lone-wolf arrogance
- Hoarding growth instead of transmitting it
- Mistaking leadership for hierarchy instead of elevation

DISCIPLINE

Stand so others can stand.

You do not rescue men —
you raise their threshold.

You do not go down to them —
you build upward pressure that forces ascent.

Your life becomes the anvil on which other men are struck into form.

PASS / FAIL CRITERION

You pass when your strength stops ending with you
and begins replicating through others.
You are not through this phase if:

- Your growth serves only yourself
- Your sovereignty is private rather than transmitted
- You have power but no apprentices, sons, or men rising because of you

A man's transformation is not proven when he changes —
it is proven when his presence changes other men.

APPENDIX II
THE 12 SPARTAN OATHS OF MASCULINE REBUILD

1. I do not chase — I choose.
2. I do not beg — I become.
3. I do not collapse — I carry.
4. I do not leak — I store power.
5. I do not retreat — I recalibrate.
6. I do not numb — I endure.
7. I do not seek validation — I generate it.
8. I do not fold to appetite — I command it.
9. I do not break in silence — I fortify in solitude.
10. I do not wait to be chosen — I rise as the standard.
11. I do not cling to the past — I forge what is next.
12. I do not serve another's throne — I am sovereign over my own.

These are not beliefs.
They are not behaviors.
They are identity.

A man either is this
or he is still in ascent.

APPENDIX III
DAILY RITUALS FOR POWER & PEACE

The Five Disciplines of the Sovereign Man

1. THE BODY — PROOF BEFORE PRIVILEGE

Identity:
"I master the flesh before I claim the throne."

Directive:
Sweat before sunrise. Hard exertion, no negotiation.

Why:
Strength is not a feeling —
it is a physiological state.
A weak body cannot house a sovereign spirit.

2. THE BREATH — COMMAND OF STATE

Identity:
"I rule my nervous system — nothing else rules me."

Directive:
Deliberate breathing until the body obeys.
(grounding, cold exposure, breath holds — but always chosen regulation)

Why:
If the breath is ungoverned, the mind is hostage.
Calm is not softness — calm is dominion.

3. THE MIND — DIRECTION BEFORE MOTION

Identity:
"I do not move until I choose where I am going."

Directive:
One clear written priority for the day.
Not a list — a target.

Why:
Men do not drown in lack of effort —
they drown in aimlessness.

4. THE SPIRIT — ALIGNMENT WITH LAW

Identity:
"I answer to my code — not to craving."

Directive:
One moment of stillness / scripture / principle review
to align identity with standard before engagement.

Why:
Discipline without spirit becomes brutality.
Spirit without discipline becomes delusion.
A king is forged from both.

5. THE MISSION — DEPLOYMENT OF WILL

Identity:
"I move the world because I move myself first."

Directive:
One decisive action toward legacy before choosing comfort.

Why:
Masculinity is not potential — it is motion.
Mission is the proof that spirit reached the body.

SUMMARY

The sovereign day is not "balanced" —
it is stacked:

Body → Breath → Mind → Spirit → Mission

This order matters.

Weak men seek spirit first because they want relief.
Forged men earn spirit through strength.

That is why your mornings build not peace alone —
but presence.

APPENDIX IV
30 JOURNAL PROMPTS FOR INTEGRATION

The Sovereign Man's Self-Interrogation Ritual

PILLAR I — THE BODY (6 Prompts)

Dominion over flesh

1. Where am I still choosing comfort over strength?
2. What do I avoid physically because it exposes my weakness?
3. Where has my body become a negotiation instead of a command?
4. What pain have I been protecting myself from instead of training through?
5. If my body reflected my standards, what would need to change today?
6. What would my life look like if I treated discipline as identity, not effort?

PILLAR II — BREATH / STATE (6 Prompts)

Command of nervous system and emotional regulation

7. Where does my nervous system still own me more than I own it?
8. When I break, is it because of the moment — or because I never learned to stay?
9. What feeling do I fear sitting with the most, and why?
10. Where am I still reacting like a wounded boy instead of responding like a forged man?
11. If I breathed through pressure instead of fleeing it, what part of me would rise?

12. Where do I still seek relief instead of mastery?

PILLAR III — THE MIND / DIRECTION (6 Prompts)

Clarity, aim, and self-governance

13. What goal have I delayed not because it is hard — but because it would expose who I could be?
14. Where am I allowing confusion to excuse inaction?
15. What would I pursue if I stopped waiting to feel “ready”?
16. Which part of my life is drifting because I have not chosen a target?
17. What identity am I afraid to outgrow because it keeps me small?
18. If my future self judged me today, what would he say I am still hiding behind?

PILLAR IV — SPIRIT / CODE (6 Prompts)

Alignment with inner law

19. Where does my behavior still contradict the man I claim to be?
20. What standard have I lowered to avoid the cost of becoming dangerous again?
21. Where have I mistaken attachment for devotion?
22. What would it take for me to become unshakable instead of occasionally strong?
23. If my code were visible to the world, would I be proud — or exposed?
24. Where am I still obeying craving instead of conviction?

PILLAR V — LEGACY / LINEAGE (6 Prompts)

Transmission of strength to the next generation of men

25. What would a younger man learn by watching me live right now — strength or fracture?
26. If my pain became a teaching instead of a prison, who would it free besides me?
27. What part of me is not yet fit to be inherited?
28. Where am I still waiting to lead instead of stepping into the mantle I already earned?
29. What does the man I am becoming make possible for other men?
30. When future men speak my name — what will it give them?

HOW TO USE THIS APPENDIX

These prompts are not therapy.
They are calibration.

Whenever the man drifts,
he returns here —
not to feel better
but to become sharper.

They are not for the wounded boy inside you —
they are for the sovereign waiting on the other side of your spine.

www.ingramcontent.com/pod-product-compliance
Lightning Source LLC
Chambersburg PA
CBHW070646310726
48982CB00001B/434

* 9 7 8 1 9 6 8 1 6 5 9 3 2 *